The Boys from Hog Heaven

A novel by
Grant Williams

Grant Williams

This book is a work of fiction. Names, characters, places, and incidents either are the product of the author's imagination or, are used fictitiously. Any resemblance to actual events, locales, or persons, living or dead, is entirely coincidental.

Copyright Library of Congress Grant Williams 2006

All rights reserved including the right or reproduction

ISBN: 0-9764666-8-6

Cover by: Krystal Neuhofel

1110 West 5th Street
Coffeyville, Kansas, 67337
www.tanosbookspublishing.com

Printed in the United States of America

The Boys from Hog Heaven

Dedication

I would like to dedicate this book to all of my magnificent seven, who read my poems and short stories. With your encouragement I fulfilled a dream and wrote my first novel. Throughout my life I have been fortunate enough to have people encouraging me and pushing me to different levels and hopefully I will continue and get better. To my friends and family, this book is for you and truly not about you. I love you all.

Chapter One

The Beginning

Tarleton J. McGregor grew up where the Spanish moss hung down over country roads. The humidity, so thick, that sometimes during the summertime the folklore had it whereby catfish would leave the ponds and just fly about for a while until they spotted a fisherman with a net. If they could not find what they were looking for, they would disappear into the murky backwater ponds of the southwestern Georgia landscape. Tarleton grew up with the knick name of tar baby or to his family, just simply Tar. The family lived in the big white two-story house on the edge of the small town of Carver named after a confederate soldier thought to have been a Georgia hero. The house had big green shutters and a grand porch that encompassed the front. Tar lived there with his Mother, Father and his Grandpa James. Tar had an older sister named Betty a southern beauty in high school. He also had a younger brother, Carver, two years younger named of course after the famous confederate who bore the same name of the town.

The McGregor's farm produced onions with a section for an orchard where they raised peaches for market. Tar had a favorite place to get away, where the backwater ponds and the thick forest met. The rumors were the biggest wild boar ever to roam this part of Georgia living in those woods. Tar wasn't forbidden to play in those woods, but he had been warned to not spend all of his time there besides he was not allowed to take Carver grew up. Curiosity interested Tar and he would plan many adventures to the woods while in his bed at night.

Spring planting would come soon with onion plants being put into the red earth. Again this year, Tar would help as his father would give him some hard earned money for his own use. Tar's father would sometimes hire black families to assist in the planting of the onions. Contrary to some of the myths and

The Boys from Hog Heaven

stereotypes, Tar enjoyed his time working with the families. Some of the black children went to the same school with Tar until they were forced away from their farms. Tar enjoyed the stories he heard about the great wild pig that lived in the forest and then the uncommon things that happened when the wild pig would be around. Although Tar's father warned him about not believing everything he heard, it was harder for Tar not to believe the eyes of the story teller, which would sparkle with excitement as the stories were being told.

Tar enjoyed springtime and looked forward to the planting. Tar's father, John McGregor, known for his generosity also had a temper. Stories had been told he would sometimes whip the workers with his braided leather bullwhip but stories even though seemingly stretched, forced Tar to realize that his father's respect had been earned, sort of like a throwback to the old south.

Tar remembered-apparently, a young teenage black man whistled at Betty and since John was in range, he struck out with his whip. Now, depending on where you hear this story, John either struck the young man or he missed him. Nonetheless, a fear is present and people do know have thoughts relating to John McGregor's family. Over the years, Tar heard this story many times but would never ask questions or for that matter have enough courage to ask his father. Tar considered himself to be equal to the families who worked in the fields next to him.

As much as Tar worked with the black families he knew that there was a difference. It wasn't so much a color issue as many thought but the black elders sometimes looked upon the thought of the boss' young son working in the field as being perhaps a spy. Sometimes Tar would ask his father after working in the field why do the others look upon me as someone so different. "Son, you are different. You are a McGregor," he answered.

Tar would often wonder why his brother, Carver, didn't have to work in the fields as he. John wanted his son to be a man of the land, so when Tar turned eight years old, he would let him work by his side for an hour or so. Tar enjoyed the time

5

with his dad as they worked together. On the other hand, Mrs. McGregor, knowing Carver to be not as sturdy as Tar, had him learning to play the piano and getting more culture in his early life. It wasn't as if Mrs. McGregor didn't want Tar to have culture but Tar a strong willful lad, modeled his father more; besides he loved the outdoors. Since the incident many years ago, Betty never came to the fields but would always treat Tar with some respect as he returned from the fields with his father in the evening. There were too many distractions for a southern beauty to overcome than to be a constant pest to her brother.

John McGregor announced to the family, during dinner, the planting would start next week and Tar would be driving the old tractor. John had three tractors and even though the old small Farmall tractor was not very powerful it would certainly give Tar his badge of sorts growing up when you could drive the tractor.

John said," Tar I'll show you how to drive the tractor tomorrow after breakfast." Grandpa James smiled as he knew it to be a right to passage, but Mrs. McGregor looked apprehensive at her husband without speaking. It was a man thing and her interference wouldn't matter. Tar sat up taller in his chair and Carver seemed to look upon his brother with more respect. Betty's mind dwelled on springtime; she didn't seem to hear any of the conversation.

The old black maid/cook/housekeeper Miriam looked proudly to Tar and presented the first desert to him. It was known amongst the families that Tar was a good lad that understood working in the fields being respected by all. Now his big day would be coming and she would go back to her family and tell them of Tar's new endeavor. She smiled at Tar and looked over to John who normally would have been served first. John nodded-everything is all right.

After dinner all but Betty sat on the big porch. Grandpa was smoking his old corncob pipe and staring out toward the forest. John and Mrs. McGregor sat in their big white rocking chairs looking out over the land. Tar and Carver sat on the edge of the porch enjoying the sunset over the red land. The forest looked so black to them but they never seemed to talk much

The Boys from Hog Heaven

about it to their parents or even old Grandpa since it seemed a mystery that someday they would conquer. The wreath of smoke encircled their Grandpa's head as the boys thought anxiously of the days to come, for spring has arrived- a time of rebirth and for new life to start. At night, they had many things to dream about while they lie in their old iron beds watching curtains gently blow with the help of the hot humid Georgia.

Grant Williams

Chapter Two

The Tractor and the Fields

The early morning sun glowed over the red dirt. Tar, excited about the day, had already been up for over an hour. Today is the day he would learn to drive the tractor- one more step to becoming a man. The old rustic barn with its graying boards not only survived hot humid summers and cold wind of winters, but it back dropped what Tar had focused on-the Farmall tractor. The tractor, even through rust of its years still looked foreboding to Tar, sat idle waiting.

Tar could see the wisps of smoke from beyond forest. He knew the sharecroppers would be preparing and eating their breakfasts of grits and red-eyed gravy. They were glad they could work on the McGregor farm to supplement their meager income. Tar not only wondered what it would be like to live in the small houses but stories the older black inhabitants told intrigued him. He believed some of the stories were true making it hard for him to distinguish fact from fiction. Tar knew the families he worked with would be happy and proud as he executed his right of passage to an adult McGregor.

As Tar looked over the fields alternating stares to the tractor, his father walked by his side staring at the tractor his father walked to his side.

"Good morning Son. It is a beautiful day. Not much wind and a good day to work the fields."

Tar did not hear his father mention using the tractor. Maybe he forgot. Maybe this day would be like many others when they would not use the tractor and just walk the fields with their hoes.

"We'll need to make sure we fill the gas tank before we go out," said John nonchalantly.

The excitement quickly built in the young boy. Tar knew where the gas was located and sometimes he had even got the can for his dad.

8

The Boys from Hog Heaven

"Let's eat breakfast first. I may be a long day today. We have got to get the fields ready to plant tomorrow," said John to his son.

Tar nodded, he had almost forgotten breakfast. Breakfast in the south is a very important meal. The cook would offer fresh biscuits with peach blossom honey. There would be plenty of ham or bacon and of course there would be plenty of grits and eggs. At the McGregor home breakfast allowed time to discuss the days work. The children would discuss their school work, their social life and listen to Grandpa give his daily advice.

Planting time is special since it gives the local young men a break from school. It replaces winter boredom and allows the Georgia boys to get out of the classroom. For the southern girls it is a time to prepare for the upcoming dances and proms, which would start after the springtime break. They would go to the towns with their mothers and shop, they would talk on the telephone to their friends and they would sit around reading poetry of beauty and intellect. Some girls would be going off to girl's school or girl's college at the end of the school year and preparations were being made. The sharecroppers and some of the black families looked at planting time as a time of looking to the future. They dreamed and prayed for a good crop and how things would be better than the previous year. But for all it was a time of rebirth, a time for hope.

Tar often would eat more than most boys his age. He loved the southern breakfasts' allowing family time. He even enjoyed the lessons his grandpa tried teaching them. Today is different. Today Tar's mind, not on the food or conversation and he didn't jump into the conversation as he would do with his grandpa. He picked at his food as he looked out of the kitchen window at the shiny and rusty Farmall tractor. Soon he would sit tall on the old metal seat and show all of the people in the field that he belonged.

Ruth McGregor, Tar's mother is a southern lady. She attended a fine finishing school and at a springtime dance she had met John. They danced and laughed. That summer John courted Ruth and at Christmas he asked Ruth's father for her hand. They were engaged for a year and had a June wedding

Grant Williams

that is still talked about in the circles of women of the county. Ruth moved to the farm with John and watched it grow. The children came and Ruth made sure all of the children would have culture. Betty, now growing up a southern lady taught in the ways by her lovely mother. Tar and Carver were allowed the run of the farm but Carver seemed to be more protected by his mother. The boys were taught manners. They were taught to read and to explore the wonders of books. They were taught the importance of the church.

"Tarleton is there something wrong with your breakfast?" asked Ruth who always addressed him by his proper Christian name.

"No, Ma'am," answered Tar realizing he was playing with his food, not a gentlemanly thing to do. "I was just thinking."

"Now is the time to eat. You can think after breakfast. Do you think Miriam cooked this lovely breakfast for you just to play with and not eat?"

"I'm sorry mother," said Tar looking at his lovely mother and smiling.

The smile seemed to be enough of an apology and John changed the subject.

"Tar is going to disc that ten acre field today."

"John do you think he is old enough?" asked Ruth in her southern mothers most syrupy voice.

"He's worked hard in the fields and now is the time to learn how to move on with the stewardship of the land. He's a big lad, and he is very responsible."

Tar beamed with pride.

Grandpa chimed in. "John was only six years old when he would ride on the tractor with me and he learned okay."

"But Tar is just a boy," said Ruth in her protective motherly way.

"He'll do fine, my dear," assured John as he finished his last biscuit.

"Be careful, dear," said Ruth not looking at John but straight at Tar.

The Boys from Hog Heaven

"I will mother. Father will show me and I will be all right."

Carver being the youngest looked at his older brother with pride for he realized his mother would never let him do this. Betty, her usual self, seemed not interested in the farm or any other such physical work. She thought all work produced sweat and to sweat was heathen. She told her mother that she would marry a man from the city, perhaps a banker or lawyer. Grandpa James knew he wouldn't have to philosophize since today is an day of passage for his grandson and therefore his opinion wouldn't be needed.

Finally breakfast ended, Tar and his dad walked side by side toward the barn and the old Farmall tractor. Tar looked at the old tractor as if it was a steed in the "Knights of the Roundtable".

"Well son, we need to make sure there is plenty of gas and the oil level is okay in this good tractor. My Father taught me on an old tractor just like this one when I was younger."

Together they checked the gas and oil as John showed his son where to look and what to look for. John told Tar that he used to crank the old tractor but now he just had to push the starter button.

"Make sure you don't have the tractor in gear," said John showing Tar where to put the shifting lever.

"You move this lever if you want to accelerate," he pointed to the lever on the steering column.

"You will be disking the field so you won't have to shift out of slow gear and after you start you put the tractor in low gear by putting in the clutch and moving the shifting handle. When you want to stop you push in the clutch and put the tractor back in neutral and put on the brakes, which are the two pedals on the right. Got that?"

"I think so," said Tar now not so confident.

"We'll take her out and I'll show you?" said John as he smiled at his now not so confident son.

"Thanks Dad."

Tar stood on the axle of the tractor by his dad's side as his dad went through the instructions again. John acted patient

11

Grant Williams

with his instructions as he repeated showing his young son. Once they got going, they stopped a few times and started over just to make sure everything Tar understood everything. When the two reached the other end of the field John put the tractor in neutral and shut it off.

"Okay son, it's your turn now," s aid John firmly.

All of the instructions whizzed through Tar's head but he remembered to stay calm and took a deep breath. The ideas now came orderly and the tractor started. Tar then put the tractor in gear, raised the throttle arm on the steering column and they were off slowly down the field as the discs cut through the red earth. John, standing next to Tar, didn't say much as he watched the work begin for he was having a moment remembering when grandpa first let him drive their tractor.

At the end of the row John told Tar to stop the tractor and let him off. He told him how to work the field from one end to the other overlapping the rows to make sure all the earth was being prepared for the planting. John also told his son that if he needed him he would be working the other onion field with the workers and the other tractors. Tar would be alone.

Tar waited until his dad was safely away from the Farmall before he started. Tar looked back at the big house and thought he saw someone peering out of the window from behind the curtains. He thought it must be his mother or maybe it could be Carver wishing him success on today's journey. In any event, he didn't acknowledge that he had any indication that someone from the house watched. Tar, anxious to resume, turned to the task at hand and slowly moved the tractor down the rows. It is a good day.

The sharecroppers arrived and went with John to the other fields. They were happy to have an opportunity to work for some cash early in the season. John normally only hired two families and they were kin to Miriam the cook. Miriam's brother Will and her cousins Virgil and Junior would always come along for the spring planting and then later for the harvest. They could work for the McGregors and still farm their acreage

The Boys from Hog Heaven

Will, the first to see Tar driving the old tractor down the rows of the ten-acre field said, "Mr. John it looks like the boy is doing a fine job on the tractor."

"First day Will, we'll see how he likes the tractor when it becomes a job."

"Yes sir, Mr. John, but Tar is different he has a feel for the land already. He can work beside us all day."

"I know Will but he is still just a lad. We should have the other fields ready by the end of the day and if Tar gets his field ready we can plant tomorrow."

"Yes sir, Mr. John, we'll be ready. I'll get the onion sets ready. Virgil and Junior can get the fields ready. We'll need another man for the planting tomorrow. There is this fellow, a white boy about thirty that just moved into the house next to mine behind the trees. He is needing a job and I think he'll be all right. He has two kids and will need some help getting started. I'll stand up for him."

"Bring him around tomorrow. We can use all the help putting the plants into the ground," said John knowing he could trust Will and his family.

"I'll see him after work today."

"Look at that boy go," said John proudly as he watched his son turn over the fresh earth.

"Doing a fine job, sir," said Will approvingly.

Tar now had gotten the feel of the tractor and his confidence grew. The trips down the field were getting too commonplace and repetitively boring. Tar was starting to lose interest. Tar started to lose interest allowing his mind to change the tractor to other things. Sometimes it was a racecar speeding in the Indianapolis 500, a race that Tar had read about in a magazine. Sometimes the old Farmall was not a tractor in Georgia but a war machine Tar read about in history books. World War Two ended a few years before Tar was born but he still managed to see a lot of the pictures at school and in the library. These thoughts would pass the time as the sun rose higher in the sky and the work became more monotonous.

During one of the moments, the tractor became a tank and went the end of the row came up, Tar suddenly swerved the

13

tractor just in time to miss the old wooden fence. Tar was driving toward the end of the row and Tar was deeply involved with his thoughts of driving a tank in the war the end of the row came up suddenly. The discs just missed the fence and Tar quickly came back to reality. He instinctively shut down the tractor and jumped off to check the equipment. His father and the crew were far away in the large field and they wouldn't need to know of this transgression.

The discs seemed to be all right and the trusted old tractor was okay with no dents or signs of drifting off the track. Tar walked around the equipment for a moment before he spotted something in the ground close to the fence. 'What was this that was uncovered by my trip off the path?' thought Tar as he looked at the metal objects in the new plowed field. Excitedly, Tar bent over and picked up a piece of an old revolver, a tin box and several buttons with a rebel insignia. On the back of the buttons were carved rustically the initials 'G. Mg.' Tar carefully picked up the items from the earth and placed them by the fence post. He couldn't tell anyone about them yet or he would have to tell them he had strayed from his duty of discing the field. He decided he would go back later tonight and get them. He waited a few moments and looked some more. He would look more later in the evening after the work had finished.

After putting the items in a safe place by the fencepost and covering them with several rocks, Tar climbed back on the tractor and started it up. He slowly put the old vehicle in gear and started back down the rows.

Tar felt glad he brought his old hat for the sun. The cool water from his canteen refreshed him for a while but when his father arrived to let him know it was time for lunch he was glad to step down from the tractor and sit in the shade.

"Hungry son?" asked John?, and then added. "The field is looking good. Is the tractor running okay?"

"It's running real good. Hope I can finish before it gets too late. I am getting a little hungry."

"Well Miriam must have known for she made you some fried chicken. She doesn't usually do that for lunch. She made one of your favorites."

The Boys from Hog Heaven

The food smelled so good to Tar. He didn't realize he became so hungry. The adrenalin had worn off and the tediousness of work had set in. The bumps on the old metal tractor seat now were part of work instead of excitement. For some reason, the tractor didn't look as shiny as it did before but Tar was still proud that he accomplished something and knew his father was proud of it.

John sat with his son under one of the large oak trees guarding the gate to the ten acre field as they ate their lunch and drank the cool sweet tea.

"How long have we farmed this field?" asked Tar looking across the half cultivated field.

"The McGregors have farmed this field from when George McGregor got this farm right after the War Between the States. He got this farm from some Yankees soon after a battle was fought on the property. There have been stories told that he buried his uniforms and gear then, on the sympathy of the Yankees obtained this land. They thought he was just a dumb old boy that wanted a little ground to farm on and since the war was ending it didn't matter much to them."

"Did grandpa know George McGregor?"

"No, George married and had a son who was grandpa's daddy and thus the farm was passed down. Grandpa's daddy bought the land around here that we now own and the forest."

"Did George own any slaves?"

"No son, George worked side by side with the negro men and cleared a lot of the land. Most of the others left the south except for some of the sharecroppers. George stayed the course and made this land so prosperous for us."

"What do you think is in the forest?" asked Tar as he consumed another chicken leg.

" There are wild boars around here and if you hear some of the families on the other side of the forest they will tell you stories about the boars eating children and other tales that I don't know if they are true or not. The stories get bigger each time I hear them."

"Have you ever seen a wild boar?"

Grant Williams

"I did see a big pig near the forest one day but it was just for a minute."

"Was it big?"

"Yes son, it was big. Why all of the questions?"

"Just wondering," answered Tar not revealing his secret cache of the buttons and the old revolver.

"Bring the tractor back to the barn when you finish. We'll need to wash some of that red dirt off of it before we put it up tonight," said John as he put the picnic basket under his arm and headed back to the larger field and the other workers.

Tar stretched and climbed back up on his steed. The old tractor would have to entertain him for the entire afternoon, as the field must be finished to allow the planting tomorrow. Tar suddenly felt grownup and saw a new respect in his father's eyes. Today is truly a special day, a day he would not soon forget.

The Boys from Hog Heaven

Chapter Three

Onion Planting Time

After breakfast the next day John assembled all of the help down by the barn. Will had brought the new man with him. The new man told everyone to just call him "Bubba" because everyone from his home had done it for years. Bubba a tall gangly man with bib overalls having seen a lot of work were faded, patched several times and shorter than the others. His flannel shirt no longer bright but muted with the days in the sun and plenty of washings.

John set us up in teams of two on the planting equipment where Will would work with the new man and his brother Junior and Tar would work with Virgil and with his father. Will and John would drive the tractors while the rest of them would put the onion sets into the red Georgia earth. If they were lucky they could have the fields planted by the end of the week. If the help were lucky there would be extra plants for them to take home for their own crop.

This experience wasn't fun for Tar since he had done a little of this last year where John had let him work with Will for a few hours. Tar remembered how hot the sun would get and how his back hurt from bending over. Tar also remembered all of the stories that Will told him and how he had hung on every word. There were so many stories and mysteries happening around the forest by the end of planting season Tar didn't know fact from fiction. Tar knew he would hear more tales again this year.

The men met in their groups and headed out to the freshly plowed and disked fields. The ground now soft and the plants went softly into the tilled earth without much effort. The truckload of onion sets always taken to a place between the two fields where several crates could be unloaded onto each planting machine. The aroma of the sweet onions in the air with the

17

Grant Williams

knowledge soon the fields would be full of the plants spurred the men on to the job at hand.

The planting machines now loaded and Virgil and Tar took their places on each side of the low planter. The onion sets now put on the planter where the crew could put them into the ground, as the tractor drivers drove slowly down the rows. The work tedious now but soon it would get hotter. Virgil and Tar became good partners and worked well together mostly because Virgil considered Tar as an equal on the job. Virgil started to sing some old hymns and spirituals as the tractor moved slowly down the field. The sound of Virgil's deep baritone voice seemed to sooth the repetitions of the odiferous crop going into the red soil.

It seemed within an hour that Tar began humming some of the sainted spirituals along with Virgil. John with the task in hand just looked out in front of the tractor concentrating at the task at hand.

"Swing Lo Sweet Chariot" sang Virgil, "coming for to carry me home."

"Virgil, did you ever see a wild pig down by the forest?" asked Tar right out of the blue.

"I done seen a great pig. One night when we had finished hoeing in the field I was walking down by the trees. It was getting dark and it was hard to see. I done heard a loud noise in the trees and when I looked up I saw a great boar hog. He had tusks that reached out about a foot and a half and he was breathing smoke out of his nostrils. He looked at me and I looked at him, then I ran to the house to get my rifle."

"What happened?" asked Tar excitedly missing a plant or two in the row.

"When I got back with the gun the pig was gone. I looked on the ground where the pig was to try to find some tracks and I saw a sign."

"What was the sign?"

"I saw the letters V and W scratched into the ground. Virgil Washington."

"What did you do next?"

The Boys from Hog Heaven

"I ran into the house and took my bible and kneeled down and prayed that we would be safe from this demon," said Virgil with his eyes getting big and excited.

"Did you ever see the pig again?" asked Tar as he now was in a good rhythm as he put the new young onion plants into the ground.

"I carried my Bible with me ever since. I have heard the crashing about in the trees but the devil pig never crossed my path again. It is evil. I know if this creature would come around our house it could eat anyone of us."

"Have your brothers ever seen the pig?"

"A long time ago when a group of hunters from the north came down and they were asking for help in finding some game Will told them stories about the wild boar and they wanted to find it. Will had seen the pig one day at the edge of our peanut patch where He swore the pig looked at him and spoke. He claims the pig buried something but would not let Will close to the spot."

"Did you ever find out what was buried?"

"We will someday. Maybe we'll try to find out what it was after the crops are in the summer heat is here. I don't think the pig will come out in the heat and sunshine of the mid-day."

"I heard that some children were missing after someone had spotted the pig many years ago?"

"Don't know. After a family spotted the pig many years ago the next day they were gone. It isn't known around these parts if the family just left and went up the river or they were eaten by the pig."

"What are you guys talking about?" asked John as he came to the end of a row.

"Nothing Daddy," said Tar as he looked over at Virgil who now was concentrating on getting the plants ready for the next row.

"Hear that noise in the forest?" asked John as he looked at some of the trees shaking and a loud unfamiliar animal sound came from the woods.

Tar looked at Virgil and Virgil looked toward the heavens for guidance. Is there really something to fear in the thick

19

wooded area or is it myth, is it a deer in rut or is it the sounds of the wild boar looking for redemption from the people of the area?

The two men on the planter didn't answer John and John turned and headed the tractor back toward the other end of the field.

When the group reached the other end of the field John stopped the tractor and got some cool water from the truck. The men took long drinks from the metal dipper and wiped the red dust from their sweaty brows. It would be a long day and a long week. It would prove to Mr. MacGregor that Tar was ready for his first steps into manhood. The other tractor pulled up with the crew.

"How's it going?" asked John knowing the standard answer.

"Going good, boss," answered Will in his gentle strong voice.

"How are you doing, Bubba?" asked John as he looked at the new man.

"Doing fine, sir," said Bubba not looking John in the eye.

"How's your family? Do they like it here in Carver?"

"Wife likes it fine. We got some chickens and she started a garden. The girls haven't met hardly anyone. They will be in school after the spring planting. The oldest will be in high school and the youngest is twelve and has so much curiosity. Don't have any boys so the girls have to hoe in fields too."

"It won't hurt them, Bubba."

"No sir, it's good for them to learn and work. They can help their Momma too."

"I need help to finish planting the onions and then we will plant peanuts. I could use some help along with these guys," offered John.

"I'd be much obliged, Mr. McGregor."

"You get with Will when we finish today and he'll let you know when we need to be in the fields. It'll be at least to the end of the week before we get all of the onion sets into the ground barring a rain storm."

"I'll be here when you need me."

The Boys from Hog Heaven

Will wiped the sweat from his shiny dark black skin. His face always shined and he looked so powerful with his snow-white teeth. John always admired Will for his loyalty, his work ethic and he respected the fact of Will's faith in God, his devotion to church and family. Will respected John for his helpfulness in the lower class community. Will always appreciated that John McGregor always hired him and his brothers and help them by giving them left over onion sets and to help plant peanuts. There were always fresh vegetables for the Washington family and sometimes Ruth would send some good hand-me-down clothes back to the families through Miriam the cook. The fact is the rumor of John McGregor's temper never came into being amongst the two families.

The rest of the day went without anything unusual with Virgil would sing his hymns and spirituals. Tar listened and dreamed about the treasure he would collect from the field. Tar knew he should tell his father but for now he didn't want to interfere with the planting. The other team of Will, Junior and Bubba seemed to get along just fine and the rows were taking shape as if they were an army lining up for a parade.

At the end of the day the men rode back toward the barn on their tractors. Tar so glad the day was over knew Miriam would have a real good supper cooked. It would be good to just jump into the old pond behind the house and get the red the Georgia dirt off his young body. It would be nice just to sit on the front porch and listen to his grandpa tell his tales.

As the tired crew of workers approached the barn Tar noticed there was a young girl standing by the barn and waving. Bubba waved back and announced.

"That's my young'un. I guess she came over to walk me home."

As the group came nearer to the barn Tar noticed the girl was around his age dressed in a light blue cotton frock with little white flowers. The dress washed many times and some of the flowers were now faded and hardly distinguishable. She was about Tar's height and her sandy hair, put up into two pigtails, tied at the ends with bits of cloth or maybe it old ribbons. Tar noticed the girl had freckles.

Grant Williams

"That's my daughter Charlotte," announced Bubba. "She's a good girl but mighty curious. She probably wanted to know what I was doing and with whom."

"Fine looking girl, Bubba, why don't you introduce her to us?" asked John

"Charlotte, this here is Mr. McGregor and his son. You know Will, Junior and Virgil."

"How do you do sir," said Charlotte as she dipped a little as if she was curtseying.

She then looked over at Tar and just kind of gave him a little wave of the hand.

"Charlotte this is my son, Tarleton, we all call him Tar," announced John.

"How do you do sir," replied Charlotte directing her eyes toward the young lad.

"Just call me Tar," said Tar quietly as he tried to show her as much respect as required.

"Just call me Char," said the young girl.

John laughed and said out loud. "Char and Tar, what a pair of names, I hope you will come by again Charlotte. It is always good to see your neighbor's families."

"Thank you sir, I like to walk and to be with my daddy," said the girl so sincerely.

The father and daughter started to leave and John looked at Tar and said, "Son, now you be polite and say goodbye to the young lady."

Tar was a little embarrassed for he was staring at the girl and checking her out. After all she is a neighbor and who knows he might see her again.

"Bye, Miss Charlotte," said Tar politely and as his father had asked.

"Bye, Mr. Tar," answered Charlotte as she smiled at her new acquaintance.

Tar stood there for a moment and watched the father and daughter walk down the path toward the trees and the wisps of smoke on the other side. The three brothers Will, Junior and Virgil were leaving too. They too would disappear behind the trees and soon they would be home to tend their own business on

The Boys from Hog Heaven

their own little acreage. It would still be several hours for them before they would finish their day.

"Nice girl," announced John to his son as they walked toward the big house.

"Seems all right," replied Tar not looking at his father.

"Maybe she can come over to the farm and help out some day?" asked John trying to get an idea of his young son's thoughts.

"Maybe she can help Miriam. She probably has a lot to do at her own house," answered Tar as if it was nothing.

"I'll bet you are tired?" asked John as he put his arm around his son while they walked toward the big house.

"I could use a bath or a dip in the pond before supper."

"I could too. It has been a long day."

As the two approached the house Miriam announced dinner would be served in a half hour and they could cleanup enough for the evening meal. Tar knew he would have to wait for the dip in the pond. He now hungry could smell the food from the kitchen.

The family assembled as requested by Miriam in a half hour in the dining room. It was known that if Miriam said a half-hour that you had better be there or hear the wrath of the old cook. Miriam always so faithful to get the food prepared and to make such a wonderful feast for the family each day it is not wise to be late.

John and Tar had cleaned up as well as they could in the short time allowed. Ruth and Betty were dressed for the evening meal, Carver now clean and had his hair combed nicely and Grandpa is already sitting at the table when the others arrived. Grandpa knew he would never cross the cook.

Miriam started bringing out the food consisting of collard greens; brown beans, pork backbone or what many northerners called chops and plenty of homemade bread and butter. Miriam also had fried up some potatoes, always a hit with the men.

The family bowed their heads and John asked for the blessing of the food. Miriam always stayed in the dining room while this event took place. It is so important to her that the farm, the food and family were in touch with God.

23

Grant Williams

"This looks great Miriam," announced John loudly," e very day you just out do yourself."

Miriam beamed a big smile on her broad black face knowing her role in this family is appreciated. She knew she is loved too just like any other member of the family.

"Don't forget Mr. John that we have banana pudding for desert," smiled Miriam at the head of the household as she finished putting the food on the table.

"Did you have a good day in the fields today?" asked Ruth looking at her husband."

"We had a splendid day planting today. Didn't we Tar?"

"Yes sir," said Tar as he continued filling his mouth with the meal.

"Ruth, we met a new neighbor today, Bubba's girl. You know Bubba is the new man that Will brought over to help?"

"How old is she?"

"She's about the same age as Tar and seemed very nice. You could tell she is used to hard work."

"It's just another Sharecroppers kid? I hope she doesn't want to hang around here?" questioned Betty in her snobbish southern way.

"Hush you mouth," said John, not to happy with his daughter's comments. "We are all God's children."

"Your Daddy is right, Betty. We should be nice to all people," said Ruth.

"I don't have to hang around with those kids, do I?" asked Betty looking at her mother and not at her father.

"You can pick your own friends but you should be nice to everyone," replied Ruth to her daughter.

"What did you think, Tar?" asked his mother.

"She seemed to be okay. May I have some more bread, please?"

The conversation veered off from the new girl and Tar was glad it did. He wasn't used to answering questions about a girl. The talk went on about the planting and the farm. Ruth mentioned to John that she would be going into town soon with Betty before school started up again since Betty wanted to look at some spring clothes and some clothes for her high school

24

The Boys from Hog Heaven

spring dance. Grandpa wanted to talk a lot about the old days and the days before World War II when most of the farms were flourishing with crops that were sold in the big city. He didn't get into the War Between the States but had enough to say about the old days on the McGregor farm.

After the banana pudding was devoured and the dishes were cleared Tar took some clean clothes and went to the little farm pond behind the barn. The water clear and cool making it a good time to clean up so with no one around a he stripped naked and dove into the tepid water. The water had warmed quite a bit during the day and as Tar came out of the water he could feel the coolness on his skin. It had been a long day and now he could sit on the porch for a while before retiring. Tomorrow would be another long day.

Maybe Charlotte would come over and meet her dad after work. He wondered why he thought about the girl at all. So that night as he laid his head on the goose feather pillow he kept thinking about the new girl. It had been the first time that any girl had ever caught his eye. He then tried to sleep and as he drifted into the night he saw those freckles and little pigtails before his thoughts moved to the treasure he had buried near the ten acre field and fell asleep with the mystery still unsolved.

Grant Williams

Chapter Four

The New Girl

The sun had just risen and was peaking in the window of Tar and his younger brother when Tar heard a knock at his door.

"Tar, it is time to get up. I'll meet you at the breakfast table. I've got to put some gas in the tractors and check the oil," said John McGregor from the other side of the door. "The men will be over after breakfast."

"I'll be right down, Daddy," s aid Tar sleepily.

Carver still in his bed with the covers pulled up around his neck but Tar didn't care since he knew his brother wasn't old enough or strong enough to work in the fields. Tar also knew it would take quite a feat for his father to recruit him from his mother's clutches. Carver actually is a good brother and a good boy ad soon after the planting Tar would show Carver the treasure he had found in the field.

Tar put on his work shirt and pulled up his work blue jeans. It took only a moment to put on the high top work shoes and tie the strings into the neat bows his mother had taught him as a little boy. Tar now could smell the bacon frying and the aroma that wafted up to his room tantalized his taste buds. Mother and Betty wouldn't be at breakfast and they would eat later with Carver but Miriam didn't mind since she enjoyed cooking for the men folks and their conversations about the farm and the land. The farm was a big part in her life too and the McGregors accepted Miriam as one of their own family.

Tar bounded down the stairway skipping a few steps on the way. He ran into the kitchen. "Morning Miss Marion."

"Where are you going in such an all fired hurry? Your Daddy just went out to the tractors to check the tanks."

"I'm going out to help him," s aid Tar going out the kitchen door and letting it slam behind him.

"You tell you Daddy that breakfast will be ready in about ten minutes, You hear."

The Boys from Hog Heaven

"I'll tell him."

"Seen your grandpa this morning?"

"I'll check out here Miss Marion."

"Don't forget, breakfast in ten minutes."

Marion had been with the McGregors ever since Betty was born and helped Ruth raise the children. The children now accepted Marion as more than a Nanny more now as one of them. They wouldn't always see eye to eye with Marion but wouldn't dare cross her or argue with her. Marion never married but raised the MacGregor children as if they were her own. Marion at one time had a suitor but he started drinking and Marion sent him on his way. On her day off she usually spent it at the church and singing in the choir. No wonder her brothers always were singing hymns and spirituals. John and Ruth had grown to accept Marion too not only as a hired person but as a loyal friend.

Tar met up with his dad just outside of the old barn where John is filling the gas tank of the old Farmall.

"Miriam said breakfast in ten minutes," said Tar. "Need any help?"

"Everything is done here. We'll be ready when the men come over from their homes."

"Seen grandpa this morning?"

"Oh, he was up early and went out to the fields to check on us. He wanted to make sure we were planting the rows straight."

"Here he comes." said Tar pointing toward the ten-acre field.

In a few minutes Grandpa was standing with the two. "Rows look straight."

"A few more days and we'll be finished planting the onion sets."

"It won't be long till the peanuts will go in."

"I'll get the brothers to help since Tar will be back in school."

"What about that new white man?" asked Grandpa?

"We'll see, when the time comes," replied John.

"Good worker?" pried Grandpa.

27

Grant Williams

"So far he's doing okay. Will said he would vouch for him."

"That should be good enough."

"We had better get to the house. Miriam will have breakfast ready and we better not be late."

The three generations walked together to the house and entered the back door just in time. They enjoyed the morning meal and eating together in the kitchen since it is a time of planning and a time for farming affairs. Tar enjoyed now being included in the daily ritual along with Miriam, so proud of her white family.

"Miriam, I swear I'm going to gain ten pounds this spring if you keep feeding me like you do. These pancakes are the best in the county I do declare."

"Yes ma'am the best in the county," echoed Tar as he poured the sweet corn syrup over his stack.

"Mighty good breakfast, Miriam," said Grandpa too.

"Tar, why don't you and the new man trade places today? I'd like to see how this man works and get to know him."

"I don't mind. I like working with Will and Junior."

"The new man moved into the old Wilson home," said Grandpa. "I heard he has a couple of girls and a hard working wife."

"Where did you here that?" asked John quizzically.

"I do get around sometimes. I do hear things. I'm not dead."

"You certainly are not and I guess you do get around. Been around the forest lately?"

"Not since I saw that giant pig," said Grandpa then pointing to the top button of his shirt. "He was this tall and fire was coming out of its nostrils. He had tusks almost two feet long."

John looked down at his plate and said to Grandpa, "I guess you won't be going back for a while then?"

"If I was younger we'd be eating that hog. I just can't get around as easy as I used to. I'm going out in the barn today and make up some more crates for the harvest. We'll need more

28

The Boys from Hog Heaven

peach crates before the fall. If I start now we'll have enough by then."

John happy his dad found useful things to do around the farm and making the crates would help out a lot by not taking up some of the field time. Grandpa happy too he still could contribute to the welfare of the farm.

Tar always interested in the stories about the big pig and it seemed even in his short lifetime the stories of the boar got larger and the pig got bigger. He had heard the stories from his Grandpa and stories from the sharecroppers so they must be true at least to some degree. Tar and his brother would sometimes sit in their bedroom and talk about this creature that supposedly lived in the dense forest. Carver sometimes would have trouble sleeping after they talked and crawl into bed with his big brother. The boys never told anyone else that they too were somewhat involved with the legend of the big pig in the forest.

"Time to go Tar," announced John as he put his coffee cup back on the table. "It was a mighty good breakfast, Miriam. We'll be working in the same place today."

"Thank you sir, I'll bring lunch for all you men at twelve," said Miriam happy in the fact her employer and friend was so pleased.

"That would be good."

"Thank you, ma'am," said Tar as he followed his father out of the kitchen door.

Miriam just looked for a moment and thought back to when she took care of Tar as a baby. Mrs. McGregor had quite a time with Tar when he was born and had to stay in bed for some time. Miriam got to bathe and dress the young man, she got to diaper him and feed him. He still is special to her since she had no children of her own. She had watched Tar grow from a red scraggly baby to now a fine looking young man, even though he is always the curious one and the one who is fond of the sharecroppers. Tar understood the land and God's order to be a steward to the land even at this early age. She heard the tractor start and turned back to the tasks at hand. The table would have to be cleared and the dishes done. Soon Mrs. and the girl

Grant Williams

would be up and Carver too would be up and about. Carver is such a good young man but so much different than Tar. Carver would be a true southern gentleman with all of the refinements and culture. He would probably go off to a good southern college and return a Doctor or as a professional man. Carver being not as special to Miriam as Tar always is but she loved him just the same.

The men were at the barn and John announced that Bubba and Tar were trading places today. The men didn't question the decision and didn't even look at each other when it was announced.

Tar didn't mind with whom he worked for he loved the songs and the stories from the three brothers since their company passed the day by much more quickly. Today is a little overcast and the clouds are heavier in the sky. It didn't look like it would rain but John had concerns he knew a strong storm could wash some of the freshly planted onions from the ground. It still would take a few days to get all of the sets planted in the rich red soil.

The planting machines were loaded and the men were now at their tasks of planting the sets. Tar and Junior now sitting astride their planter as Will drove down the rows. John drove the other tractor with Virgil sitting on one side of the planter and Bubba on the other side as the went down the rows.

The work had begun and as the rows of onions filled the fields the stories started to unfold.

"Did I ever tell you about the time that Will and I went to Atlanta?" began Junior.

"I reckon not." Replied Tar knowing he would hear the story anyway.

"It was right after the big war and we had an old uncle who had passed. It was decided that Will and I would go to the funeral. Miriam was just young and had just started working for your folks and couldn't leave. Virgil didn't want to go and would take care of the acreage. I think Miriam was taking care of you since you were just born around that time."

The reached the end of the row and Will slowly turned the tractor around to start down the next.

30

The Boys from Hog Heaven

"What was it like in Atlanta?" asked Tar. He had seen pictures of the big city and had heard his mother and father tell of their trips there.

"It was strange to Will and me. Public places had three bathrooms, one for the women, one for the men and other said colored. We couldn't eat at a restaurant on the trip but could get food from the restaurant by using the back door. When we got to the city, we rode on the big busses but always had to sit in the back. It was so much different than here in Carver."

"What did the city look like?" asked Tar.

"We stayed at our relatives and we went to the old Negro church for the funeral. The city was big and had big buildings. There were plenty of motorcars and many stores for the white folks. Most of us colored folks just stayed in a different area. I do remember the music and hearing the blues for the first time in person. There were lovely black girls there to try to take Will's and my money. They liked to drink cheap liquor and dance all night on a Saturday. It was too fast for Will and me but it wasn't too long when we were headed back here. We did buy some city store bought clothes and a new hat for Miriam to go to church in."

"Did you see a baseball game?"

"There was baseball and the only games we could go to was games in the Negro leagues. We didn't go but we drove by the old wooden stadium. The white folks had a team too and I think it was called the Georgia Crackers."

"I'd like to go to Atlanta someday," Said Tar, I would like to see the big buildings and the stores. I saw pictures but I would like to go there myself."

"I like it here. Not so many problems. We don't have problems with the people."

"The people, you know a black and white thing."

Tar most of the time never thought of his neighbors being black. They were his neighbors and of course Miriam was like a mother to him sometimes. Tar had seen how his daddy had treated all men. There is difference and Tar realized that too. There lives as friendly as they were would never run the same course and he would always have the advantage in this part of

31

Grant Williams

the world. The class difference never questioned and mostly understood by all, even though they heard things were different in the north and in big cities.

"Did you ever see the Klan?"

"Don't want to talk about them, boy," said Junior looking down at the plants. It's good for us folks to be concerned about those folks."

"My daddy said the same thing."

"Your daddy is a good man."

Tar's face filled again with pride for he knew his father as a friend to all the people in the area. Someday Tar knew he would hear more about the Klan and maybe then he would know what they did. Now it's more important being a young man.

"Tar did I ever tell you about the big pig?"

Tar always interested in the lore and legends of the wild boar wanted to see the big pig and someday maybe it would be him that captured the monster.

"Did you see the wild boar?" asked Tar.

"I reckon so. One day while I was working in our field next to the trees I had to relieve my self and went to the edge of the forest. I hear some crashing around but thought it might be the wind or a bunch of deer. I was doing my business when I looked up and there was the pig. It was huge and had red eyes. It made a terrible sound and pawed at the ground. It had tusks that were at least two feet long and were twisted up passed its cheeks."

"What did you do?" asked Tar excitedly.

"I started singing"

"Singing"

"You know songs I learned at church."

"What did the pig do?"

"He looked at me and then up to the sky. He stayed just a short time and I kept on singing. I knew I was a goner."

"Did he attack?"

"I think he liked the music and stayed a while before crashing back into the trees."

"Did you ever see him again?"

The Boys from Hog Heaven

"I think I hear him several times but each time I got near the trees I would sing those old songs. I think it was God's will that I wasn't attacked that day."

"Do you ever think anyone is going to capture that pig?"

"I think me and my brothers won't. We try to stay away. It was told that years ago the pig came to one of the small houses and took a baby and ate it. I know several families left suddenly at different times. Maybe the pig told them to leave or ate one of them."

"Do you think the pig would eat us?" asked Tar now with his eyes wide open.

"That pig is evil. Oh Lord, keep us safe from the pig," cried Junior.

Will turned and looked at his brother and then at Tar. They both had their eyes wide open and had stopped putting the sets into the red dirt. Will seeing this stopped the tractor and said. "Enough of these stories, you done missed a bunch of sets and you can do those by hand."

Junior and Tar quickly obeyed and before long they were back on the planter seat and back in rhythm. Junior started singing again and was soon joined in by his brother Will and with Tar.

Tar continued his help during the day but thought of the pig in his spare thoughts. He knew someday he would find the pig or maybe just see the pig. He maybe could go to the woods some day when he was allowed to hunt and carry a gun. Maybe he could be a hero and kill the evil pig. Tar also thought of school starting back next week and seeing his old classmates again but one thought that kept crossing his mind was that new girl Charlotte that had come over to the farm just to walk with her dad back to their humble sharecropper's house. As much as Tar tried to dismiss the thought he face would flash in front of him. He tried to think of the treasure near the ten acre field that he had carefully had hidden away. He knew he would have to retrieve the treasure soon before someone else would find it. There were a lot of thoughts going through the young man's mind. The testosterone of becoming a man was taking affect on the fabric of his young body and mind.

33

Grant Williams

The day now coming to an end and soon they would be heading back to the barn to put away the tractors and call it a day. Tar being very tired, knew his time in the fields was limited. He was hoping to work at least one more day with the men but he knew also that might be up to his mother. Sometimes Ruth would take her two boys to town for a haircut, new shoes or some school clothes and the spring vacation was one of those times. Sometimes John would take them to town and then pick them up at the noon break from the fields.

John and Will drove the tractors back toward the old barn. The big house looked so inviting to Tar and he knew soon he would be in the comforts of home and Miriam would have a wonderful dinner for the family. The men talked amongst themselves as they tediously walked up the trail worn by the tractor tires. It had been a good day and they knew that John MacGregor would take care of them after the planting. They would have some needed cash to run their own small acreage. The brother's knew that there would be some onion sets left over this year and John customarily would give them what was left over. This would help them sustain their own farms and the profits from the onion harvest would help them throughout the year. Bubba was tired but seemed as if he too was satisfied that whatever income he would take in from the planting would go a long way to help him and his family make it through the upcoming year.

As the men got closer to the old barn Tar noticed the young girl was there again. Charlotte he thought is such a good southern name. He knew that Charlotte is the name of the main character in the book "Gone with the Wind" and that book is a renowned book of the south and the War Between the States. Tar's heart seemed to skip a beat and for some strange reason he was getting short of breath. He had walked the path to the barn plenty of times and new was short of breath before. Why today? Tar walked to the opposite side of where the young girl was standing and with little attention to the task at hand tried to help his father with the planter on his tractor.

The Boys from Hog Heaven

"Tar aren't you going to say hello to Miss Charlotte?" demanded Tar's dad trying to remind Tar that manners and southerners should be synonymous.

"Yes sir," said Tar pretending to do more work than he was actually accomplishing. "Hello Miss Charlotte."

"Hello Mr. Tar."

Tar's gaze never left the box of onion sets that he took off of the planter. His mind really wasn't on the sets or the planter and dropped the box. He watched the young plants scatter and with red face of embarrassment started picking up the plants and started putting them in another crate nearby.

Charlotte seeing the dilemma that her new friend was in came to the rescue and kneeled down beside her new friend Tar. "I'll help."

Tar didn't acknowledge but happy the young girl was there beside him. The others didn't seem to pay much attention to the events and let the young ones work together. Tar saw the freckles seemed to dance on her face and her adult teeth were coming in and filling the gap in the front of her mouth. Her pigtails were perfectly parted and the bits of ribbons on the ends seemed to highlight her sandy hair. He glanced over to look at her without her knowing just in time to see her look at him and he saw the light blue eyes that seemed to dance with excitement. She had looked at him too straight in the eyes. Quickly they two young people looked away.

"I'm going to have to walk Pa home." Said Charlotte trying to start and finish a conversation.

"Thanks for helping me." Said Tar "I'm glad you came over today."

"I'm glad I came over here too," answered Charlotte not looking in Tar's direction. "I'll be here tomorrow to walk with Pa. Will you be here?"

"I think so?"

"Bye, Tar."

"Bye Char."

Tar stood and watched the new friend and her father walk away toward the forest. He knew it wouldn't be long before they would be safely in their little house. He was glad the girl

35

Grant Williams

would be coming back tomorrow and hoped tomorrow wouldn't be the day he would have to go to town with his mother and his little brother.

The Boys from Hog Heaven

Chapter Five

The Last Day of Onion Planting

At dinner Ruth McGregor told her husband and Tar she would like to take the boys to town. She explained how they both would need haircuts and new shoes for the rest of the school year. With school starting up after the break there wouldn't be much time to get this done. Tar didn't want to have to leave the farm at least for tomorrow because he knew that Charlotte would be over to walk her daddy home from work. He knew he could not protest but John so proud of the work that his son was doing saved the day for his son.

"Ruth, we are just about finished planting the onion fields and I could use Tar at least another day. Maybe we could all go to town on Saturday. I could go with you too. Tomorrow will be busy and with Tar's help we should be finished at the end of the day. Saturday I'll have Will and the others come over and clean everything up."

"I guess we can wait another day. It would be very nice for you to come with us," answered Ruth. "I'll get the shoes and haircuts with the boys and you can get your business done at the farming store and maybe we can then get some ice cream or go to the movie show."

"Good ideal Ruth, will Betty be staying at the house with Grandpa?"

"Betty is going to her friend Louise's house in town. You know her, she is Dr.Handly's daughter."

"Miriam can leave some food for Grandpa unless he wants to go with us."

"I'm staying home," interrupted Grandpa. "I'm capable of taking care of myself."

"I didn't mean any harm," said Ruth in her finest southern voice. "I know you can take care of yourself."

37

Grant Williams

"Bring me some more nails for the crates, John," said grandpa rather gruffly and trying not to let everyone know he would be happy just to be at the farm by himself.

Tar and Carver both thought a movie would be so great. Most times there were westerns playing or sometimes there were mystery stories. They had been to the movies several times and got so exciting seeing heroes on the big screen. Tar and Carver knew their daddy a big fan of the motion pictures would enjoy the day. This would be great especially for Tar because he could also see his new friend Charlotte tomorrow.

Ruth happy too since it is an opportunity for her to socialize in the southern community. During the planting and harvesting times on the farm she didn't get to go out much and visit the townsfolk. She and John would go to the Christmas parties and the holiday dances. They would go to the town's celebration after the peach harvest and participate in the carnival, the pageants and the festival. Since she had lived on the farm only seldom she would have her own party or entertain the townsfolk. This practice would most likely change now that Betty was entering her last years of high school and would be going off to college. It would be time for Ruth to entertain the debutants and their young men before they would leave their southern homes to take on the world.

Miriam had heard the conversation and became happy to have some time off. She still had to wash the clothes for her and her brothers but after she would probably get one of them to take her into town. The brothers would like to go to town sometimes and once in a while would get hold of some corn liquor and have a few drinks with the city black folks. They would have to hide this from Miriam or hear her wrath of the fire and brimstone that would follow them. The fire and brimstone would most likely be better than the vocal beating by their beloved sister. It would be a rare trip since the family seldom ever went into the town of Carver.

Tar happy his daddy would have him stay at the farm today. It might be the last day he would see Charlotte for a while. He knew also after the planting his father would get the men together and give them all a pay envelope. This time he

38

The Boys from Hog Heaven

would get one too. Maybe he would have enough to get a gun so he could go hunting. Maybe he could get a gun to try and kill the pig. He knew it would be soon that his father would be taking him along on his hunts in the fall.

The day warmer than normal caused the tractors to stop a little more frequently for water. Tar getting concerned with all of the stops they wouldn't finish today or have to work into the early evening. In either case he got anxious that he might not get to see the girl.

"I'm going to town tomorrow," said Tar as the last few flats of onion sets were loaded onto the planter.

"What are ya'll going to do?" asked Junior. "We might go to town too."

"Daddy said we might go to the movie show. Did you ever go to the movie show?"

"One time a traveling preacher brought a movie show to the church. We can't go to the movie in Carver unless we sit in the balcony."

"Maybe it will be a western movie with all of the horses and outlaws?'

"Maybe it will be a love story," joked Junior.

"If it is I won't go," said Tar sounding a little perturbed and as if Junior was thinking that there was a romantic connection with him and Charlotte.

"Are you going to the store while you are in the town?"

"I want to look at a rifle so when we go hunting I can get that pig."

"Forget about that evil pig," said Junior very seriously. "That pig will cause you nothing but misery."

"I can use the gun to hunt deer too."

"Maybe but forget about that pig."

"What are you going to do?" asked Tar as they continued down the row.

"We'll take Miriam with us and we'll go to the store and maybe we'll meet up with some old friends. I might even look for a wife."

Tar never thought of the three brothers and Miriam being alone and none of them being married. The brothers were very

39

Grant Williams

eligible bachelors in the black community. They had a parcel of land, didn't drink much and went to church regularly. They were respected for their honesty and hard work.

"Why haven't you got married before?" asked Tar in his youthful innocence.

"Don't know," replied Junior. "Guess I never thought about it much."

"Don't you get lonely sometimes?"

"Never thought about it," said Junior as he looked off into the end of the field.

"I'm not going to get married either," said Tar. "There's too much to do without a woman around."

"What about your Ma and don't you think your daddy is a happy married man?"

"It is not for me. I've got too many things to do."

Junior started to ask the young man what he thought of the new girl but maybe it wasn't his place to ask, especially coming from him a local black sharecropper.

Will turned around on the tractor seat long enough to ask "What are you talking about?"

"I was asking Junior why he wasn't married?" laughed Tar.

"The truth is Tar that Junior just is too plain ugly."

Junior taken by surprise started stuttering and stammering. "I am not to ugly."

"Are you pretty?" asked Will.

"Well no but I'm not ugly. There are plenty of girls who would take me down the aisle."

"If you're not pretty then what are you, Junior?"

Will just laughed and Junior was getting angry. Tar laughed too. Junior just started putting the last of the plants in the ground with much more energy and didn't say another word.

"I'll show you when we go to town. I'll find me a girl," exclaimed Junior. "She'll want to marry me."

"Will she be ugly too?" Asked Will and laughed so hard he almost fell off of the tractor.

"You will see my dear brother. She will shine like a piece of fresh cut coal and smell like the magnolia trees in spring."

The Boys from Hog Heaven

"But will she be ugly?"

"You'll see my big brother."

The tractor nearing the last row and the last plants were being put into the ground. They finished on time. The plants now looked like soldiers lined up in even rows and marching on the red Georgia dirt. The men were proud of the accomplishment and glad the planting is finally over.

In a few minutes the two tractors and the men were heading back up the path to the old barn. Soon they would be heading back home and with a little cash in their pockets.

As they approached the barn Tar noticed that Charlotte wasn't there waiting for her daddy. A sudden emptiness filled his stomach. He had looked forward all day to seeing his new friend. Tar and the men were putting the extra crates of onion sets outside near the entrance of the barn. Tar tried to hide his disappointment that Charlotte wasn't there.

"Everything all right?" asked his father.

"Yes sir, just a little tired, I reckon," said Tar as he helped the others put the flats of the odiferous young plants outside.

"Will, Virgil, Junior, Bubba," said John as he beckoned the men together. "Here is your pay for the planting and each one will divide and take the extra sets home."

Each man received a closed envelope in which contained the cash for the work done. The onion sets would help provide some cash again at the harvest for the families. The men would wait until they were alone to open the envelopes.

Bubba turned to Will and asked. "Could you drop me off on your way home? I need to get my truck to cart these plants home."

"Sure Bubba," answered Will. "I think we could make room for the plants in the back of our truck."

Tar looked at the two men hoping that Bubba would return to pick up the plants.

"I need to get my truck anyways." said Bubba. "Just a ride would be fine."

The men loaded the sets for the brothers and with Bubba and Junior sitting on the bed of the old truck they headed off to

Grant Williams

their homes. It wouldn't be out of the way for Will to drop off Bubba since they were neighbors and only just a quarter mile away from each other. Tar watched the men leave and stayed for a while putting Bubba's plants neatly together near the door of the barn.

"Are you coming in?" asked John as he headed for the house.

"I'll come in soon. I think I'll wait for a while and help Bubba load the plants if he comes back."

"Don't wait too long. We'll have to clean up for dinner. You know how your mother feels if you are late."

"I won't stay long," said Tar as he continued putting the flats of onion sets together in a group.

As Tar watched his father go up into the big white house he heard the sound of a truck coming down the lane by the barn.

Tar wanted to see if Bubba came but most of all if Charlotte came with him. Tar wasn't disappointed and watched the old pickup truck approach him. It is Bubba and on his right is his daughter.

When the pickup pulled up to the barn Bubba got out and in his hand he had what looked like a pie covered with a cloth.

"My wife wanted me to give this to you' all for the plants and the work." said Bubba looking down at the ground and uncomfortable in the role of the social graces of giving a gift.

"My Mother and Father are at the house and I know they would appreciate the gift. I'll load up your pickup with the plants while you are gone."

"Charlotte you help old Tar while I'm gone," said Bubba as he took the covered dish toward the big white house.

After Bubba was half way to the house Charlotte said. "It's a sweet potato pie my Mama made and it is real good."

"I'm sure it is," said Tar, as he wouldn't look directly at the young girl. "I'll put these flats in your truck while your daddy is up at the house."

"I'll help," said Charlotte as she reached for a flat.

"No need to," said Tar as he took the flat from the young lady. His hand brushed hers and it felt cool and soft. He quickly moved his hand away and continued his task.

42

The Boys from Hog Heaven

"Will you be in school, next week," asked Tar as he put a flat of onions into the bed of the truck.

"Yes it will be my first day here. We were in school over in Jackson County until we moved just before the spring break. How is the school? Are the teachers okay? Are there a lot of children?" asked Charlotte non-stop.

"School is good, the teacher is good and there are a lot of kids our age."

"I'm glad you will be there. You are the only one from school that I met so far."

This statement encouraged Tar. He then asked the blue-eyed pigtailed girl. "Have you ever been down by the woods? I heard there is a big old pig in the trees."

"My daddy told me and my sister to stay away from there since we heard sounds in there at night."

"Maybe someday I can come over and we can walk around the outside of the trees."

"Maybe someday you can come over and meet my Mama and my sister Tara. Tara is in high school and won't be living home much longer."

"I have a sister in high school too. Betty is such a socialite. She is at all the dances and goes out a lot with the high school crowd."

"I guess the sisters won't see each other much being from the big farm and all I reckon your sister wouldn't have time for Tara."

Tar didn't really want to admit it but the statement was true. His family was a different status in the community.

"You'll still be my friend, won't you?" asked Tar trying to make up the differences of the two families.

"Mr. Tar, you will be my friend until you tell me to go away. I hope you will show me the town, the school and the farms."

Tar felt a lot better as he struggled through the social graces. He still tried not to look into Charlotte's eyes and when he spoke to her he would look down. He felt nervous and anxious inside. After running out of things to say and Charlotte staying close to him he hoped Bubba would soon come back but

Grant Williams

also somewhere inside he hoped it would be later rather than sooner.

"I like you, Tar. You are a nice boy. There were some boys at my old school that made fun of my clothes and me. They made fun of me because my family is poor."

"I won't let that happen here in Carver," said Tar chivalrously. "I'll see you at school on Monday."

"Here comes daddy" said Charlotte as she watched her father amble down the path to the truck.

Tar put the last flat of onion sets in the back of the pickup truck.

"Nice folks, Tar," said Bubba. "Thanks for putting the plants in the truck."

"Glad to do it. I hope you will come over sometime with your family." Said Tar in his trained southern manners.

"I hope so too, "said Charlotte too as she climbed into the old truck.

"See you at school, Charlotte."

"Bye, Tar." Said Charlotte as the truck started to leave down the path toward the trees.

Tar watched for a while until he couldn't see the pigtails bouncing in the wind that blew briskly through the window. He watched the dust from the old road finally obscure the vehicle as it turned behind the forest.

Tar happy but tired as he walked to the house, it had been a good day in the fields and all of the onion sets were planted. It looked as if it might rain within the next few days and that would give the plants a good start.

The talk at dinner that night was about the trip to town tomorrow. Ruth is happy that she could go into town with her family, Carver happy that all of the family could go excitedly talked about going to a movie show. John too in his own way is happy to take his family on an outing because he too is proud of his family. Grandpa is happy to be alone at the farm because sometimes he felt he was a burden to the family and had to be taken care of all of the time. Tar hungry and didn't talk much he still was thinking of the old pickup driving off to the little

The Boys from Hog Heaven

sharecropper house by the forest. He could still envision a little head with pigtails bouncing down the path.

Ruth served the sweet potato pie that Bubba's family had brought over for them. It is such a good pie and with each bite Tar thought about his new friend.

"That was a very nice gift from that family." said Ruth "Maybe when we get back from town, Tar, you can take the pie pan back to them and thank them."

Tar didn't want to seem too anxious but this was his opportunity to see Charlotte again. "Yes mother, I will if you wish."

"It would be a nice gesture since you know Bubba and his daughter."

"It would be proper. I'll take the dish over to them Sunday afternoon after church."

After dinner before the family excused themselves to the porch John had an announcement. "Tar this envelope is for you. You worked side by side with the other men and this is your share."

The family all looked at Tar and realized this was validation of his growing up. It now is a time when he felt like a young man and not a boy. Ruth even though she didn't like her boys working with the hired hands was proud of her son. Grandpa didn't say anything but he too looked at this event with pride. Carver now looked at his brother in a new light and saw he is growing up into a young man.

Tar didn't open the envelope in front of the family but thanked his father before leaving the table. He would wait until he went to his room to look at the money. Maybe he would have enough to look at a rifle to hunt with his father and Grandpa. Maybe he could buy the gun to hunt the big pig. He knew his daddy could convince his mother of the necessity of a young man carrying a gun. It was part of growing up in the south and particularly in this part of Georgia.

As the family went out to the porch to enjoy the evening Tar went up to his room alone and opened the envelope. He surprised but pleased that his father had given him a full share. He lied on his old iron bed and looked up at the white ceiling.

45

Grant Williams

Maybe he could look a new rifle while they were in town tomorrow. Maybe his daddy would help him find the right gun. But as the thoughts of the money, the rifle and the trip into town rolled around in his young mind he then thought of the girl with the blue eyes and the little pigtails. Sunday he would have an excuse to see her again. It is good to live there with the red dirt of Georgia and a wonderful place to grow up.

The Boys from Hog Heaven

Chapter Six

Trip to Town

Everyone was up early at the McGregor house. John had already gone out to the fields to see the rows of onions. Ruth arose early to dress for her trip to town for it is known that any southern girl must always look their best while in public. Betty up early too preparing for her friends from town who would pick her up in the morning also at the farm. Carver excited and didn't have to be coaxed to get up and get ready. Tar too up early and had gone out to meet his father in the fields.

John standing at the end of the rows in the ten-acre field looking down toward the other end as if in anticipation of the onions growing right in front of him.

"The rows look good," said Tar as he walked to his father's side.

"Need rain son," said John as he looked toward the sky. "Forecast is that we should have rain within a few days. We need it soon."

"Do you think we'll have a good crop this year?" asked Tar.

"If it rains, we don't get floods or weeds we should have a very good crop. The plants this year were very healthy and should bear some good Georgia onions. Those Yankees sure like our onions and so do those city folks from Atlanta."

Tar thought that Yankees were foreigners that were bold, brash and with few manners but liked to do business with the southerners. He couldn't recall if he had ever met a Yankee in the flesh.

"We better get up to the house. I know your mother, sister and brother will be up today and Miriam won't have the patience with everyone up so early. We better get ready to get to town too."

"Daddy, can I look at a rifle when we get to town today?"

47

Grant Williams

"You know your mother won't approve. She thinks you are just a boy. Maybe we can look at one when we go to the farm store. I know a good place to find one but I'll have to tell your Mama something or not tell her at all. If we find one you let me handle her."

Tar looked admiringly at his father the southern gentleman and farmer. He knew his daddy was proud of him and would see fit if he could get a gun. John proudly knew Tar had done a lot of work in the planting.

The two walked together up toward the big house with John's strong hand on the shoulder of his now young man, always such a good feeling for both.

Miriam had breakfast ready for the family. The biscuits were hot from the oven when John and Tar walked into the house. Today there would be some ham and eggs with plenty of grits on the side. The biscuits would melt the sweet butter and leave room for plenty of peach jam. Miriam wanted everything to go well for today so she could also go to town with her brothers and the sooner the family was fed and on their way the sooner she could leave too.

"It should be warm today," said Ruth. "I don't think that you boys will need a jacket."

Ruth dressed in a very nice long light blue cotton dress that accented her beautiful figure. She would wear a hat, a staple of southern culture for the women of that time. Her makeup always just enough but not too much and put on precisely and yet delicately. John always looks proud when he watches the way his wonderful wife carries herself in the company of the southern families. He is glad to take her to town where he could show off her beauty and her class.

Carver looked the part of a southern gentleman even at the early age of ten. He didn't look like Tar and didn't look like a southern farmer. Even at this early age he looked as if he was going to be a doctor or professional man as his mother predicted and groomed him toward. But even though he was different than Tar he did understand he is Tar's brother and so glad of that fact.

The Boys from Hog Heaven

Tar is Tar as some of the families' closest friends put it in their conversations. Tar is a gentleman even at the age of twelve but also loved the land, the people and loved the fact he lived there in Georgia. Tar even though a popular child in school and is a leader amongst the other students. Tar did get good grades but always more interested in the history of the area and in the people of the county. Usually what ever Tar said to the other students would stand and many arguments were avoided by doing this. The girls liked Tar because he came from a good upstanding family, he was a good-looking lad and he is such a leader amongst them. Tar had not really paid much attention to the girls in his school since to him they were too frivolous and fickle.

Today they would take the big sedan into town. John had bought the car only a year ago and it wasn't used too much. The war is now over and the car builders are building big cars. The harvests were good and John felt it was time to drive his family around in a classy sedan. The Buick so clean and the black paint sparkled in the morning sun and there is no sign of any Georgia red dirt on the car that morning.

After breakfast the boys went out to the car with their father while Ruth had some final instructions for Betty and had time to fix her makeup for the last time.

As their mother came out to the car Tar held the front door open for her. She looked so elegant as she slipped into the front seat beside her husband. After Tar and Carver got into their places in the back seat John guided the big sedan down the road toward town with a boost of power.

The dogwood trees had just opened their blossoms and the whites looked so bright around their brown eyes. Some of the spring flowers had come up and were showing their bright colored heads along the road. The big car wound down the road at a comfortable speed enabling the family to view the countryside but it wasn't long before they passed the few little houses of their sharecropper friends. Will standing by his truck as they passed his house waved as John honked the powerful horn on the Buick. They all waved at their friend and neighbor and then they saw the next little house coming into view.

Grant Williams

"That is Bubba's place," declared John as they approached.

"I wish I would have remembered to bring the pie pan," said Ruth.

Tar glad she didn't because it would give him a chance to go over and see Charlotte maybe tomorrow. The pie pan could be the best excuse for the moment. As the MacGregor car approached the little farm, Tar's eyes were glued to the view out of his window hoping to see Charlotte. Bubba's little house needed repair and the little porch even though it looked comfortable had a few shingles missing from the attached roof. Tar could see that behind the house there was a garden patch and a larger field. He could see two people working in the field. It is Bubba and it is Charlotte bending over and putting the onion sets into the ground. Tar now so happy his daddy had given them some of the extra plants for he knew it is difficult for the small farms to make a living without the help of the large farms. John also saw the father and daughter working in the field and honked his horn. Charlotte and her Daddy looked up as the car passed by and they both waved. Tar waved and hoped that Charlotte would see him. Tar continued to look back at the little farm at the figures of the father and daughter standing there in the red Georgia dirt. He watched out his window until they disappeared into the landscape. He then smiled to himself knowing it would be a good day.

The town of Carver wasn't very big and had quite a history during the War Between the States. Most of the town was spared since the Yankees only held it for a short time and until the boys in blue left for Atlanta. The town consisted of streets forming a square with a beautiful park in the center and the center is a place where the old courthouse once stood so proudly. Now the more modern courthouse and city building stood by itself on the street leading toward Atlanta. The town square still had many of the old buildings built in the cotton heydays prior to the war. Some of the original families still owned some of those structures and took pride in the southern tradition. There is the department store that carried many of the things desired by the southern women of the community; there is

50

The Boys from Hog Heaven

a five and dime store serving some sandwiches and ice cream, there is a bank that had been there around a hundred years. There are several other small stores and a doctor's office and there is a buyer's office for the crops that were sent out of town such as the onions and peaches. The side streets had the normal businesses such as the farm store, the car dealer and a local tavern.

Tar had never been on the street behind the old baseball park since it is the place where most of the black people would congregate. It too had a general store where the customers could buy anything from flour to liquor. It is a place where the black women could buy their beautiful hats they would wear proudly to their church on Sunday. The black men who were mostly sharecroppers and small farmers would congregate at the back of the store and drink some corn liquor made by local people away from the sight of the law. Tar had heard a lot of stories of the arguments and the frequent stabbings of jealous men trying to just be macho. He had heard of the dice games and the gambling. He also had heard of the prostitution that is overlooked by the local authorities but he was taught to never talk about that part of town since it didn't concern him. He knew this is where Will and his brothers would be tonight and Miriam would be visiting her friends in the store and going to the church singing.

John entered Carver with his family in the big Buick and of course is recognized right away. Many of the local citizens knew John and Ruth McGregor were very prominent people and were responsible for much of the onion and peach crops in the area. They knew it is important to invite the McGregors to the parties, dances and weddings.

"Ruth, I'll drop you off at the Department store with Carver. Tar and I will be at the farm store for a while. We'll meet you at the store in an hour," said John as he pulled the big car up to the front of the store.

"Thank you John, I'll find some shoes and maybe some clothes for Carver but I'll need Tar back here soon so he can try on some new shoes."

"We'll be back soon."

Grant Williams

Carver had jumped out of the car and had opened the door for his mother. Carver knew someday he would go with his father but now it is all right to be the guardian for his mother as his daddy and brother went on to the farm store.

It is so obvious Ruth McGregor was highly though of in the community because when the storeowner seeing the McGregor car come up to the door came out to greet his favored customer and held the door open for her as she walked proudly into his establishment. John smiled at the attention his bride received and knew he could stay as long as he wanted at the farm store with the other farmers. He knew Ruth would get a lot of attention and would be able to shop at her own speed without having to drag her loving husband around as she perused the dresses and other women's items.

After Ruth disappeared behind the doors of the department store John and his son went directly to the farm store. John knew he had better not forget the nails for grandpa and then he could visit with the other local farmers and friends. It is a coming out for Tar because in the past years Tar knew he would be walking down the aisles of the department store with his mother but today he knew he would be treated like a man.

Tar followed his daddy into the farm store and it had everything a Georgia farmer would need. There were even some items that were rumored to be in the store right after the War Between the States. Tar walked a few steps behind John as they came upon a couple of neighboring farmer.

"Hey, John who is that following you?" called out the heavyset man in the straw hat.

"Ephraim, this is my son Tarleton. We call him Tar," said John proudly. "Tar worked a lot on the tractor and with the planting   this   year."

"Do tell, I didn't think you had a young'un old enough to help out," said the man John called Ephraim as he filled his mouth with some Red Man chewing tobacco.

"How are things going over at your place? Have you got all of your onion sets in the ground yet?"

The Boys from Hog Heaven

"Another few days I'll be finished if it doesn't rain. I lost my blackie for a while. He's at the county for stabbing a man last week. I think I have found some other help."

"I know a couple of men if you need someone. Let me know by Monday and I'll see what I can do."

"You might just do that, John, you got to get those sets in the ground before it rains." Then the man turned to Tar. "How do you like working in the fields?"

"It is just fine sir," answered Tar directly and politely.

"What are you going to do with all of your money?" asked the man.

John interrupted the conversation knowing the man might be making fun of his son, "Tar needs to buy a rifle to hunt with us this fall. You don't know where he can find one."

The old man tipped his straw hat back on his balding head and scratched his chin as a sign he was thinking. "You know there is a real nice gun that Jim keeps under the counter. It is a special gun and he would only sell it if it went into the right hands."

"What kind is it?" asked John.

"I think it is a 30/30. It looked like a good deer rifle."

"Maybe we'll take a look at it before we leave. I've got to get some things for grandpa McGregor before I forget. Don't forget if you need help to call me I know I can find you a couple of good men."

"I might just do that," replied Ephraim as he walked to the door and spat some tobacco juice onto the street.

Tar wanted to ask his daddy if they could look at the rife but didn't want to seem impatient but he knew sooner or later that his father would get to it. As John talked with the Jim the manager and weighed some nails for grandpa, Tar walked around the store. There is about anything any of the local farmers could ask for. Tar walked back to the counter where his daddy was still talking with the manager. The talk didn't interest Tar but seemed to be of importance to his father. Next to the counter stood an old display case and in it were artifacts of the War Between the States. There were several old rebel hats, a pistol and rifle, a bayonet, a folded flag, a book, part of an old

Grant Williams

uniform and some uniform buttons. The map of the area included the McGregor farm, the wooded area and the surrounding area laid in the case

The pistol and the buttons were of particular attention to Tar since these items looked just like the one's he found near the ten acre field. The pistol is in better shape than the one that Tar had hidden but of the same make and shape. The buttons looked the same and Tar noticed on the button in the case there too were initials or letters scratched into the backs of them.

Jim the store manager looked over at Tar as he carefully looked over the artifacts and said. "Do you like those things that we found from the war? All of those things were found around Carver."

"Sir, what are the letters on the back of the buttons mean," asked Tar.

"Young man, some of the soldiers would carve their initials into the buttons for better identification in case they were killed or missing. Most of the men in the company around here would do this. Some of them would give a button to a favorite girl or their wife when they would leave for the war."

This fact of history really excited Tar and he knew there's some significance to the treasure he had found. He needed to investigate more about his find before he made the treasure known to his family but for the secret would have to stay with the twelve-year-old boy.

"Do you want to hold the pistol or the rifle?" asked Jim.

Tar looked at his father and asked. "Is it all right if I do?"

John Macgregor nodded to his son with approval and Jim took out the old rifle and handed it to Tar. Tar carefully pointed the rifle away from the two men and handed it back to the storekeeper.

"I heard that you have a real nice rifle that you might want to sell?" asked John rather offhandedly.

"You need a good gun, John?"

"I am looking for a good gun for Tar. I want to take him hunting with me this year."

"Need a deer rifle or are you going boar hunting?"

The Boys from Hog Heaven

"Deer rifle, I don't care to go pig hunting with the thoughts of that big one that is supposed to be in my woods."

"Always good to have some venison in the winter," said Jim as he reached far under the counter. "Been deer hunting before?" looking at Tar.

"No sir, not yet but my daddy said that I should go with him this year," said Tar as he wouldn't take his eyes off the store manager.

From under the depths of the counter Jim pulled out a gun case and laid it on the counter. He carefully unzipped the leather case and took out a clean rifle with a dark walnut stock. It was an impressive piece and Jim was proud of it too.

"What do you think?" asked Jim with a big smile plastered on his broad face.

"Nice gun," said John McGregor trying not to show any excitement knowing that any indication of it would cause the price of the gun to go up.

"What do you think, Tar?"

"It looks good, Mr. Jim," answered Tar also trying not to show the excitement he felt.

"I'd sell it for the right price," said Jim trying to get some kind of a read from the faces of the two persons in front of him.

"Maybe later on," said John.

Tar started thinking that his father wasn't interested in the rifle and started getting anxious. The boy in Tar coming out now but still he didn't want to show his disappointment to his father who had bragged about him now being a young man.

"You want to touch it again. Go ahead and pick it up," encouraged Jim as he looked at Tar. Tar put back the antique gun and with the deftness of a horse trader Tar said "No thanks, Mr. Jim. I think I'll look at the new magazines."

Tar walked away and he didn't hear what had transpired but John McGregor had the gun case under his arm and Jim was smiling too.

John and Tar walked to the car, opened the trunk and put their prized possession into the vast compartment.

"Tar, you don't go telling your mother about this. It is you gun and we'll keep it locked up in the big box in the barn

55

Grant Williams

until the right time comes and I can tell her that you are the owner of a really nice deer rifle."

"How much do I owe you?" asked Tar knowing he had money from the planting.

"You keep your money, help me cultivate the corn and onions and the gun will be yours. You have to remember to always be safe and only use it when it is right," said John looking so proudly at his son for it seemed as if it was only just yesterday when his dad had given him his first gun."

"I will daddy; I will work and help you. Thank you for trusting me and getting the gun for me."

"It's okay and it was fun just negotiation with Jim. He's happy and we are happy so it was a good deal."

Father and son went back into the store, picked up the nails and other supplies. The two then loaded the items into the trunk trying to obscure the gun in case Ruth happened to look in. They felt good and now could meet up with Ruth at the store. They knew that she is no stranger to finding a way to buy new clothes and shoes for she after all is a southern lady.

It is not one of life's greatest pleasures for John McGregor to shop at the department store. Those duties were always left up to Ruth and his daughter Betty. Today would be different because Ruth would have most everything done and the time in the store wouldn't take so long since Carver would already be fitted with his new shoes and new clothes. Ruth had picked out some clothes for Tar and some shoes for him to try on. Ruth always had something for John too but today it was just some work shirts and a couple of pairs of socks. This is good news for Tar too since he wouldn't have to stay in the store much longer either.

The shoes were tried on the bought all of the accounts were settled up with the proprietor and the packages were brought out to the big grand Buick.

"I'll put those packages in the truck, dear," said John as he and Tar carried the items out of the store. "Carver please open the door for your mother."

Ruth always proud of her sons and pleased Carver is becoming a proper southern gentleman and pleased John and

The Boys from Hog Heaven

Tar were taking care of the packages. It is still some time before the movie theater would open and it is a good time to eat some lunch. John knew Ruth just adored the little tearoom next to the bank building. Being a little feminine the tearoom is not always comfortable for John but today the four would dine there.

The tearoom is quite a quaint little place where it serves small sandwiches and special soups. Today there weren't any black-eyed peas or country ham but a refined menu that would tickle the pallets of any southern lady. Today the men would tolerate the small cucumber sandwiches and watercress salads. They would drink their tea and watch the happiness of the matriarch of the family. Today is a special day for all of the MacGregors.

The white linen tablecloths and white cloth napkins were very nice and the service impeccable. The family treated as royalty and as if they were not in that little town in Georgia. The boys remembered their manners and made their mother very proud.

The time for the movies came and the boys didn't want to bring up the subject but they were getting anxious to go and anxious to leave the little tearoom. John broke the ice.

"I bet we can make the matinee at the movie house if we leave soon. I heard there was a pretty good movie playing. It is called the "Song of the South". Maybe it is about us," l aughed John.

"I think we are through here, John," said Ruth. "We wouldn't want to miss the cartoon."

Tar thought 'what no western' and Carver is just happy to go and see the big screen.

The short drive to the theater took little time and there were plenty of places to park. The show is starting in twenty minutes and there would be no problem getting into the building and finding good seating. John bought each boy a big bag of popcorn knowing the little finger sandwiches they had for lunch didn't fill their growing stomachs. The theater wasn't very hot as it could be at time and the three ceiling fans were whirling around and in each revolution made squeaking sound. The seats were covered in a maroon velveteen type material and matched

Grant Williams

the large ropes that hung across the entrance to the aisle ways. The three male members of the McGregor family made sure that their mother had a good seat with the best vision. Tar sat on one side of his mother and Carver sat on the other and between the parents.

Tar noticed in the theater balcony there were others sitting but they were all black folks. He knew at that time in Georgia that there were differences but had learned to respect all people. He had just worked hand in hand with Will and his brothers and he saw Miriam everyday and considered her a member of the family. This discrimination in the theater bothered Tar but he knew better than to bring it up. He knew his father and mother treated all people well but still had the training of the differences in their blood. Tar knew it is not wise to turn and look up into the balcony for this might upset his mother but he wondered if Will, Miriam, Virgil or Junior were up there.

Tar's thoughts also wandered and he thought of Charlotte. He thought someday he could bring her to the movies and they could see a good western movie. He wondered if Charlotte ever went to town and if she had ever been to a movie before. He thought of the pie pan and if his mother would still let him take it over to her tomorrow. As he thought of her and her little pigtails the sound of the movie came on and the lights started to dim.

The cartoon was funny and even Ruth had to laugh out loud as the hunter chased the crazy rabbit. There was a little delay between the cartoon and the feature but just enough time to play the upcoming events and movies that would soon be at the theater. There is going to be a western coming soon. Tar now hoping he and his little brother might be able to go but they would have to wait and see. Today would not be the time to ask.

The movie came on the silver screen and the wonderful music filled the little theater. As the movie went on Tar recognized the characters because "Uncle Remus" was a book that Miriam had read to him when he was just a little boy. The part about the Tar Baby made the entire MacGregor family laugh because that was how Tar had gotten his nickname. The

58

The Boys from Hog Heaven

movie compelling had a lot of how it is in the south and how it still is now. As John and Ruth didn't see some of the indiscretions Tar and even Carver did and knew they should not talk about them with their parents. The movie was very entertaining and Ruth knew her lads would be singing "Zippidy Do Da, Zippidy A, my o my what a wonderful day" for a long time back at the farm.

The trip back to the farm that afternoon became such a nice drive. The sun just started going down in the west with its bright oranges and purples lighting the sky. Carver had fallen asleep on the seat next to Tar and as the big black Buick steadily moved down the road toward the farm each one of the family was contented and happy to be their in their part of the world. Tar just glanced out of the window as the car passed Bubba's little home. He could see a light in the window but no one moving about on the outside of the small abode. They passed Will's place and there was no activity. Tar just imagined Miriam singing with her church group and the men were there on the back street of town talking loud and having a little corn liquor.

Soon Tar knew he would again be safe in his bed and could dream of the fine rifle that his daddy had bought for him. He would dream of the fine movie and how much his family and he had enjoyed the show but most of all he would dream of little pigtails and blue eyes knowing that tomorrow he would see Charlotte again. As the quiet Georgia night approached Tar knew he was where he should be, right there in the red dirt of western Georgia.

Chapter Seven

The Treasure

As a habit Tar up early knew he would have to get ready for church after breakfast. He dressed quickly, ran outside in a matter minutes and met his father who just came out of the barn.

"Morning Tar, I see you are up early."

"I wanted to look at the onion fields before we went to church," said Tar lamely looking for the right thing to say.

"You want to look at the new rifle?"

Tar's pulse quickened because it really is what he wanted to see.

John continued, "I put it in the lock box in the barn. I haven't told your mother about it but I will in good time. Let's take a look, okay?"

Of course it is okay as Tar raced ahead of his father to the big wooden lock box on the wall of the barn and waited. John took out a key ring, carefully found the right key and turned it in the old lock. As the door opened he saw the gun case with the fine leather shining in the morning sun.

"Take it out Tar. It is your gun or will be your gun."

"Can I daddy," said Tar as he looked into his father's approving eyes.

"Yes son, you can take it out."

Tar carefully opened the shiny leather case and felt the supple leather. The case felt good in his hand and felt expensive. Being hand tooled showed the case had a great deal of care put into the fabrication. Nestled in the case he saw the rifle with the barrel clean and the wood on the stock so shiny from being polished with a good grade of polish.

John watched his son carefully take out the fine deer rifle and point it out of the doorway and away from them.

The Boys from Hog Heaven

"Be sure to always put the safety on when you are not using it," said John as he showed his son how to lock the gun. "Too many unloaded guns have killed people."

"What?"

"Don't ever assume the gun is empty. Too many people have assumed and got shot. Here, I'll show you how to load and unload the gun," beckoned John as he asked for the gun.

After doing what his father had told him, Tar became a master of loading and unloading the gun.

"Maybe next week we can take the gun out and do some target shooting. First of all I will have to explain it all to your mother. For now don't tell her and leave it up to me. She knows I intended on getting you a gun soon but a mother will always have some worry no matter how old you are or how mature."

"Thanks Daddy, I will take care of the rifle and I will use it safely," said Tar as he put the gun back into the leather case and secured the safety.

John locked the door of the big wooden box and put the key back in his pocket. But Tar also knew of another key hanging on a nail on the back of a two by four near the front door. Tar had seen grandpa get the key and open the box before but had never told anyone about the extra key. Now would not be the time to tell his father he knew where the other key was hidden.

"We better get back up to the house and get ready for church. Your mother will cook breakfast this morning since Miriam had the day off. We don't want to be late."

When the two got back to the house Ruth happily making breakfast for her family had arose early to make sure her family would eat a good meal before church. Ruth a good cook but only cooked once a week on Miriam's day off. There would be no biscuits this morning but Ruth loved making pancakes.

The family always enjoyed Ruth's cooking and even volunteered to do the dishes and clear the table while their mother got ready for church. Carver excused himself right after he cleared the table to get ready for church. It wasn't long before the whole family with their neatly combed hair and Sunday clothes headed out the door.

Grant Williams

Grandpa too always got ready for Church early especially now since church is his social life now since he rarely goes into town. His age starting now to slow him down didn't seem to change his opinions about most everything. After all his family had been going to the same church ever since it was built before the War Between the States and feels his opinion in the church is paramount. Grandpa has seen many weddings and funerals transpire behind the doors of the old white building. He also has seen many preachers come and go even though he liked some of the preachers and with some he disagreed. But ultimately he saw them all and they all knew him well especially since Grandpa wasn't bashful about letting them know his opinion. He liked the preacher they had now and remarked how this preacher is a good old southern boy. He also said this is the preacher who will bury him.

The church service interesting as the preacher talked a lot about how to treat your fellow man. Most of the congregation dressed in their finery nodded approvingly many times during the service including a few Amen's from the men of the church. Tar wondered if Miriam and her brothers listened to the same kind of sermon at their church since there are no black people here and most likely no white people at Miriam's church.

Leaving the church is also an event it is where the preacher of course would greet the families. The families of the community would meet and greet after speaking with the preacher. Tar's sister Betty who had come with the family of her friend did sit with the MacGregors because it was the proper thing to do for a southern family. It is so important for many of the women to meet after the service and Ruth always became the center of activity because of her popularity in the community. The other women always wanted to be associated with Ruth McGregor. John always cordial to the other families he would see after church but would much rather be sitting on a tractor or on his own front porch. Grandpa always a person of importance and a fixture at the white church enjoyed the fuss over him and his tenure there. The younger children sometimes would run about and the girls would always try to chase Tar but Tar would much rather be at home too.

The Boys from Hog Heaven

Tar hoping the social visits wouldn't last too long so he could take the pie pan back to Bubba's family this afternoon as he promised his mother. He most likely would see Charlotte at least for a while even though her parents would be there. But Tar knew too that he would never interrupt the activities after the church service for to some it is a matter of posturing in the community and to others it is the pecking order of the town. Tar wondered if Charlotte went to church and where she went to church when she lived in Jackson County. Tar's mother taught him it is important to go to church and to live up to the standards of the other southern families. He knew it is very important and it should be important to Bubba's family too.

Finally the family left the neatly landscaped white church but they could still hear the sounds of the church bells in the distance as they drove their shiny black Buick back toward the farm. Ruth now smiling for this part of her culture and part of showing off her family to her is so important. Soon they would be home and Miriam would be there too. Miriam would leave her church and come directly to the McGregor household because Sunday dinner is always an important ritual in that part of the South. It is traditional on most Sundays it would be fried chicken, mashed potatoes and southern white gravy, corn or string beans with some of Miriam's famous biscuits or homemade bread. The family would dine and usually spend the day on the porch where John read the Atlanta Sunday newspaper and looked out over his fields, Grandpa usually took a nap, Betty would usually find a telephone and talk to her friends from town, Carver and Tar would either play or lay on the front porch in their play clothes and read comics and Ruth would either knit or sew and watch over her brood with pride.

Today Tar knew it would be different for him for he put on his best play clothes and combed his normally unruly hair. It is obvious that his sudden need for good grooming had an ulterior motive but Ruth didn't mention that sensitive issue to her son.

"Do you have plans this afternoon?" asked Ruth as she looked over her now growing up son.

Grant Williams

"You told me I should take the pie pan back to Bubba today," said Tar trying his best to look nonchalant.

"I sure did," answered Ruth. "That was a very wonderful pie and a very fine gesture. You tell them how much we appreciated the gift. Walk on the road and don't go through the woods and be back before supper."

John looked over at his son and his wife and interjected, "Tar's a big boy now." followed by the comment. "Listen to your mother, Tar."

"I will come right back and I'll be home before supper. I will thank them for the pie. It was good," said Tar anxiously trying to get going.

"The pie pan and the cloth are in the kitchen, and you mind your manners and be home before supper," said Ruth looking proudly at her son as he went back into the house.

In an instant Tar had retrieved the pan and the cloth. He looked at his image in the glass door panel as he left the house and smoothed down his hair again. Then down the old road he went with nothing but the thought of seeing Charlotte on his mind.

The road is about a mile to Bubba's house but the distance could be cut in half if he would take a short cut through the forest. He thought then decided not today because he had promised his mother to take the road and didn't want to disappoint her by disobeying her. The afternoon sun getting higher and now warmer, which made the trip seem longer than a mile and whether it is from the heat or just the anticipation of seeing the girl it just seemed longer. Tar finally saw the little house in the distance and his heart started to race a little with each step toward the dwelling. Tar took out his clean handkerchief and wiped the sweat from his young brow. He thought maybe they are not there or Charlotte won't be able to see him. Many other thoughts crossed his mind as each step he got closer to the little house. As the house came clearer into Tar's view he noticed some activity on the porch where it looked as if the whole family is sitting on the front deck. Tar could see Bubba's big frame sitting in an old chair and he could see some other people there too. As he got closer he could see the outlines

64

The Boys from Hog Heaven

of the three other persons. Next to Bubba is an older woman who must be Charlotte's mother and the two sitting on the steps must be Charlotte and her sister Tara.

The old mongrel hound dog spotted Tar first and started barking. Bubba looked up and saw the figure of a young man walking down the road and announced to his family that someone is coming. Charlotte immediately noticed Tar and ran to meet him.

"Hi, Tar. Did you come over to see my Pa?" asked Charlotte.

"I really came over to give your mother back the pie pan and cloth that she had sent over," said Tar not indicating that he actually is happy to see his friend.

"She is on the porch. Come on and I'll introduce you to her and my sister Tara. You already know my Daddy."

Tar walked with Charlotte to the front of the little house.

"Hello Tar," said Bubba as he threw a stick for the old dog to fetch.

"Tar, this is my mother and this is my sister Tara," said Charlotte as she introduced them.

"Pleasure to make your acquaintance," said Tar in his most grownup voice. "My family enjoyed the pie you sent over and my mother wanted me to especially thank you for your kindness. It was a real good pie."

"Thank you Tar," replied Charlotte's mother happy the well to do family in the big white house enjoyed the simple cooking. "We wanted to thank you and your family for the onion sets. They will help us tremendously at harvest."

Tar looked over a Tara and saw as a teenager she had bumps and curves. He tried not to look at the pulchritude of the young lady but he being a young man started to notice such things. She didn't have any makeup on like his sister Betty did most times but the freshness of the skin and lips didn't seem to warrant any. Her hair too put into pigtails and when the sisters stood together they were unmistakably sisters without any doubt. Tara didn't have any thoughts about being with such a youngster and excused herself. As she got up and stretched Tar

65

Grant Williams

felt his manhood challenged but for a moment until he heard Charlotte's voice.

"Ma, can I show Tar where we planted the onion sets?" said Charlotte.

"You young'uns go play and yes, Charlotte you show Tar where we planted those sets," answered her mother as she took the pie pan and cloth into the little house.

"Come on Tar," said Charlotte. "It is out back."

"See you later Tar," said Bubba as he too went into the house. "Tell your folks we are much obliged for the plants and one of these days Ma will make another pie for Ya'all"

The two walked out into the backyard. Tar noticed right away how different it is here than on his big farm. He noticed how all of the land is so important to the family. The clothesline moved gracefully in the wind even without any clothes hanging on it. The little shed housing the small amount of hand tools for the farming was between the field and the house. In the filed behind the house he saw an old model A Ford pickup truck without any wheels facing the house.

"We can sit up here," said Charlotte pointing to the back of the pickup that overlooked the field. "I got some old boxes and put some old cloth over the tops up here in the back of the old truck. It is my special place to just sit and think sometimes."

"Okay, I can stay a little while," said Tar happy for the invitation.

"Here Tar, you sit on this box. It is bigger and for the men," said Charlotte pointing to the large peach crate that sat turned upside down.

He though about what Charlotte just said, 'for the men' and knew she meant him. He sat proudly there with her.

"Sometimes I come out here all by my self and look over the land. I think of coming here from Jackson County and how happy I am here."

Tar looked over at Charlotte as she spoke and watched her blue eyes sparkle when she talked about the land and about her family. Her little blond pigtails bounced with excitement sometimes when she talked. She just wasn't like the other girls he knew from school or church. She is definitely different.

The Boys from Hog Heaven

"I saw you and your daddy in the field the other day as we passed by in out car on the way to town."

"We were planting the onion sets that you gave us."

Tar then proceeded to tell her of the gun. He told her of the adventures he expected when he could hunt later on that year and how he would get some meat on the hunt with the grownups. He told her that someday he would kill the big pig that lived in the woods. He then told her about the movies and the excitement on the big silver screen. Her eyes watched every syllable that came out of Tar's mouth. She could feel the excitement from his words.

"I would like to go to the movies someday," said Charlotte. "We don't have much money for those things my Mama said."

"Maybe someday I'll take you," said Tar not thinking of a date or committing to a time. He wasn't even thinking of a boy-girl thing. He just wanted to show her how exciting the movie could be.

"Will you. Tar," said Charlotte as she hugged arm gently.

Tar now feeling so grownup and so good inside answered. "Yes someday."

"What about the hunting? Is there really a big pig in the woods? My Daddy said that he has heard sounds and Junior told him that he should stay away because it probably was the wild pig. My Daddy won't let my sister or I go into the woods. I think he is in fear the pig will take us."

"I'll get that pig, Charlotte, so you won't be afraid anymore. You'll see. When I go on the hunt I will get the pig."

They stopped talking as a crow flew over the field and into the wooded area. They both most likely were thinking of the bird and the pig together either as friends or as dinner.

"Can you keep a secret?" said Tar as he looked at his new friend.

"I don't know. What is it?"

"It is nothing bad but we can't tell anyone just yet. Can you keep a secret?"

"If it's not bad I guess I can."

Grant Williams

"Will you spit in your hand and shake mine after I spit in it to keep the secret."

"I won't tell," said Charlotte as she spit in her little hand and extended it to Tar.

They shook hands. The deal is done.

"The other day when I was driving the tractor I uncovered some things that I haven't yet told anyone about. I dug up several things in the ten acre field and left them by one of the fence posts."

" Well what were they?" asked Charlotte excitedly as he interrupted her friend.

"I'm getting to that" said Tar who now a little perturbed by Charlotte's anxiety.

"When I ran the tractor a little close to the fence I saw that the disc uncovered something shiny. So I got down from the tractor and there they were."

"What was there?" asked Charlotte excitedly.

Tar in a quiet secretive voice went on, "I found an old pistol, an old box and some buttons with initials carved on the back."

"Were they new?"

"When I went to the farm store Saturday I saw some of the things that Jim the storekeeper had kept in a glass case from the War Between the States. The gun was the same and there were buttons too."

"Did the buttons have initials on the back?"

"They had initials on the back too. Jim said that the soldiers would carve initials on the back for identification if they were killed and some sent a button to their girl friend or their wives as a reminder of their devotion."

"Are you going to tell anyone about your find?"

"Not yet but I thought I would go and get the goods after school tomorrow. Would you like to go with me? Do you think your Daddy will let you come over?"

"We can meet after school by corner of the forest. I can't go in the woods but I can meet you on the road. My Mama will have some chores for me first but I can meet you at four thirty."

"Don't tell anyone, remember your promise."

The Boys from Hog Heaven

"I won't tell anyone. I swore an oath. We shook hands."

"Okay but we need to keep this quiet until we find out what is in the box."

Charlotte looked over a Tar and knew she had trust in him. She now seemed very happy as they sat on the boxes in the back of the old pickup. It didn't matter to her that Tar lived over at the big white house. As they looked across the fields of onions they were equal and they were friends.

***

That night while the two brothers lay in their beds Tar explained what he had found to his little brother and made him promise not to tell anyone. Tar told Carver tomorrow he and Charlotte would go to the ten-acre field and get the treasure. They would bring the treasure to the farm and keep it a secret until they found out more about the find. Carver spit on his hand and shook his brother's hand and promised he wouldn't tell anyone. Carver seemed so happy his brother included him in this adventure.

***

School not something that Tar is always excited about but he enjoyed the teachers and the other students and not always did he enjoy sitting in a classroom when the weather outside was warm and inviting. Today it would be different.

Carver always got up early on a school day and today Tar got up early also. The two brothers came down to the breakfast table together. Betty got up early and had fastidiously put on her makeup and combed her hair.

"Do I have to ride to school with the boys?" asked Betty knowing her father would make them all ride in the same vehicle.

"Of course you will, but I'll drop them off first at their school before we go to the high school," answered John McGregor.

"Would you drop me off at my friend Darla's? We can walk to school from there," asked Betty hoping that she wouldn't have to be driven to school by her parents.

69

Grant Williams

"We'll see," answered John. "Let's eat breakfast first."

"Miriam" said Betty. "I'll just have some toast and coffee."

Miriam looked over at the teenage girl disapprovingly but answered "Yes Miss Betty."

John looked at Miriam and then at Betty and said. "You should have a better breakfast than that. Miriam makes such good food."

"I've got to watch my figure. I want to look good for the upcoming prom."

Ruth and John didn't answer but returned to their own breakfast.

"Are you glad to get back to school?" asked John looking over at Tar.

"Yes sir, It isn't so bad," answered Tar.

"Better than working in the fields?"

"Working in the fields is all right but school is all right too," answered Tar trying to please both mother and father.

"How about you Carver?" asked John.

"We are going to study about state of Georgia and the multiplication tables. I think it will be an interesting week," answered Carver.

School is like a profession to Carver even at this early age. His parents were always proud of his interest in school work proved out by the grades he brought home on his report card. School to Tar had been a necessity and even though he did all right he didn't have the zest for it like his brother. Today it became an exception as he looked forward to getting to school and seeing his new friend Charlotte. Today should be different for Tar.

As promised John dropped off the boys at the local Carver elementary school and Jr. High school.

When the boys walked into the school Carver looked at his big brother and said, "Are we going to go look at the treasure after school?"

"Yeah, but don't tell anyone even your friends. Okay?"

"I won't Tar, I promised."

"Run along Carver, don't be late for class."

70

The Boys from Hog Heaven

Some of Tar's school friends when they saw Tar come into school quickly gravitated to him. He being a leader amongst them became important and it became important in the class order to be Tar's friend.

"Hey Tar, how was your spring break?" said his old friend Mason.

"I worked on the farm. Helped plant our onions and had to drive the tractor for my daddy."

Driving anything was a point of passage to manhood and Tar knew it impressed his longtime classmate and friend.

"Wow, was it hard to drive?"

"Not really, but working in the fields doing anything isn't easy."

"I went to Atlanta with my family," said Mason that seemed not so impressive since his longtime friend had actually drove a tractor and worked with the men.

"Oh, did you have fun?"

"It was okay. We got to see a lot of things."

About that time the new girl walked into their view. Tar glad to see Charlotte had arrived and didn't mind that she wore less expensive clothes and shoes than the other children. It didn't matter to him that she a girl and from a poorer background than most of the students for she was his friend. Charlotte's pigtails bounced a little as she came closer.

"Hey, Charlotte."

"Hey, Tar."

"Mason this is my friend Charlotte, Charlotte this is my old friend Mason"

"Hey Mason," said Charlotte with a big welcoming smile.

"Hey Charlotte."

A few of the other classmates passed by and especially the girls from town made sure they said hello to Tar so they could check out the new girl. After they were out of earshot they young girls seemed to talk more and Charlotte knew it had to be about her. Mason too excused himself and headed to the classroom wondering about how a girl now came into Tar's life.

"You know the girls are jealous that you are talking to me," stated Tar feeling important.

71

Grant Williams

"Maybe they are jealous that you are talking to me," answered Charlotte inflating Tar's ego a bit, "Are we going to look at the treasure this afternoon, after school?"

"You didn't say anything? You didn't tell anyone?" said Tar looking straight into Charlotte's eyes. After he made his point he quickly looked away because looking in her eyes made him feel a little uncomfortable.

"I promised I wouldn't tell didn't I."

"Yeah you did. I'm sorry I questioned you."

"It's okay. Are we going?"

"Can I meet you somewhere after you get home? Will your mother let you go with me?"

"I can go after I do my chores when I get home. They'll take about a half hour or so. Maybe we can meet an hour after school by the woods but on the road."

"Okay, I'll meet you there after school," said Tar as they walked into the classroom together.

Tar seemed anxious all day to get home and meet Charlotte away from school. Charlotte loved school and not shy or demure as many of the girls from the south were taught. She loved the history, the math and especially the writing assignments. Charlotte wasn't afraid to ask questions and to raise her hand to answer queries from the teacher. Her outgoing nature by any means alienated her even more from the proper southern girls. Her image did not present herself as a typical southern belle. Tar admired her courage and the fact that she was different from the other young ladies. The boys in the class seemed to like Charlotte for being honest and unafraid. Even though Charlotte would like to have more female friends it didn't matter as much as her friendship with Tar. She knew her friend liked her even amongst the others he had known so many years.

The day would seem to drag by with the anticipation of the meeting after school especially with the warm day and the sun shining into the tall windows of the old school house. Charlotte happy to be in the classroom although not accepted warmly by the other girls it didn't seem to matter much to her. She had a friend and a friend of importance to her. It didn't matter that Tar was popular with both genders. It is only

The Boys from Hog Heaven

important that he is her friend. Tar, too, glad to see his old classmates but now he had a new friend just as important as all of the others but different in a strange way. The big clock above the large blackboard moved so slowly but eventually the clock struck three and a buzzer went off filling the old school building. School finally ended for the day.

Tar hurried to see Charlotte before he had to leave to meet his ride.

"See you at four-thirty," said Tar excitedly.

"I'll meet you on the road by the forest," smiled Charlotte.

"Bye," said Tar as he ran down the front steps of the school to meet his father waiting in front of the school in the pickup truck.

Tar so glad that most of the time he wasn't picked up in the Buick because he didn't want to feel superior to the others by riding in such a fancy car. The pickup similar to what most of the other families drove didn't seem out of place. On the other hand if Betty complained if she got picked up in the old truck, she seemed embarrassed by the work vehicle. Most times Betty would ride home with a girl friend or a new beau. Carver didn't care who picked him up as long as he had a ride so that he could bring many of his books home with him.

"School today?" was the first question from John McGregor as the boys piled into the Ford pickup.

"It's different than working in the fields," replied Tar

It was great," chimed in Carver as he put his many books under his feet.

John smiled as he thought how much different his boys were and how strong each was in his own way.

"It is Grandpa's birthday on Friday," said John. "We should get him something nice."

"Why don't we get him a new pipe? He chews the ends off of the old corncob pipe all of the time," said Carver.

73

Grant Williams

"Good idea Carver. What do you think Tar?" asked John.

"I'll have to think about it. I still have my money from working in the fields," answered Tar.

"Your mother wants to have a birthday party but I don't think Grandpa would be up for that. You know how grouchy he gets when we fuss over him."

"I think we should have a surprise party and don't tell him," said Carver. "He really likes to have someone fuss over him but he won't admit it."

"Maybe that is a good idea. Your mother can invite a few of his old friends from the area. His old friend Robert would come and so would Doc from town and a few others. We can't make it too big but make it grand enough for a true southern gentleman."

"Miriam can bake a cake and we can have some punch," said Carver.

Tar smiled at the thought of his grandpa pretending to be angry but enjoying the family and friends fussing over him. He knew too how much this would please the old gentle man and also how much it would please all of the family to recognize grandpa on his birthday.

"Tar, the onion sets look real good. That little bit of rain really stood them up today. It looks as if we'll have a lot of onions this year. We'll need to cultivate the rows soon. Do you think you could drive the tractor and the cultivator on Saturday?"

"I think so. You'll just have to always look ahead when you cultivate and make sure you drive between the rows. If you look back at the cultivator you'll run over the rows ahead."

"I'll remember, daddy," said Tar thinking of what his father had just told him, 'Never look back to go ahead'. There must be part of growing up in that statement. He would remember if that what it would take to drive the tractor again.

"We'll see how the weather is first," said his father.

"And how everyone is feeling after grandpa's birthday party," laughed Carver.

John laughed along with his son, "And how everyone is feeling after the party and what is in the gentlemen's punch."

The Boys from Hog Heaven

"Daddy, I want to take Carver out to the ten acre field this afternoon. Is it all right?"

"Sure" answered John looking suspiciously at his youngest son. "So you want to look at the crops too?"

"Tar wants to show me some of the farm. Maybe I can learn something?" answered Carver.

"Don't go into the forest. I heard some noises in there today. It might be that big pig."

"We won't daddy," said Tar. "Did you see the pig?"

"No."

"Did you ever see the pig?"

"I saw something one day and it looked like a cow or a big animal. It wasn't very clear but it was big. It was soon after that I heard one of the little black kids was missing."

"Do you think the pig ate the kid?" asked Tar excitedly as he and his little brother looked toward their father for an answer.

"That's what the Negro families think. I don't know. I know there was a big hunt and the pig wasn't found. After that incident several families left the area."

"Do you think when I get older that I can hunt the pig?" asked Tar.

" You can never alone. Maybe someday someone will kill the pig. Who knows one of us might someday kill that wild pig. Now don't get ideas, Tar. We'll hunt later this year but deer hunting, Okay?"

"Okay daddy but who will hunt the pig? Oh sometimes some Yankees come down here and we take them hunting pigs but always over at the Dixon farm. Charlie has a lot trees down over the hill by the river. Sometimes we find some boars in the trees. I think there will always be some pigs over there since they breed well there."

"If you go with the Yankees this year can I go with you? I have my own gun."

"Carver you don't tell your mother that Tar has a gun. I'll tell her. Maybe you can go but I'll have to ask the other men first," answered John.

75

Grant Williams

The sight of the farm still in sight and the boys had their adventure ahead of them. They knew they would have to kiss their mother and tell her about school first, and then change out of their school clothes before going out to play. They knew their mother liked it very much when the boys did things together but Tar didn't mention to his father that Charlotte would be going with them but he thought it would be okay so why ask. Tar knew his brother would enjoy being with them and it would be a good experience. Tar knew too that they would have to do their business and be home for dinner on time so they wouldn't be questioned or feel the wrath of their beloved Miriam.

The boys changed their clothes quickly and talked with their mother for a short time. They explained their day at school and all of the wonderful things that they learned. Ruth always excited about education and always so happy her sons were good students. She knew her daughter would go on to a fine southern women's college or a fine finishing school and didn't worry much about Betty's future. She knew Carver would be a professional man someday and could already see it in his personality and even in his demeanor even at his young age. Sometimes she worried about Tar but knew his manners were fine, he got good grades in school and his popularity is never questioned amongst his peers. She knew Tar would become more like her husband and father-in-law. She knew he loved the land also.

"Mother" said Tar, "I am going to take Carver to the ten-acre field. I want to show him what I did the other day."

"You be careful Tar, you know your brother is not the man of the land that you are. You watch after him," replied Ruth.

"I will mother, we will be home well before supper. Can I take a few cookies with us? I saw some in the kitchen."

"May you take a few cookies?" corrected Ruth and then she continued, "Please ask Miriam and only take a few. I don't want you boys to spoil your supper."

"Thank you mother," said Tar as he went into the kitchen to find Miriam.

The Boys from Hog Heaven

"Thank you mother," said Carver too as he kissed his mother affectionately on the cheek. "We will be home before supper."

Loaded with some cookies and a few extra for Charlotte the two brothers ambled down toward the ten-acre field and continued down the road by the forest. Tar knew soon he would see Charlotte and then the three of them would go to the place of his treasure by the ten-acre field.

"Zippidy Do Da Zippidy- my o my what a wonderful day" sang Carver as they walked down the road, "Me and the Tar baby."

"Funny kid," said Tar sternly to his little brother. Then he smiled.

"That is a good movie. Maybe we can go again soon. I'd like to see a western with cowboys and horses. Wouldn't you?"

"Maybe daddy and mother will take us again soon. We can't go this weekend since it is grandpa's birthday. What do you want to get grandpa?" asked Tar.

"Remember I said we should get him a new pipe. Maybe mother will let me give one to him," answered Carver.

"I don't know what I'll get him but it will be special," said Tar as he picked up a rock from the dusty road and flung it toward the trees ahead.

"Do you think there is a wild pig in the trees, Tar?" asked Carver since he too had heard many stories and tale of the big pig.

"I think there could be but I promised not to go into the forest alone. Someday I will find the pig if he is in there and I will shoot him."

Carver looked proudly at his older brother and believed that this could happen. He knew if his big brother put his mind to something he would succeed.

"Do you think that Charlotte will come with us today?" asked Carver as he looked ahead toward the trees.

"She said she had some chores but could come with us when she was done. She will be her," answered Tar confidently. "I know she will come."

77

Grant Williams

It seemed like hours but from down the road Tar and Carver saw a figure coming toward them. As the figure got closer they could see the bouncing little pigtails. It had to be Charlotte. Tar seemed so relieved but didn't want to show too much emotion in front of his little brother.

"There she is," shouted Tar as he waved vigorously.

The boys could see the figure getting closer and recognized the figure as Charlotte. She had changed from her school clothes and now dressed in a pair of faded bib overalls with the pant legs rolled up a few turns wore a boy's flannel shirt that also had the sleeves rolled up. The shoes she wore were not feminine little girl shoes but were boy's shoes that had quite a bit of wear from working in the fields.

"Hey Charlotte, this is my brother Carver," said Tar when Charlotte met them on the road. "You probably saw him at school."

"Hey Carver."

"Hey Charlotte," answered Carver who had never seen girls in work clothes before. Being so accustom to seeing his sister and mother always dressed in the fashion of the southern women, Charlotte's appearance surprised Carver.

"Here, have some cookies. We can get to where the treasure is in a few minutes," said Tar, "Did you tell your mother you were going to be with me?"

"She said I could go with you since your brother was going to be there with us and I have to be home by supper time. Thanks for the cookies they sure are good."

"Did you tell her about the treasure?"

"Of course not Tar, I made a promise and we shook hands" answered Charlotte as she munched on the cookies the boys had brought.

"I knew you wouldn't tell anyone," said Tar as they walked toward the ten-acre field.

"I didn't tell anyone either," interjected Carver as he looked for approval from his big brother.

"I know you wouldn't," answered Tar realizing his brother is there.

The Boys from Hog Heaven

Tar seemed so visibly happy Charlotte came for the rendezvous. He liked her because she is different than all of the fickle, little silly girls he knew at school and church. He liked her because she is not fragile and could talk to him. He liked her because she is not afraid to be his friend and just because she wanted to be with him with no strings attached. He liked her because of all of these things but also because she is actually beautiful under the boyish exterior. He loved her pigtails and her eyes.

The trio reached the ten-acre field and walked toward the end of the field where Tar had placed his find. As they got closer Tar walked a little faster with his heart racing a little as they got closer since he wanted this find to be important and maybe to impress his friend and his little brother

The ground had flattened out some because of the rain and the mound where Tar had buried the treasure now had flattened out. He still walked to the same fence post and kneeled down, as Char and Carver looked on Tar uncovered his find.

"Wow," said Carver as he saw the remnants of the old confederate pistol. "Can I hold the gun?"

Tar handed the gun to his brother and then took out the box and the buttons he had meticulously put near the box.

"Here Charlotte you hold the buttons," said Tar, "Let's sit over there on the grass and we'll open the box."

The three youths moved a few feet, found a flat open space on the brown Johnson grass faced each other as if they were in an Indian ceremonial circle and opened the box. He had to remove the wax around the seal before he could pry the lid open. Carver now had put the revolver down on the ground between his knees and watched intently.

Slowly the lid came open with a tug by Tar revealing a little book and more buttons. On the back of each button were the initials G.M. that matched the other buttons outside of the box.

"What's in the book?" asked Charlotte excitedly.

"Yeah what's in the book?" mimicked Carver.

"Just a minute. We need to be careful when we open it. We don't want to bust it," said Tar as he slowly but carefully opened the small black book.

"What does it say?" asked Charlotte.

"It says here on page one property of George McGregor, Lieutenant in the Confederate Army, First division of Georgia."

"Wow," said Carver. "That was our Great-Great Grandfather."

"Turn the page," said Charlotte anxiously.

Tar looked at her with a little impatience but slowly turned the page and from the next page he read, "If anything happens to me in battle and I am lost to this earth please tell my beloved Mary Ellen that I will meet her on the other side. I love her dearly and do not wish for her to pine for me for I will be in the company of our Lord. I wish for my family to grow and prosper here in the wonderland of Georgia, my home."

"What love he had for Mary Ellen," said Charlotte. "It is so romantic."

"He was a soldier," answered Tar trying nervously to change the subject of romance.

"When I grow up I hope someone thinks of me like George McGregor did his Mary Ellen," said Charlotte quietly and reverently as she looked at Tar.

"Do you think this was his gun?" interjected Carver. This statement allowed Tar move the conversation from the inquiries of Charlotte.

"I think it is his gun and he buried these things after the war and when he started farming on the land."

"It must have been a difficult time for the people here," said Carver.

"They must have just started farming when George McGregor buried these things. He most likely was with Mary Ellen and their lives together were just starting again," said Charlotte.

The three new friends heard a sound from the direction of Charlotte's home.

"I think it's my Pa," said Charlotte. "He likes to have me home before supper to help my Ma. I'd better go now."

The Boys from Hog Heaven

"We'll read more in the book at another time. We'll walk you back home," said Tar being a southern gentleman.

"You don't have to Tar," said Charlotte and their eyes met.

Tar turned his glance quickly away from his new friend. "Carver and I will walk you back home. Here you keep a button and Carver you keep a button. I'll keep a button too and it will always be our link to each other."

Charlotte carefully put a button in her bib overall pocket. "I will treasure this just as George treasured his Mary Ellen."

Tar looked her in the eyes as he helped her to her feet and they both understood.

The three friends walked down the dusty road together until they reached the edge of the forest where they said goodbye. The boys watched Charlotte disappear into her yard and then they turned and started walking home.

"Zippidy Do Da Zippidy A, My O My what a beautiful day," sang Carver.

Tar put his arm around his brother as they walked home, "Don't say anything to Daddy or Mother about today. I'll put the box and the revolver in a safe place for now. We'll tell them about this some other time. It still is our secret for now."

"Okay big brother, let's go home I'm hungry."

"Okay little brother."

Then the two of them walked slowly back to the big white house still singing the song.

"Zippidy Do Da, Zippidy A, My Oh My what a beautiful day. Plenty of sunshine coming my way. Mr. Bluebird on my shoulder-------------."

Grant Williams

Chapter Eight

Grandpa's Birthday

Everyone around the McGregor house had been warned not to mention grandpa's birthday. Grandpa always enjoyed the celebrations even though he put on the appearance of being annoyed. John picked up the pipe Carver had picked out for grandpa when he went into town. Betty got some special Civil War books she had ordered from Atlanta. John and Ruth decided to get grandpa a new fishing pole, reel and lures since the old man should go fishing again and relax. From not knowing what to get his beloved grandfather put Tar into a quandary. He wanted to get his grandfather something special and not just something ordinary and commonplace. Tar knew he had the rest of the week to get something and would figure it out before the party on Saturday.

The week flew by and Tar even though he would see Charlotte at school, they were not in private long enough to talk much about the treasure. Tar realized Charlotte by being blunt and outspoken hadn't been too popular with the other girls, because Charlotte being a sharecropper's daughter also had some bearing on her status in the school. Charlotte had not been picked on or abused in any way because the class knew since she is friend of Tar it would be social suicide for any classmate to go against Tar.

Tar didn't get to see his friend after school since she stayed busy with her chores and helping her family. Tar too became very busy helping his father get the cultivator ready and even though unable to help his father plant the sweet potatoes he would help cultivate and weed the onion patches. Soon the bulbs would be strong and standing tall in the fields and the life of the farm depended a lot on the onion crop. Tar knew he would be able to help cultivate, weed and hoe this year to help pay for his new rifle locked up in the box in the barn.

The Boys from Hog Heaven

Ruth had privately planned a fairly large party for grandpa and had invited some of grandpa's old friends from around the area. She had Miriam on alert to bake a big cake and have food for the guests. John would get his son's to help watch the overnight process of cooking a pig. Miriam would make some potato salad and would have a pot of brown beans along with the pickles they put up last summer, pickled okra and of course plenty of sliced sweet Georgia onions. They brought out the ice cream machine, cleaned it and then put plenty of ice in freezer to be used on Saturday. Grandpa would know when the pig was put into the pit the celebration would be for him but for Ruth's sake he wouldn't complain until the guests were arriving.

Even Betty got involved because in her own way she loved grandpa too and proud of his accomplishments. She, always proud of his stature in the community knew it is a very positive thing socially to be a McGregor. Betty helped her mother with the calls to grandpa's friends, helped in the planning and even helped Miriam. For soon Betty knew she would be in college and even though she never wanted to admit it she would miss the family functions. She knew this might be one of the last functions for her with her family for a while.

Carver always got excited when special events came around and he too proud of his heritage and being a McGregor. Carver many times would sit at his grandpa's side and ask questions about the McGregors. He would ask many questions about the War Between the States and the McGregor history. Grandpa loved this boy's zest for learning and sometimes would bring him bit of history. Obviously Carver would inherit many McGregor historical items from his dear grandpa and this would be all right with Tar and Betty.

Grandpa McGregor even though he was not close to the black community had garnered a lot of respect from the people since he had shown a lot of respect for the working man throughout the years no matter what race they are but the local black community still did not or would not socialize with grandpa. Miriam could go a step further since she always seemed like part of the family. She could chase grandpa out of

Grant Williams

the kitchen or preach to him about the devil. Grandpa could also tease Miriam about her time off and that she should have a boyfriend. Miriam could be at a party but she and be the only black person invited.

Saturday now getting closer and Tar had not gotten his grandpa his birthday gift. He began getting worried and asked his brother for some ideas. He also had a chance to talk to his dear friend Charlotte at school about his dilemma and she had a wonderful idea. Tar knew after their conversation what he would give his grandpa.

Friday afternoon after school John drove his two sons to the market in town and parked the pickup at the back of the store. John told his sons to wait in the truck and he would be right out.

In a few minutes John and the storekeeper returned out of the back door with a big package wrapped in butcher's paper.

"That's a nice hog, John," said the Storekeeper. "I'll be there to sample it tomorrow night."

"Thanks, we'll be glad to see you and so will our guest of honor, grandpa. You come hungry. You hear."

The boys could remember how tasty the feast was the last time the family roasted a hog in the pit. They didn't or weren't allowed to help then but this will be a treat for them as part of growing up and being responsible. They knew the package in the back all neatly wrapped in the white paper would be a feast. They were happy that their father took them to the store and this was a thing they could do together.

"Daddy, can we invite Bubba and his family to grandpa's birthday party?" asked Tar as the pickup moved down the road toward home.

"Well Tar, I think you should ask your mother since she has put the guest list together."

"They are our neighbors."

"I know son but we can't invite everyone but we'll ask you mother when we get home."

"Tar's right, they are our neighbors," chimed in Carver trying to support his brother's request.

The Boys from Hog Heaven

"We'll see," answered John as he directed the pickup down the dusty road.

It wasn't long before the trio got home and John with the help of his sons hung the pig in the barn until later where they would fire up the pit after supper and then they would put the pig on to slowly cook through the night.

After Supper John left for a while. He took the old pickup down the dusty road toward town. He left instructions to his boys to have all of their homework done by the time he would return so they could start the pig roast. The ladies of the house were happily working on the preparation for the party, even Miriam stayed a little while later and worked beside Ruth and Betty. Grandpa went out on the porch for a while sensing something is going on but not fussing yet. As grandpa sat in his rocking chair a wisp of smoke came out of his old corncob pipe. The sky still blue but the moon is now rising over the forest. The aroma of the new crop of onions permeated the evening air and the flowers on the peach trees just starting to come out would soon take the place of the aroma of the onions.

It wasn't long before the old pickup truck idled into the yard. The boys had finished their homework and were talking with their grandpa on the porch. John and Grandpa talked awhile and soon grandpa disappeared into the big white house.

"Well sons," asked John, "are you ready to get the pig roasting?"

"We're ready," they answered in unison.

The boys had seen this ritual many times before but were never asked to help. This is an honor for them especially to participate in such an event. Grandpa always had been considered cornerstone in the community of Carver and any celebration including him is very important.

Seasoned oak and hickory wood had been stacked by the smokehouse building. In the building louvered sections in the ceiling had to be opened for the heat and excess smoke to escape. The pit large enough to accommodate a pig or a half of a steer and with the old spit that ran efficiently by an electric motor, pulley and fan belt it could handle a large carcass. The spit hinged so it could be swung out over the fire and locked there normally is handled by two men. The trick is always getting the pig on the spit because it took the two men.

The three of them carried the pig to the smokehouse building and laid it down on the table beside the pit.

"First of all we need to season this little shoat," said John as he took down an old coffee can from one of the shelves along the wall and poured some of the contents in an old tin pie pan. "You boys rub these spices in the inside of the pig while I get some wood for the fire."

What a responsibility thought both young men as they rolled up their sleeves and rubbed the aromatic spices into the inner pink part of the carcass. The smell of the dried onion, garlic and sage permeated the air in the smokehouse building. The sharpness of the dried pepper filled their nostrils as they continued their tasks and the salt worked its way into the little cracks in their skin. They felt so good being able to help and for grandpa.

John returned with an armful of the seasoned wood and strategically placed it in the pit.

"Remember it is very important to get the fire just right and to put the wood where it should be, now watch," he instructed his two eager boys.

They watched intently as their father put the rest of the wood in the pit and with a little help of some paper and kindling wood started the fire.

"Now my good lads, you' all need to help me truss this old pig on the spit rod. Do you think you can lift it with me?"

The question being rhetorical needed not to be answered as the boys and their father in unison lifted the pig to the spit and place the bar down the center of the carcass.

Quickly and deftly John tied the pig to the spit with some butcher twine and some small gauge wire.

"Good work boys. Now let's swing the pig over the fire. The coals won't be hot enough yet but it won't take long. We'll just have to wait and add wood during the night. Do you think we can do it? We'll just have to take turns watching the fire and make sure the spit keeps turning."

The Boys from Hog Heaven

The pig now pushed over the fire when Tar responded first.

"Daddy I can stay up during the night and watch the pig."

"I can too," e choed Carver now feeling grownup himself.

"First of all you boys go wash up. You need to get those spices off your hands and arms. Then you' all come back here and I'll show you what we have to do. Wash up outside by the well pump. Miriam and your mother would have a fit if you brought all of those spices into the house."

Soon the boys returned with their clean hands and arms. The coolness of the water made their hands feel much better after the harshness of the spices. John had brought to the smokehouse a big pot with some liquid mix and a three-foot mop made of twisted cotton and a hardwood handle.

"This is important," he said to his young offspring. "You must put mopping mixture on the pig every once in a while and not let the pig dry out. The sauce will make it tender, juicy and give it the right flavor. Do you understand? You just can't let the pig dry out."

Both of the boys nodded that they understood.

"Carver you will take the first watch and you will be relieved by Tar at Eight o'clock. Tar you will take the second watch till midnight and you will be relieved by Will, Virgil and Junior. I will take the morning watch at four and then we all can come back here when you get up. Always make sure there is wood on the fire and only put a piece at a time when it gets low. Make sure to mop the pig and don't let it get dry."

Now six- thirty, an hour and a half would be a long time for the youngest boy but Tar had proven himself in the onion fields and John knew he could take the four-hour watch before going to sleep. Will, Virgil and Junior had volunteered to help in grandpa's party and is a good way to help and show their respect. They were not close to the old man but still had utmost respect and admiration for him but most of all they were very good with bar-b-queing and wanted to help in a special way. John always being an early riser saw no problem getting up an hour early for his shift.

Grant Williams

"If you have any problems you call me, you hear," said John with a smile to his youngest boy.

"Yes sir," answered Carver tentatively but willing to give it a try for this is an important step for any young man to be trusted by his father, especially in the south.

John and Tar left the old smokehouse and headed for the house. They could see the light in grandpa's room and knew he must be reading or secretly getting ready for his birthday party. They met Ruth on the porch and sat for a while where they all looked out over the land. John and Tar knew they couldn't go to the smokehouse to check on Carver and understood it is his time to start growing up and to be trusted.

Carver stared at the pig as it made its revolutions on the spit and concerned that he wouldn't have enough mopping liquid on the pig and it would dry out. Would the wood his father put on the fire be enough until Tar relieved him? So slowly Carver sitting in the old building got the hang of the fire and the mopping. He kept thinking of tomorrow and the party for grandpa and he could help. He thought when he grew up and became a doctor or lawyer he would get a smokehouse and have grand parties and roast his own pigs. Happy his father put the trust in him, the youngest son smiled as he continued with his tasks.

About ten minutes to eight Tar arrived at the smokehouse wearing the same old shirt and blue jeans he wore when he worked in the fields. He knew the smoke would soon be part of this attire.

"Hey Carver," announced Tar as he entered the rather dark building, "the pig looks good. You did a good job."

"It should taste good tomorrow. I can't wait for the party."

"Me neither," said Carver as he mopped the turning pig. "Grandpa won't admit it but he likes to be fussed over."

"He'll be happy with the birthday feast and seeing many of his old friends. You watch and you'll see him and some of the old men sneak off behind the barn and taste some of the corn liquor."

The Boys from Hog Heaven

"I think they don't know if anyone sees them but they sure return a lot happier. Remember old Ephraim and grandpa singing last time we had an outdoor party?"

"They couldn't sing a lick," said Tar as he took the mop from his younger brother's hand. "Maybe this year at least they can sing "Dixie". I can take over now, Carver, if you want to go up to the house."

"If you don't mind I'll stay a while. I'm not tired," answered the little brother.

"Suit your self," said Tar as he continued spreading the mopping liquid over the roasting pig.

"Do you like Charlotte?"

"Of course I like Charlotte, why do you ask?"

"I mean do you like her, I mean like her like a girl friend?" stammered Carver.

"She is my friend. I like her. She isn't like the other girls in school, all silly and all of that."

"Is she your girl friend?"

"I told you she is just my friend," answered Tar seemingly annoyed.

"It's all right if she is. I won't tell anyone. I like her too."

Tar envisioned his friend in his mind as he now began mopping the pig without any liquid, not realizing he was daydreaming. He thought maybe she is more than just a friend.

"Do you think she will keep our secret?" said Carver looking intently into his brother's face.

"Of course she will. We made a promise," answered Tar glad that his brother quit questioning him about Charlotte being a girl friend.

"Have you read anymore in the book you found?"

"I will after grandpa's party. I want to know more about George McGregor."

"I do too," said Carver. "I want to know everything about the farm and this part of the country."

"I want to know why George McGregor buried his pistol. You would think a man from the army would keep it."

"I'm sure we will find out."

"Do you want me to carry in some more wood for you?" asked Carver.

"I'm okay. Do you want to go up to the house? I think there is some banana pudding left."

"Maybe I will," answered Carver thinking of the delicious way that Miriam always made the desert.

"See you tomorrow," said Tar as he watched his little brother slowly walk toward the big white house. Tar always so proud of his little brother and knew someday he would have his own profession with a big sign with Carver McGregor printed on it sitting in front of his offices.

The pig now turning slowly over the coals and Carver had done a good job keeping the fire burning and the coals hot. The pig shined in the dimly lighted room as it turned and dripped fat and juices onto the coals. Tomorrow the pig would be tender and juicy and the skin would be crackly and brittle. Tar stepped out into the Georgia evening and looked up into the sky. He couldn't count the stars because there were so many but he could smell the onions in the fields. He could barely make out the lights from the sharecropper's little houses in the distance just over the woods but he could see a light on in Charlotte's house and he wondered if she is thinking of him. He couldn't wait to see her again at school. He also could see the faint outline of lights in Miriam's and her brother's house. Soon it would be dark when he would be alone with his thoughts and the pig.

The night came suddenly and Tar alone with the pig and with his dreams thought about Charlotte, the treasure and grandpa's birthday. He watched the pig now getting slightly golden from the heat from the pit. Tomorrow they would eat the pig and celebrate and honor his beloved grandpa. He had gotten a gift and wrapped it and had put the gift in his drawer with his underwear. He knew the gift would surprise everyone at the party and knew his grandpa would like his gift because it would be very special.

Ten o'clock and the last of the lights in the big white house went out. Tar alone in the smokehouse with its dimly lit bulbs knew he would have to bring in some more hardwood for the fire soon. A walk outside would make Tar appreciate the feel

The Boys from Hog Heaven

of the cool spring night air. Tar looked up again at the beautiful Georgia sky as he proceeded to the woodpile near the smokehouse when suddenly he heard a terrible noise. It sounds as if someone is getting killed in the forest. It didn't sound human but more like an injured animal. He thought of the big pig immediately came into the mind of the young man. Maybe he smelled the roasting of a relative or maybe he is just letting me know that he is still in the woods. Tar quickly returned to the safety of the interior of the old smokehouse with his mind racing. In his haste he had dropped several pieces of the hickory wood and would get them later. Now he is safe but alone in the building.

Tar put the pieces of wood that he had managed to carry into the smokehouse into the firebox. He would wait a while before venturing out again to pick up the rest of the wood. Someday he thought 'I will take my new gun and I will bring back the pig to the farm and we will roast it on this fire'. Tonight he would not disturb the big pig for there were other tasks to do for it would still be about two hours before Will and his brothers would be over to relieve him. Now he knew he would have to make sure he mopped the rotating swine and make sure there were plenty of hot coals.

The sounds from the forest finally calmed down and Tar again thought of Charlotte. He would see her again soon and they could again spend some time together and look over the treasure and the old book again. The thought of her quelled the anxiety of the noise of the forest but it lit a fire of its own in his belly. He knew he would have to see her again and this time it would just be him and her.

Around eleven thirty Will and his brothers arrived and prepared to spend the night. The men were experts at pig roasts and were known all over that part of western Georgia as some of the best bar-b-quers in the area. They knew how to make the meat so succulent and the skin just crispy enough. They too were happy that John McGregor asked them to help and to be at the party the next day.

"Hey Tar," said Will as he led his brothers into the smokehouse. "This here pig looks mighty good."

Grant Williams

"It smells mighty good," chimed in Junior.

"You better run along to the house and get some sleep," said Virgil. "We'll watch the pig till your daddy comes out."

"Did you hear the noise in the woods last night?" asked Tar quizzically.

The three brothers looked at each other and finally Will being the oldest answered. "It was that big pig I think. Sometimes there is a terrible noise as if it comes right out of the ground all the way from the devil's own place."

"Sometimes I think it just wants to let us know he is there and can get us if he has a mind to," said Junior as his eyes got bigger.

"Does he ever come out of the forest at night? Have you ever seen him after dark?" asked Tar.

"I saw him in the daytime once but never at night. I think he stays deep in the woods most of the time," answered Junior as Virgil brought a few more pieces of wood into the building."

"Don't scare the boy," said Will firmly to his younger brother.

"He doesn't scare me. When I get older I'll hunt the pig and we'll have a great celebration and I'll let you cook it for all of the community. We'll have a feast for everybody."

Will looked at the young son of his neighbor and somehow thought maybe he would hunt the pig. Many others have tried and failed maybe Tar would somehow succeed.

"Maybe someday you will Tar," replied Will. "Now you get along we'll watch the pig and we'll see you at the birthday party."

Tar is so pleased that Miriam and her brothers were included into grandpa's birthday party. They knew grandpa isn't prejudice against the black people but it is inherited from the past history of the south. He really liked Miriam and allowed her the privilege of scolding him when he interfered in her duties. He really liked the brothers because he knew they were honest and hard working. He also understood that it was unaccustomed for the blacks and whites to socialize very often and both parties agreed it was all right. After all it still is the south and many things were inbred to all throughout history.

92

The Boys from Hog Heaven

As Tar walked to the big white house he looked toward the forest and looked to see if he could see Charlotte's house. He listened for sounds of the forest and waited for sounds from the big pig but it is now silent. He slipped into the house and put his smoky clothes into a basket with his little brothers cooking clothes and climbed under the sheets. He saw images and shadows on the ceiling from the moon and the trees. Some of the images looked like a large pig and others of little girls with pigtails. Soon he fell asleep.

John relieved the three brothers in the smokehouse at four AM. The brothers told John they would stay if he wanted them to but he scurried them out. He told them that the party would start at one and to be back then and to be hungry. Their friendship is very important and he is looking forward to them coming back for the party..

Within an hour and a half the signs of the farm started coming alive. The old rooster that coveted his few hens started crowing with the light from the dawn. The sun is rising slowly from the east over the newly planted onion fields. Soon Miriam would arrive and walk into the MacGregor kitchen. Many mornings John would hear her sing as she made their day more pleasant with the freshly made biscuits. He is happy his family had been brought to this farm with its red dirt and peach trees and content as he mopped the roasting pig as it turned over the hot coals on the homemade spit. Soon it would be time to plant sweet potatoes and cut the grass under the peach trees in the orchard. He would miss his daughter as she went away to finishing school but knew his son would help him more in the future. Today though ultimately grandpa's day, he would make sure it is a wonderful day for him.

Miriam brought John his breakfast and John sat outside the old smokehouse and ate the ham and fresh biscuits. Soon it would be time to let the fire and coals die out and the pig rest until the pig picking and the carving of the carcass.

John let his boys sleep in but by eight thirty both of the lads were up, fed and out to the smokehouse to see the results of the hours of cooking. After all they were part of this ritual and they wanted to see the final offering.

Grant Williams

"Wow" said Carver as he walked into the smokehouse. "That pig is beautiful."

"It is golden." said Tar as he looked at his father's smiling face.

"I will be delicious. Look how crackly the skin is." John took out his knife and cut two little pieces of meat just under the skin and handed a piece to each boy.

The boys devoured the meat quickly and both wiped off the little bit of grease that had run down their chins.

"This is really good," said Tar. "Grandpa will be happy."

"This is really good, even Betty will like this," said Carver and the three MacGregors laughed.

"Not much to do until the party. Will, Virgil and Junior will be over to help cut up the pig around noon and Miriam will have all of the other food ready. Your mother and Betty were going to set the long tables out side by the back of the house. Maybe you young men could help her or Miriam?"

"Okay daddy, we'll help. Do you need us to help with the pig?" asked Tar hoping he could be part of the men folk's participation.

"Run along now and try to help. Everyone will be on edge and a little testy today so help and stay out from under foot."

That wasn't the response the boys were looking for because they thought they had passed some right of passage to manhood by helping with the bar-b-que but obediently went back up the big white house.

The women of the household were busy with the decorations and setting up the tables for the event. They really didn't need the boys so the boys didn't even ask. Tar still had to wrap his present to his grandpa and Carver wanted to get dressed for the party. Carver took his clothes to the upstairs bathroom and drew the water for his bath. Tar now alone opened the drawer of this chest of drawers and took out the present he had for his grandpa. Tar carefully put the gift into a box lined with tissue paper and wrapped the box with nice colorful wrapping paper, then took a ribbon he had been given by his mother, put it around the wrapped gift and tied it neatly in a

The Boys from Hog Heaven

bow. He made out a birthday card very simply that his mother had given him 'To my Grandpa from Tarleton.'

Around eleven o'clock the ladies came in and dressed for the event. John would come in after Will, Virgil and Junior would come over and help with the pig picking. Tar and Carver were dressed with clean Sunday clothes but without jackets or neckties. The boys just went out and sat on the porch to get out of the way. The day perfect and couldn't have been better with the midday temperature it would not be too hot or too cold. It would be very pleasant for the party for grandpa. It wasn't long before grandpa joined the boys on the porch and took his familiar place in the big white rocking chair.

"I don't see what the fuss is all about. It is just another year older for an already old man. I don't need a birthday party," grumbled Grandpa.

"Mother and Daddy want to have it for you. Maybe they need to do it?" said Tar.

"Maybe they do need it. At least we'll have some of that good pig picking. I could smell that pig a'cookin' all last night. I was tempted to go down to the smokehouse and get me a bite. I hope your Mama didn't invite the entire county," said grandpa now a little excited that he was remembered.

"You know our mother. I don't know whom they invited. She never told me or Carver."

"Didn't tell me," said Carver.

"Are the boys coming over to help your Daddy with the pig?"

"They should be here most anytime."

"Good they are good boys and work hard."

The sound of an old pickup truck interrupted the conversation. Will and his brothers had arrived and the pick picking ritual would soon commence. It wouldn't be long until the platters of smoked succulent pig meat would grace the long white table clothed tables. Miriam hearing the truck coming up the drive prepared to take out the other foods too. The pitchers of sweet tea cooled with condensation dripping on the kitchen cabinets by the sink.

Grant Williams

***

As southern tradition allowed, most guests arrived about fifteen minutes. The food looked so appetizing as it sat on the tables covered with the white tablecloths. Will, Junior and Virgil each brought a platter of the chopped pork up from the smokehouse and Miriam directed her older brother to put one of the platters in the house for later. Bowls of potato salad, brown beans and some okra were strategically placed on the table for all to enjoy. The family had presented themselves to the guests and stood at the head of the table with the guest of honor, grandpa.

John was just about to tell all of the guests to be seated when another pickup truck arrived at the big farm. Tar had been watching his grandpa secretly enjoying the event and didn't notice the vehicle. It is Bubba, his wife, and his daughters Tara and Charlotte. As grandpa's gaze wandered over to the new arrivals so did Tar's. He hadn't expected the recently arrived guests but overjoyed and happy they could come. He knew how special all of the neighbors were to his father and how important it is for his mother no to forget.

The female members were dressed in nice spring dresses made of cotton. Their hair neatly combed and of course is Charlotte's attired in her trademark pigtails. Bubba even had his hair combed and his bib overalls seemed to be rather new. The family left a gift at the table filled with gifts for grandpa and proceeded to mingle with the other guests. Tar hoping he would be able to sit by Charlotte but that didn't think it would be possible since he had to sit with his family at the head table.

"Hello," said John McGregor loudly to the murmuring crowd. "Please sit down, Hello, Please sit down.

The crowd started quieting down and seated themselves. Grandpa sat at the middle of the head table and enjoyed the attention even thought he tried to give the impression that he didn't.

"Please, my friends, neighbors and family bow your heads so I can ask the blessing on the food," and then John added. So we can eat."

The Boys from Hog Heaven

After John McGregor gave the blessing for the food and recognized grandpa's birthday the congregation of friends, family and neighbors sat down. Foods were passed and talk commenced and laughter and happiness commenced around the tables. Tar saw his friend Charlotte sitting proudly with her family at the far table. One time when he was looking too intently their eyes met and quickly they returned to their own families;

Betty turned to her mother and asked rather loudly, "Why is that new family of sharecroppers here?"

Ruth answered. "They are our neighbors and are welcome."

"Well they are just hired help and poor people. Don't they know I am going to college and will have my debutant party soon? Their daughter Tara is in my class and she is too country for me and my friends."

"They are our guests and you mind your manners, young lady," said Ruth McGregor sternly looking her daughter straight in the eyes.

Tar looked at his sister in amazement. How could she even think those thoughts? She doesn't even know them. He didn't say anything but felt bad for his friends. It didn't matter what side of the tracks the family came from they were all God's children as he father had taught him.

After plates of the feast were consumed and the sun was warm against the cheeks of the guests John announced Grandpa McGregor would open his gifts. There were many cards with nice verses and many gifts from the many friends in attendance. He got a new harmonica from an old friend from his youth. He received many gifts from pens to shotgun shells. Bubba's family gave him a real nice foot stood that Bubba had made from some walnut wood. He liked the gifts from the family and promised to go fishing with the rod and reel from Ruth and John. He loved the book from Betty and gave her a big hug in front of all. He loved the pipe from Carver and promised to smoke it. He opened the gift from Tar and his eyes got real big for he knew this is a one of a kind gift and thought. Grandpa knew immediately what it was. He looked at the four buttons in the box with the initials

Grant Williams

carved in the back GM. He knew they were from George McGregor's uniform and from the War Between the States. He carefully put them back in the box and would look at them again later on. He nodded to Tar with a tear in his old eyes and said thank you, knowing they would talk later.

The men excused themselves to smoke cigars and to drink a little corn liquor in back of the barn. The women folks would gather on the porch after the tables were cleared. The ice cream would come later when the men returned to turn the cranks of the old ice cream churns.

Tar and Carver were the only young men so they went out to the back porch by themselves. Soon their young friend Charlotte joined them.

"Tar, did you tell your grandpa of the secret of the buttons?"

"No I just gave him several of the buttons since they were from his grandpa."

"It was a good gift, Tar," said his brother Carver. "Do you want some sweet tea? I'm going in to get some."

"I would please kind sir," replied Charlotte in her own country sophisticated way.

"How about you Tar?"

"Not now Carver but thanks anyway," answered Tar.

"I'll be back soon after I can get one of the ladies to pour us a couple of glasses," replied Carver as he turned and slowly walked to the kitchen door.

"I'm glad we could come," said Charlotte. "I always like to see you."

Tar a little embarrassed being alone with Charlotte but tried to maintain his composure. He wasn't accustomed to being with a girl all alone.

"Tar when we get older and in high school will you be my boy friend? Would you take me to the dance in the springtime?" said Charlotte looking directly at Tar.

"I don't know Char. I don't know what I'm going to do in high school."

"I won't bother you know but I want you to think about it."

The Boys from Hog Heaven

"Char, you will always be my friend," said Tar.

Charlotte moved closer to her young friend and put her young strong arms around him, "I will always be your friend too."

What ever got into Tar he couldn't explain? He just looked down at her and kissed her directly on the mouth. Charlotte seemed not surprised and did not pull away even though it felt awkward but sweet. It would always be memorable but clumsy.

"I'm sorry," said Tar as he pulled away from the beautiful young lady.

"I'm not. It is my first kiss by a boy and I will always remember it. It always will be from you."

"Don't tell anyone, Please Charlotte," begged Tar.

"I won't tell anyone."

About the time of silent conversation Carver appeared with two ice-cold sweet teas, obviously he had not observed what had just happened.

"Here you go Miss Charlotte," said Carver as he handed Char one of the cold drinks.

"Just in time, Carver, and thanks. You are such a southern gentleman," answered Charlotte as she took the tea and gave it a long sip.

"It looks as if you might need a cold drink too, my brother," said Carver as he looked at his brother's flush face.

"I'm all right, I'll be just fine," replied Tar rather annoyed.

"Did I miss anything?" asked Carver.

"Didn't miss a thing," said Charlotte as she protected her virtue.

"We were just going to meet again to look at the treasure and read the book that was in the box." injected Tar.

"Let's do this next week," said Carver excitedly.

"It's a deal. I think I can meet again after I do my chores. Let me know at school."

"We can do this next week I think. I'll tell you when at school," said Tar now feeling more in charge of this effort.

Grant Williams

Suddenly there were loud voices coming from the house and out of the door came Charlotte's mother and her sister.

"Bubba" called Charlotte's mother in a loud voice. "It is time to go home."

Tar and Carver noticed that Tara, Charlotte's older sister now in tears and running toward her old pickup truck.

"Bubba, you come here right now. We are going home. Now!!"

Bubba came from in back of the building and noticeable he had tasted some of the local corn liquor. The white lightning had taken affect on him but he could still negotiate his way to the family truck.

"What's the matter?" called out Bubba.

"I'll tell you on the way home. Get your country butt into this pickup truck right now."

Without hesitation and without partaking of the ice cream to come Bubba and his family got into the pickup truck and drove quickly down the dusty road.

Tar and Carver watched from the porch of the big white house and knew they would hear what the problem was at a later time.

100

The Boys from Hog Heaven

Chapter Nine

Reconciliation

Grandpa's birthday party may have been successful for many but having Charlotte and her family leave before they cranked the ice cream disappointed Tar tremendously. Nothing had been said about the incident at the time but Tar knew by the look on his mother's face it couldn't have been a dead issue. Tar and Carver helped Miriam with the last of the dishes while John and Ruth spoke privately in the drawing room. Miriam didn't say anything about the incident but kept on singing softly different religious and spiritual songs. Tar and even Carver knew something different is going on but if they were to know their parents would tell them.

"That was some great potato salad" said Tar as he dried another dish with the white tea towel.

"Thank you Mr. Tar," said Miriam with a great big toothy smile. "You boys sure did a good job cooking that pig."

This comment made both boys smile too especially when she included them in men folk things.

"I can't wait until I shoot that big pig in the woods and all of the county will eat it," said Tar bravely.

Miriam had heard the stories about the big pig, its evil eyes and even the story that the pig had eaten some of the little black children. She was afraid of what she couldn't see and what she couldn't control. She too had heard the awful screams in the night coming from the dark wooded area between her house and the big farm.

"I hope the pig will be gone soon. You be careful around the trees. Tar, don't mess with that creature. It is a devil that God allows to live here in Georgia."

The boys could see fear in her eyes and sensed the pig pumped fear through her veins.

"I'll make sure I don't get too close and I'll be with the other men folk," said Tar trying not to upset their dear cook.

101

Grant Williams

"You just wait until you grow up. There is just too much to do until then."

"I won't hunt that pig," said Carver trying to get the woman's mind off of the animal. "Do you think grandpa had a good time?"

"He had a mighty fine time. He was so happy that his family and friends could be there. I even saw him smile when he thought no one was watching. Look's like were finished here boys. Thank you for helping. I need to get home and rest awhile. Will is waiting for me outside in our truck. Tell your Ma and Pa I'll be here bright and early for breakfast."

The boys watched their beloved cook leave and walk slowly down the path to the truck where her brother had been waiting. They always felt so close to Miriam and were so happy she helped raise them and cared for them. She is family and always will be family.

Conversations between John and Ruth are private and quiet in the drawing room and the boys without being told went straight to their room. They would hear later about their discussions and if important they would know then.

The silence at the breakfast table is not normal at the McGregor farm neither is Ruth getting up early up early and dressed as if she is going out. Betty did not come to the table either but only showed up in time to go to school. The boys ate quietly and after breakfast waited patiently in the car for their father to take them to school.

No one said a word on the way to school and the silence became deafening. Betty sat in the front seat with her father but stared arrogantly out of the window. The boys were dropped off first as usual and their father told them he would pick them up after school and to have a good day.

"What do you think is wrong?" asked Carver as the McGregor car sped away.

"Something happened at grandpa's party," said Tar as they walked together up the steps of the school.

Obvious to Tar, Charlotte wasn't there to greet him. Could it have been the kiss or is it something else, after all she

102

The Boys from Hog Heaven

and her family left in a hurry yesterday. He knew he would see her later and maybe they could talk.

"Do you think Daddy and Mother are getting a divorce?" asked Carver.

"What?" Answered Tar with a laugh. "They love each other. Didn't you see the way they looked at each other this morning?"

"But why was Mother dressed to go out today. She doesn't usually go out without announcing where she is going."

"Maybe she has to take care of some business with Daddy today. Maybe they are going to town after Daddy gets home."

"You think so?"

"Don't worry. I'll see you later," said Tar as they entered the school building and went toward their own classrooms.

Tar couldn't help thinking, no Charlotte this morning, maybe she didn't come to school today. Maybe she is sick or maybe she just didn't want to see him this morning.

Tar went into his own classroom and he saw Charlotte sitting in her regular seat. When she saw him come into the room she just looked away. It was disturbing to Tar as he sat in his assigned seat. What is wrong? He would have to find out later he though and then the bell rang and the teacher entered the room.

The classes dragged by for Tar. Each time he looked in Charlotte's direction she turned away. His thoughts were not on the class or the subjects but just on what is going on with his friend.

The bell for recess rang for the school and noisy children hurried down the hallways to freedom outside. The morning yet another beautiful day and the Georgia sun shone above in the cloudless blue sky.

By the old swing set Tar finally caught up with Charlotte.

"What is going on? What is the matter? I thought we were friends?" said Tar in a very serious voice.

"Don't you know? I'm sure you think of me the same way?" asked Charlotte making sure she didn't look Tar in the eyes.

Grant Williams

"Know what? I only know you are my best friend. Tell me what is going on?" pleaded Tar as he tried to figure out what is now between them.

"You don't know do you?"

"Please, what is happening?'

"Didn't you hear what your sister said to Tara? She called her everything but white trash and couldn't understand why your daddy invited us to your grandpa's birthday party."

"It isn't what our family feels or thinks. I am sorry. My Mother and my Daddy wouldn't have invited your family unless they wanted them to come. I don't feel that way. You know that don't you?"

"My Momma said we should stay away from your family and we are probably just poor white people that don't belong together," said Charlotte still not looking at Tar.

"To Hell with my sister, she is just a big spoiled baby. She thinks she is the queen of Georgia."

"She is your sister and she is your family."

"You are my best friend and I want to still be you best friend. Please don't take whatever Betty said as what the McGregors are all about," pleaded Tar.

"I think my mother wants me to stay away from your family for a while but I believe you for some strange reason. I will be your friend. I am your friend, Darn it."

"Charlotte about yesterday," started Tar as the bell rang ending the recess time.

"Talk about it some other time, friend," said Charlotte as she walked back into the schoolhouse.

"Can we see each other and read the book I found. You know, the treasure."

Charlotte continued back into the classroom but turned and looked at Tar for the first time during the conversation. "We will see each other soon. I'll let you know as soon as all of this blows over."

Tar thought to himself 'that was the reason Mother was dressed this morning. She was going over to Bubba's house. That was the reason that her and Daddy were talking in the study last night. That was why there was no conversation in the car

104

The Boys from Hog Heaven

that morning.' He took his seat but gave a glance over at Charlotte. She looked back and smiled.

***

Ruth McGregor knew how important her visit to Bubba's home would be. She dressed in ordinary but nice clothes. She had John drive her to Bubba's home in the pickup truck and not the big Buick. It is the right thing to do.

As the McGregor pickup truck arrived at Bubba's home, Tess Bubba's wife stood alone on the small front porch.

Having no beef with John or Ruth, Tess waited for Ruth to get out of the pickup.

"Hello Tess, may I talk with you for a while?" asked Ruth.

"If you must," answered Tess in not the friendliest voice.

"John, you come back in an hour," ordered Ruth as she turned to her husband.

John didn't want to be around for this woman's posturing and control. He obediently left and went back to the big white house.

"Please sit," said Tess as she offered the rocking chair on the porch.

"Thank you Tess. I want you to know some things and I want you to listen."

"Go ahead, I've got some time before I have to make the chitterlings," said Tess sarcastically.

"Chitterlings, do you need some help?"

"Just talking. There are no chitterlings. I thought all of you rich folks thought all that we ate was chitterlings, collards and cornbread."

"I don't think that way at all. John and I started the farm with little help. Believe it or not I helped in the early days. I became ostracized from my friends from the city and even in town being a farmer's wife."

Tess started to pay attention.

"I can't help what my spoiled selfish daughter said. It probably is my fault and I must have failed. I didn't want her to grow up being prejudice or thinking she is better than any of God's people. I can't answer for her but from me to you I am

105

Grant Williams

sorry and you and your family are always welcomed to our home."

"She shouldn't have said what she did. My daughter Tara is in high school and will never be part of the inner circle of southern ladies. Tara just wants to be accepted."

"You are right, Tess. Please have her come over some day when Betty is away. I want to show her some things. You can come with her. It will be just a day for the three ladies."

"I can't forget about Charlotte. She seems to get along well with your boys. I guess she is a little of a tomboy."

"Please bring her too. I want you to come over and I want you to understand I am not against you or your family."

Tess looked for a long time at Ruth. Ruth just looked out over the Georgia morning. Tess could see Ruth is a person of dignity but has kindness toward the common man. Tess knew she could believe Ruth.

"Would you like a cup of coffee?" asked Tess.

"Thank you. It would be nice to just sit here for a while and visit. John won't be back for an hour."

They made coffee and talked. They talked about the important things such as their husbands, children and the family life and realized there really isn't much difference in the way they feel. Tess felt much more comfortable with her neighbor as they sat there on the humble porch of the little sharecropper's home.

***

The feud between Bubba's family and the McGregors ended with the exception of Betty. Betty did know to keep her distance from the neighbors because her opinions didn't change and probably wouldn't. It would be best for Betty to live out the next few months away from the distraction of the neighbors since she would be leaving for finishing school or college. The friendship between Tar and Charlotte continued but they had not been together since grandpa's birthday party. They had not had time to see each other and the treasure book stayed locked up.

The Boys from Hog Heaven

Tess and Ruth became friends and would see each other time to time. Tess will be coming over and will be bringing her daughters the following Saturday. On this particular weekend Betty will be going to visit the campus of her attended school. The Doctor from town, whose daughter is Betty's best friend would be taking Betty along with his daughter.

Tar hurried around and did all of his assigned chores. He wanted to see Charlotte and now since they were all friendly again maybe they could read the book in the box. Grandpa took his fishing equipment and Carver to see if they could get a mess of catfish for dinner. John would be going to town later and would leave soon after the chores were all done.

"What are you going to do with all of the females around today, Tar?" asked John with a grin on his face.

"I'll probably go up to my room and read," answered Tar.

John looked astonished at his eldest son knowing didn't care to read much unless it had to be schoolwork or required reading. "Maybe you should go fishing with grandpa?"

"I think it is good for Carver and Grandpa to go together. I'll be alright."

"You want to go to town with me?"

"No really daddy, I think I'll just hang around today."

"Okay son but you keep out of your mother's hair. She wants everything to go well today."

"I know daddy. I won't bother the ladies."

"Well I'm going to say goodbye to your mother and I'll be in town today for a while. Clean up the barn a little before I get back."

"I will daddy. Ya'll have a good time and don't worry," answered Tar as he commenced his cleanup chores.

In just a few moments Tar heard the McGregor pickup move quickly down the dusty road. It wouldn't be long before Bubba's girls would be at the house so he hurried with the task of cleaning up the barn. He checked on the box and the book in hopes he and Charlotte would read it together this afternoon.

Within an hour he heard the sound of an old pickup truck coming up the dusty road and knew it had to be the ladies. He peeked out of the barn door, saw Tess and Tara get out of the

107

front seat and Charlotte jumping out of the old wooden bed of the truck.

Bubba only stopped long enough to let the ladies out and continued back toward his little tract of land. Tar had not noticed Tara much before but saw that she was a beauty too but in simple form. He knew that Charlotte had to be her sister by their common good looks. Tess seemed a little uncomfortable as she walked up to the door. The girls followed.

When the ladies arrived on the porch the door swung open where Miriam came greet them.

"Come on in Miss Ruth is expecting you."

Tar's Mother came out right behind Miriam. "Come on in. I am so glad you all could come over today. We'll have a good time. Please come in."

"Thank you Ma'am," s aid Tess.

"I'm Ruth and you are Tess. I'm not Ma'am. I am your friend and neighbor. Come on in girls. We are alone John went to town and Grandpa and Carver went fishing. Betty is away for the weekend and Tar is working in the barn."

Tar could see his friend Charlotte smile when she heard he is around somewhere.

Tar knew his chores are important since he had worked more with his Father and drove the tractor regularly. He learned how to cultivate the crops and to always look ahead. He learned very quickly when he looked back to see if the cultivator stayed between the rows the front of the tractor would go off course and run over some of the crops. He knew it is important to help on the farm and to also pay off the gun that is still locked up in the cabinet in the barn. So he knew he must do his chores before visiting.

With the women folk safely inside Tar finished his chores. He knew sooner or later he would see Charlotte again and knew it would be best to make the meeting as accidental as believable. The ladies would have their tea and coffee and then probably talk or maybe they would look at some clothes that Betty didn't want anymore. Tess and Tar were almost the same size and the two were really close to Betty's size. Tar had seen his mother

108

The Boys from Hog Heaven

milling around the closets and figured that his mother would give the ladies some nice hand-me-down clothes.

The morning was getting warmer and the sun was getting higher in the sky. Sweat had popped out on Tar's forehead as he finished his chores. He knew an hour alone the ladies had plenty of time to visit and do the women things. It would be safe for him to slip up to his room and rest a while. He could see Charlotte after he cleaned up and changed his work clothes. It would be best if he stayed as inconspicuous as possible for the time being.

The ladies were in the living room as Tar slipped up the back stairs to his room. He wanted to look his best when Charlotte would see him and the dirt on his cheeks must go. He didn't want to look too shiny and clean where it would be too obvious he only cleaned up for Charlotte but he wanted to look good with a clean face and combed hair.

Tar found a clean pair of blue jeans and a clean plaid shirt to put on before he would meet all of the ladies in the front room. He knew too other than meeting Charlotte this gesture would please his mother very much.

He gathered his clothes and walked toward the big bathroom at the end of the hallway. He knew soon he would be able to see his new friend. As he approached the door of the big bathroom he saw that it was not entirely closed. He hesitated a moment and could see a shadow in the room. Quietly he walked up to the door. Who is in there? He thought grandpa and Carver went fishing and the ladies were downstairs. He got closer and to his surprise it is Tara, Charlotte's sister. She had a pile of nice dresses at her feet and on the commode and is trying on some of Betty's old dresses.

Tar wanted to leave but his adolescence curiosity wouldn't let him go. He watched for a moment as Tara slowly lifted the dress back over her head. Tar had only seen a naked women's body before and that was in the National Geographic magazine at school. He saw the small firm breasts and the narrow waistline of the teenage girl. She had on cotton panties but could see a dark outline beneath the white cotton. His mouth became dry and he swore he could hear the boards

Grant Williams

creaking on the hallway floor where he was standing. He stood for a moment which seemed like hours and watched Tara change dresses several times. He could see the smile on her face, as each dress seemed more satisfactory than the other. He knew he had seen enough and more than he should have. He tried to slip away quietly but dropped his belt on the floor.

Tara looked through the door and saw Tar and to his amazement she did not scream or call for help but looked at him and smiled. She had only her panties on and the dress she was trying on was around her ankles. Tar didn't say a thing and he too just stood there for a while.

"Have you seen enough?" said Tara quiet enough that no one from downstairs could hear.

"I'm sorry Miss Tara, Honest I am. I didn't mean to look. Honest."

"It is only natural; do you think I have a nice body? Do you think I am pretty?" asked Tara very seriously.

"I think you are beautiful, much prettier than my sister."

Tara then grabbed the dress and covered her half naked body. "This is our secret. I won't tell anyone. Will you?"

"Honest I won't. I won't tell a soul."

"You'll tell your little friends at school, won't you?"

"I promise I won't tell a soul, on my honor."

Tar then turned, picked up his belt and took his clothes back to his room. He would dress there and wash in the kitchen or outside. He fled to his room and had to sit on his bed for a moment. This is too overwhelming and it is Charlotte's sister. It had to be a secret. He finally caught his breath and dressed quickly. He went down the back steps quietly and washed in the kitchen. He combed his hair and looked at his reflection in the glass on the back door and knew it time to visit the ladies in the parlor.

Tar walked into the parlor and saw his mother, Tess, Miriam and Charlotte sitting around with a lot of clothes in the center of the room. Tara had not returned from her dressing room, the upstairs bathroom.

"Good morning Miss Tess, and Charlotte. Good morning mother. Good morning Miriam," said Tar as he stood a man

110

The Boys from Hog Heaven

amongst the ladies. He seemed to have a new air of confidence around him.

The ladies all said their good mornings and how do you do's. Ruth glowed with pride seeing her son grow up before her eyes. Miriam too always proud of Tar and had been so glad she had a part in his upbringing. Tara came back into the room soon after the greetings had been passed around.

"Good morning Tar," said Tara as nothing had ever happened between them.
"Do you like this dress? It was you sister's."

"Good morning Tara, the dress looks better on you than it did my sister," answered Tar knowing he would tip his hand but he wasn't nervous at all. Everything is going to be all right. Tara being faithful to the promise wouldn't let on anything is different between the two, after all they were just casual acquaintances before and she is just Charlotte's sister and Tar is Charlotte's friend.

Tar could see a similarity between the sisters and happy he could go on the rest of the day without having to be so careful of what he said or thought. Tess happy to see Tara in the fine dresses of the MacGregor girl because it is so good her eldest daughter now had a couple of nice dresses and maybe someday would go to the dances and festivals dressed in finery. Ruth now happy the families made up and the girls were happy too.

Charlotte had tried on a couple of things and got tired of sitting in the house. She needed the fresh air and to get outside. Ruth could see the restlessness of the young girl and suggested to her to go outside if she would like.

"Tar, would you take this young lady outside and show her the farm. I think she is bored with the rest of us. We'll call you in for lunch when it is ready. We have more dresses and ladies clothes to try on. Charlotte do you want to try on more clothes now?"

"No, Ma'am, I think I'll go outside with Tar if it is all right with ya'all."

Tess told Charlotte. "Go on, we'll be in here for a while. Have a good time."

111

Grant Williams

"Tar you be a gentleman and show our neighbor around. We'll have a nice lunch soon, right Miriam?"

"Yes Miss Ruth, we'll have a good lunch. I'll call you children when it is ready. You get along now, you hear," laughed Miriam with her toothy smile. "You get along now."

The two friends left the confines of the parlor and felt more comfortable outside.

"Whew, I didn't think I was going to get outside all day," said Charlotte.

"Me too, Too many women" answered Tar. "You wanna go look at the old book and the box."

"You bet. Do you think it would be all right with your mother if we were alone in the barn?"

"Of course my dear Charlotte I do give a damn," laughed Tar as he quoted "Gone with the wind".

"You know me and my sister were named after that book. You know "Gone with the Wind.""

"Well you are a treasure of the south my dear little lady," said Tar as chivalrous as he thought was necessary. "My mother trusts me and you can trust me too."

"Well in that case let's go," said Charlotte as she extended her hand to her friend.

Tar took her hand and found it cool but not cold. He held it gently until the two descended the steps of the porch. He wanted to continue holding her hand but he knew this is not the time so they walked beside each other to the old barn.

They felt comfortable as they sat on old peach crates.

"Are you going to get the box and the book?" asked Charlotte.

"Hold your horses my southern belle. I'll get the book."

The two friends sat quietly as Tar took the old book from the old box. The cover in fairly good shape considering how long the box had been in the ground, the cover tattered but the pages though fragile were still functional and serviceable. Tar slowly opened the cover and then looked at Charlotte. He saw the excitement and anticipation flowing from her presence.

Tar opened the book and they again looked at the first pages where it gave the particulars of George McGregor and his

112

The Boys from Hog Heaven

status in the First Division of the Confederate Army. They went to the page where he had left a message for his beloved Mary Ellen.

"Tar read me that part when George McGregor wrote all of the romantic stuff about his Mary Ellen."

"Let's go on to the rest of the book," answered Tar trying his best to get by the mushy stuff.

"I like to hear how much George loved Mary Ellen. Don't you?" asked Charlotte looking directly at Tar.

"It was a long time ago and they were at war," said Tar trying to go on with the book.

"Would you have some things to say to me if we now were at war and you would have to leave?"

"That was different then. I don't know what I'd do now."

"I'd write you letters if you went away."

"Let's see what is on the next page," said Tar as he turned the old page carefully.

"Look it is a map and it looks like the forest and the farmland. See the town. It was very small then. It is our town before it really was a town."

"George had a big X near where your house is now."

"He must have got this land right after the war."

"You think he knew that the south was not going to win and the slaves would leave and go north."

"I think he knew he would have to farm the land himself and make the best of the lack of help."

"Did I ever show you my new rifle?" asked Tar excitedly.

"I didn't know you had a gun," said Charlotte. "Is it big?"

"I can't tell anyone. If I take it out my daddy will take it away from me. Someday I am going to shoot that big pig in the forest but my daddy said I could hunt deer with him this fall."

"I won't tell," said Charlotte knowing this is a big secret that had to be kept. This idea of her young friend having a gun sounded so grownup. "Maybe you should wait until your daddy gets home."

"No you can see it but then we need to put it back in the case."

Grant Williams

Tar went and got the hidden key and opened the big locker. The gun case shined with its brown leather absorbing the sunshine. Tar carefully opened the case and pointed the gun away from Char. The metallic blue from the barrel and the well polished wooden stock impressed the young lady.

"You weren't kidding Mr. Tarleton, it sure 'nough is a big gun. Someday will you shoot it for me?" said Charlotte looking at her hero.

"Guns ain't for women folks but someday I will shoot the gun for you. I've got to put it up now before we get into trouble," said Tar. "Do you want to touch it first?"

"Can I?"

"Be careful. It isn't loaded but we still need to be careful," said Tar in an unusual protective way.

Char handed Tar the rifle and watched him put it back into the big box and lock the door.

"O Tar. You are such a big man and so brave. I won't be afraid if I am near you. I am not afraid when you are near me now." Char then grabbed and gave Tar a hug.

Tar did not resist the hug but slowly moved out of the firm grasp of the young friend. "We had better put up the box and the book. I'm going to study the map that George McGregor left and I let you know if I find out anything."

"Do you think the map means anymore than the land here in Carver?"

"I don't know. We had better get up to the house before the others think we are doing something wrong."

"Do you think they would think we would do anything?" laughed Charlotte as she looked at Tar.

Tar's face began to redden and his thoughts went back to the first kiss and then strangely went back to his encounter with Tara in the upstairs bathroom.

"Let's go. Miriam is a great cook and I know my mother wanted you ladies to have a good day. I am going back out in the fields after lunch and leave you alone. You girls should have the day to yourself."

114

The Boys from Hog Heaven

"Don't you want to be with me? "asked Charlotte trying to embarrass her friend. "Don't you want to hold my hand and if I let you don't you want to kiss me again?"

"Let's go," s aid Tar as he took her hand and escorted her to the big white house. Of course he wanted to be with her and of course he wanted to kiss her again but this is not the time. He became confused and bewildered as any adolescent would be. Maybe next time she dared him to kiss her he would. He would show her. He would let her know who the boss is.

When the two youngsters walked into the kitchen the ladies were just coming in for their lunch.

"Hi, Tar," s aid Tara smiling at the young man. "Having a good time with all the ladies here?"

The sentence from Tara made Tar very nervous and wondered if Tara would keep her secret. He didn't want Charlotte to know what happened, at least not yet. Tar grabbed a couple of sandwiches and headed out the door and said goodbye to the neighbors as he let the screen door slam behind him.

"Guess he didn't want to be around all of women," s aid Ruth laughingly.

Chapter Ten

The Yankees

The McGregor family and Bubba's clan became friends with the exception of Betty. The society world that Betty lived in did not include sharecroppers or other poor people. Betty tolerated the Black community and its people but didn't have anything to do with people that could not embellish her steps up in the social circles of the area.

The McGregor clan put up with their PRIMA DONNA and knew she didn't represent the entire family in their views. Being springtime, the proms and spring dances were coming up and the time of a young debutante's life. Betty wanted to be included and she would be. She had the stamp of approval from the community by being the daughter of John and Ruth McGregor, always accepted too because she is the friend of many influential person's daughters and sons in that part of Georgia. Her life's mission is to go to a good college and finishing school and eventually become the wife of someone important in the south.

The small but affluent country club controlled by the local influential people held a springtime dance where Betty would attend even though now she didn't know who her date might be. It never became a problem for Betty to find someone to take her. The only issue is to make sure he is the most eligible and someone who would accent Betty as an accessory similar to a piece of jewelry. Louise Handly, daughter of Dr. Handly, and best friend of Betty would go together with whomever they chose.

Of course Betty would have to have a new gown for the evening and John would not argue about this. It is so important his only girl would have the best even though he always didn't agree with her new kind of thinking. Ruth would make sure the McGregor family represented themselves in the proper fashion to the affluent and the country club set. Tar and Carver knew it

116

The Boys from Hog Heaven

is not the time to deal with their sister's moods whenever a function such as a dance would come up. The boys knew to stay away as much as possible.

Excitement grew around the house, as the date of the dance got closer. It would be within a month when the family again could relax until the next crisis in Betty's life.

"Got a call a while a go from a fella who was here a while back. He wants to go hunting again," said John one evening as the family sat on the front porch.

"Where is the man from, John?" asked Ruth as she sipped a cup of tea.

"He's from up in Pennsylvania, somewhere around Philadelphia," answered John. "We all were hunting over at Ephraim's place. Nice young man. He said a few of his friends want to come down with him and wanted to know if we all could go out again."

"Will he be here long?"

"He said he would only be here for ten days or two weeks depending on the hunt and the weather. I thought we could get together with Ephraim again and see if we can find another pig. If not we'll take the group fishing for some bass? Grandpa can go with them, after all they are Yankees."

"Yankees, daddy, maybe I can go with them too. I need to learn how to hunt. If Yankees can go then I should be able to go too?" asked Tar as he worked his way into the conversation.

"I don't think Tar is ready to go yet. Do you John?"

"After all the Yankees won't eat him or harm him. They won't get him too drunk and won't have him rape too many girls," laughed John.

"That's not funny John," said Ruth in a rather scolding manner, "I mean Tar is just still a young boy."

"He's growing up good and proper, Ruth. After all remember he helped with the planting this year. He worked right along side of the other men. Anyways I'll be there too to make sure he won't get into too much trouble."

"We'll talk about it later," said Ruth as she looked at Tar.

Tar knew it meant his father would try to convince his mother all is well and his mother would try to convince his

117

Grant Williams

father that he is still a little boy. If his daddy insisted, his mother wouldn't put up too much of a vigorous fight. It would be a good chance he might be able to go on a real hunt.

"The hunt is planned at the same time of the Country Club dance, Ruth. It might be good that there are some things for us men folks to do."

"You might be right John. You just might be right."

***

John McGregor made plans for the Yankees to come down to Georgia for the hunt. He had contacted his friend Ephraim to see if he would oblige having the hunt at his property since there were wild pigs in the area. Ephraim overjoyed to have the hunt and always glad to take the Yankees' money and tell them the tales of the south and who really won the War Between the States. John also had made plans for the three young men to stay at the only boarding house in Carver. The boarding house always had been known for its great reputation and congeniality. Mrs. Tucker who had been widowed for over twenty years would be glad to have people stay at her place and could use the extra money too.

John called the contact in Pennsylvania. His name was Walter Krucek, a son of a man who had made his fortune in the steel industry. Walter became the financial officer of the company and even at the young age of twenty-three was very capable of watching the wealth of his family and the family business. Walter explained he was having two friends come along for the hunt and their names were Bill O'Hara and Jeffrey Fitzgerald. John outlined the details of the trip to his Yankee friend. John also told Walter he and his friends would have good accommodations and a good hunt. So the arrangements were made and agreed upon. They party would arrive a week before Betty's big dance and leave shortly after, a thought that brought happiness to John McGregor.

The issue now settled about Tar going on the hunt and even through some weak protests by Ruth it had been agreed. John would take his son out to target practice and have him ready for the upcoming hunt. Having the preparation for Betty

The Boys from Hog Heaven

and the Country Club dance would be enough for Ruth to handle and having Tar with his father seemed to settle Ruth's nerves.

Tar excited he could go on the hunt with his father and with the Yankees. He knew the Yankees were similar to the southerners since he had seen pictures of many of them in the newspapers and magazines. He also had heard the tales of the War Between the States and the monstrosities of their visits. He heard that they talked different and somehow had different manners. Tar would have to tell all of his friends in school and he would have to impress Charlotte.

Miriam knew too that even with the upcoming dance John and Ruth McGregor would want to entertain the guests from the north at least one evening. Miriam knew her time would be desired to cook a southern dinner for the guests with all of the nice china and glassware. It would be an interesting few weeks for her. Miriam knew too the McGregors would compensate her richly for her efforts but she knew she would have done it for them anyway.

Betty became a little miffed at not being the entire center of attention. She had not got a date for the dance. She and here friend Louise had talked that they might just go unattended, an idea against all southern custom. She still had to get her gown, her shoes and accessories and that alone would take possibly a whole day with her mother. Didn't her parents realize this is her time and she should be on the center stage at the McGregor household?

Grandpa just sat back and enjoyed all of the activity. He had seen his granddaughter in action before and her selfish fits. He had seen his son and his son's wife spoil that girl from a child. He became excited about the Yankees coming to Georgia for the hunt and if he felt up to it he would go also. He would at least take the boys on a day of fishing at the lake for some stripped bass. The big ones were just starting to bite and they would have a good time. He looked down at his new pipe Carver had given him, felt the buttons from Tar in his pocket and knew he was loved.

Grant Williams

***

Time came quickly to the McGregor household with the hunt coming up and the men from the north arriving today. The Yankees would situate themselves at the Tucker boarding house and would be guests of the family in the evening. Miriam had been cooking all day and decided they would have southern fried chicken, sweet potatoes, turnip greens, butter beans and plenty of home made cornbread. Miriam had baked a velvet cake for dessert. The dinner would be served with sweet tea and cordials would be served for the adults later.

Tar and Carver were told to dress in their Sunday clothes and even grandpa would wear his suit and tie. Betty had picked out a very pretty light spring dress which showed off her fine figure. Betty also spent a lot of time putting on her makeup and preparing for the invasion of the Yankees. Ruth happy to entertain and as always was very proud to show off her family.

John dressed early and went to town to pick up the visitors from Mrs. Tucker's boarding house. He is happy to bring the men to his home in the newly polished Buick and to show off his little piece of Georgia but mostly he is proud to show off his family.

The three men were ready when John arrived and they climbed in the shiny Buick.

"Hello John, remember me, sir? "Said Walter Krucek holding out his hand with a smile.

"Yes sir, How are you Walter?" answered John and shaking Walter's hand vigorously.

"John McGregor I would like to introduce you to these two friends of mine who will be on the hunt with us. The tall one is Bill O'Hara and my other friend is Jeffrey Fitzgerald."

"Welcome to Georgia and a pleasure to meet you," said John in his most proper southern voice.

When the handshakes were made and the formalities were done John put the Buick in gear and headed out toward the farm. The sun now setting and the sky bursting with a beautiful sunset highlighted the red dirt in the fields and on the sides of the road. It is a good time of the year where the evenings were pleasant and very comfortable.

The Boys from Hog Heaven

"Are you all from Pennsylvania?" asked John.

"I am from the mining area of western Pennsylvania," answered Walter. "But I live and work in Philadelphia now. Bill is from the country just west of Philadelphia and Jeffery is from New York."

John looked at Jeffrey a little suspiciously since many people in the south though all persons from New York were either Gangsters or shysters. Bill quiet and seemed to enjoy the ride from town whereas Jeffrey seemed anxious and nervous. John seemed to like Walter right away. He liked the way he carried himself and liked his friendly way but not too friendly or overbearing. John liked the way Walter asked about the land and the farm but most of all that he asked about his family. Bill was quiet but Jeffrey seemed to talk too much and how he thought the people of New York would view this part of the world. Walter had dark brown hair parted just left of center and had a tan complexion for someone who worked mostly in offices and banks. Walter handsome, well built and well mannered and his flashing dark brown eyes sparkled with excitement when he talked about the trip and the upcoming hunt. John was glad he was here.

The Black Buick rolled up the dusty road and passed the sharecroppers houses. Will and Junior were on their porch when John passed the simple little house. John honked the loud horn of the Buick and waved. Will and Junior waved back. Walter looked at John as this transpired and knew the men were all friends. This made Walter more comfortable with John. They saw no one at Bubba's house but lights were burning through the windows. They soon passed the forest and saw the big white house in the distance. They all knew this would be where they would be spending the evening.

The Buick drove directly to the front porch and the four men got out. John walked them up to the front door where Ruth McGregor greeted them.

"Gentlemen this is my wife Ruth," said John as he proudly introduced them. "This is Walter Krucek, Bill O'Hara, and Jeffrey Fitzgerald," pointing to each one individually as he announced them to Ruth.

121

Grant Williams

Each man with his finest manners acknowledged their introduction to Ruth and then she escorted them into the house. Tar and Carver had been peeking out of the window near the door to see if these Yankees had horns or looked like evil demons. As the men came into the house the boys had scattered into the study.

Ruth led the men into the study and introduced the men to Tar and Carver. The boys as they were told to do shook each man's hand and said their howdy-do's in their best southern behavior.

"I will check on dinner and see if my daughter is dressed. John will make you comfortable and get you a drink or a cocktail. Tar, Carver please seat your guests," said Ruth so elegantly as she left the room.

The boys doing what they were told showed the Yankees to a seat.

"How about a drink, boys," said John to his guests. "I don't have any of those fancy city drinks but I've got some good old Southern Comfort."

Each man took a drink and sipped it slowly.

"Tar, Carver," said John "That fella there is from New York," pointing to Jeffrey.

"I'm not really a gangster," said Jeffrey as he walked over toward the boys.

Tar and Carver didn't say anything but kept watching as Jeffrey walked closer. When Jeffrey got close to Carver he reached up near Carver's ear and produced a coin.

"It isn't black magic. I just know a few tricks," said Jeffrey trying to ease the southern boy's anxiety, "See there is a coin in Tar's ear too."

The magic fascinated the boys and Jeffrey did a few more tricks for them. He had their attention as John talked to Walter and Bill.

"We'll go out to the hunt tomorrow and get with old Ephraim. You remember him don't you Walter, the old man who chewed a lot of tobacco?"

"Good old Fellow, are we hunting in the same area that we did before?"

122

The Boys from Hog Heaven

"Same area. Ephraim said he saw a couple of boars there a few days ago. Grandpa wants to take you fishing before you' all leave. There are some big stripped bass at the lake now and it would be ashamed if you 'all didn't take one back and show them in the city what a big fish looks like."

About that time Grandpa entered the study, "Did I hear my name? And where is my drink, John?"

Introductions were all passed around and Grandpa wanted these Yankees to know who he is and that he is a southerner from a family who had fought in the War Between the States and his Granddaddy was a war hero right there in Georgia. With some skepticism Grandpa talked with the men and soon was telling them tales that may or may not have been true. Tar and Carver loved it when Grandpa would go on with his tales and stories.

The door of the study opened and Ruth entered followed by her daughter Betty. The men quickly stood and were mesmerized by the beauty of the young lady especially Mr. Walter Krucek. When they were introduced the eyes of Betty and Walter met for the first time and quickly Betty lowered her eyes. There seemed to be an immediate attraction and it was obvious by all in the room.

"Gentleman dinner will be served in the dining room. Please come with me," said Ruth as she took the arm of Bill O'Hara. Walter took the arm of Betty and Jeffrey walked with the two boys as Grandpa and John followed.

Seating at the table included John and Ruth at each end, Grandpa at the right hand of John, Walter sat on the left of John with Betty on his left and Bill next to Ruth. Jeffrey sat on left of Ruth with Tar next to Jeffrey and then Carver between Tar and his Grandpa.

The table set very elegantly with the best linen tablecloth, china and silverware. The good crystal glasses were used and nice short bouquets of flowers were placed in the center of the table. Miriam came in with the food to be served family style and to be passed around. Miriam introduced to the Yankees by John told the guests she proudly served them some of the best food in the south.

123

Grant Williams

The dinner, absolutely great, and the Yankees enjoyed the feast put before them. Even Grandpa enjoyed the young men even though he was a still skeptical of Jeffrey coming from New York. The young men told stories of their lives, families and their business. Betty became extremely impressed with Walter being so young and so in charge of much of the family business. He is handsome, well mannered and rich, what more would someone such as Betty want in a man. She became infatuated and so was Walter. After dinner as the men folk went on the porch for cigars and a little whiskey Betty took Walter for a tour of the grounds around the house and settled on the back porch as it looked out over the onion fields. Ruth joined the men after she had dismissed Miriam and made sure Miriam had plenty of leftovers to take back to her brothers. Will picked up his sister in the old pickup truck and slowly drove back to the little house near the woods.

Grandpa now after a few whiskeys for some strange reason became fond of Jeffrey or 'New York' as he called him. Jeffrey showed Grandpa and the boys some card tricks that grandpa swore he knew but it was obvious that he didn't understand any. Tar and Carver were still in awe of the Yankees being all different in voice and especially with all of the entertaining tricks. Ruth enjoyed Bill O'Hara talking about his family and growing up on a farm such as theirs. John knew the night was a success especially when Jeffrey went over to Ruth and pulled out is handkerchief and when he shook it, out came a wonderful rose that he gave to his hostess. The sweetness of the peach blossoms mixed with the pungent aroma of the onion plant now growing strong gave the Georgia night a special appeal.

It wasn't long before Betty and Walter appeared on the front porch. It became obvious to Ruth that Walter would not be a stranger to the McGregor house for the next ten days. Betty looked happy and seeing Betty happy made Ruth happy too. Grandpa seemed happy and would have a great time with the Yankees on the fishing expedition. Tar and Carver were finding out that it really didn't matter where you came from but who you were. They would all have pleasant dreams that night.

The Boys from Hog Heaven

John finally had to take the men back to the boarding house since Mrs. Tucker wasn't too fond of her guests keeping late hours. She of course would more understand tonight since the men were visiting the McGregors. The trip back was pleasant even though Walter had little to say. The plans were made and they would meet tomorrow at ten o'clock and go to Ephraim's place and get ready for the hunt. It would be a busy day and most likely go into the nighttime hours.

The Buick purred as it pulled away from the old boarding house and as John accelerated he rolled down his window and felt the cool night air rush across his face. It is so good to be alive, have such a wonderful family and live in such a paradise. Tomorrow he would see the Yankees again.

Chapter Eleven

The Hunt

At ten sharp two pickup trucks arrived at Mrs. Tucker's boarding house. John had Tar in his and the other truck was Ephraim's. The Yankees were ready to go. They had their hunting gear on and hunting boots. Each man had a fine looking new rifle and several belts of ammunition. John and Tar took Walter with them while Bill and Jeffrey or now know as 'New York' went with Ephraim. Being Saturday and Tar happy to be out of school but couldn't wait to see Charlotte to tell her all about the Yankees. Maybe there would be a lot more to tell Charlotte after the hunt and he of course would see her at school on Monday.

It wasn't a very long ride to Ephraim's place by the river but there were a lot of trees and the roads were not in very good shape. The gravel roads were bumpy and uneven but added even more ambiance to the hunt. The guns bounced up and down in the beds of the pickup trucks but never left the truck but finally they arrived at Ephraim's humble abode safely.

"Enjoy the ride 'New York'?" said Ephraim as he parked the old pickup truck.

"Just like riding down Broadway," answered Jeffrey as he brushed off his new hunting duds.

"We'll get the dogs and then start the hunt," announced Ephraim. "Bring those two blue tick hounds," pointing to the biggest hounds in the dog run.

"Washington, get a move on. You and Johnny take the dogs ahead by the river. We'll follow. Let's go!" growled Ephraim to his two black hired hands.

As Washington and Johnny took the dogs ahead Ephraim said, "I can hardly get those men to move. They are just plain lazy sometimes. You know some of these black folks are just too slow."

The Boys from Hog Heaven

These statements seem to bother the Yankees but they were told that this might happen and they couldn't change things so just go on. It surprised Tar to see the look in his father's eyes when Ephraim went on about the lazy blacks for John McGregor always respected his fellow man no matter of color of wealth. John knew too he wouldn't change Ephraim or other of his fellow southern farmers but in time he knew things would change.

"Tar, got your gun loaded and the safety on?" asked John.

"Yes sir, daddy, I am ready," answered Tar.

"You walk beside me and Walter. If you see the pig make sure it is in the clear and you get a good shot. Make sure the others are clear. Got that?"

Tar had been told over and over again about how to stalk and how to shoot at the game. Safety was always first. John also told his son to let the Yankees shoot first since they were paying for the hunt and Tar understood, just to be out with the men folk made the hunt worthwhile.

"Ready Walter?" asked John McGregor. "I don't think we'll see anything for a while but as it gets closer to the evening some of the pigs will come out to get water. You'll see the boars will be more aggressive and are a better looking kill."

"I'll be ready Mr. McGregor."

"Walter, please call me John. We'll see each other all week so let's not be so formal."

"Okay, John," said Walter as they started toward the river.

Walter wanted to ask John about Betty and if he could see her again soon but thought he would have plenty of time in the next ten days. He could see how intent John had become so they would have a good hunt and bringing up his daughter now wouldn't be the best thing to do.

Tar walked patiently beside his father and with the rest of the group, so proud to be with the men folk and that his father had asked him to go with them, especially with the Yankees. He could see Ephraim's two black men walking ahead with the dogs and all was rather quiet now.

Grant Williams

Jeffrey seemed a little out of place with his new duds but managed to keep up with the others without complaining. Bill O'Hara had been on hunts before and seemed very comfortable in the woods. His Pennsylvania country upbringing must have accounted for this degree of familiarity of the outdoors. Ephraim just hustled along and spat his chewing tobacco on the trail as he walked with the others.

Ephraim motioned to his two black helpers to turn right into a thicker part of the forest. The trail began getting smaller and the river was still to the left of the men. As they would go deeper into the wooded area and into thicker brush, they still would be between the water and the creatures they were hunting.

"Slow down," hollered Ephraim to the two black men. "Look for the signs."

"What does Ephraim mean daddy?" asked Tar.

"He means look for signs of the pigs routing in the ground, eating tender bark from the trees or signs of pig hair on the brush or the bark of the trees."

"Oh," answered Tar as if he should have known that fact. "I'll look too."

"Make sure you keep the barrel of your gun pointed down when we go through the brush," said John to his son, "Don't want to shoot anyone especially a Yankee."

Tar looked at his father quizzically. Then John laughed and so did Walter.

Tar didn't say anything since he knew he had been had but did make sure he had pointed his new rifle toward the ground. Walter looked at the younger McGregor and smiled knowing he too had been had. The group walked a little slower and the dogs seemed to be tiring a bit too.

"Let's take a break up yonder by the old cottonwood tree," Ephraim commanded to the other members in the group. "The dogs will need a break and so will my boys."

Surprisingly Jeffrey still had enough energy to sneak up behind Ephraim as he sat beside the cottonwood tree and snort like a pig. Ephraim jumped up and grabbed his gun and turned, pointed between Jeffrey's eyes and said where everyone could

128

The Boys from Hog Heaven

hear. "You're lucky 'New York' you could be a dead pig right now."

Everyone looked at one another and John McGregor finally laughed and then everyone else laughed too.

"That Yankee got you Ephraim," said John.

"I about got me a Yankee too," said Ephraim trying not to be outdone.

The two black men and the Yankees were happy that now they all were a little more equal.

"You think we should camp by the river tonight, John," asked Ephraim. "Them there pigs will come out for water tonight. Maybe we should find a place now and feed the dogs. We could set up camp and start some vittles for our own selves."

"Not a bad idea. I'll scout around for a good place and we'll set up camp. Tar come with me. Ephraim have your men tie up the dogs and feed them when we set the campsite. Walter, you and your friends can set up your tents when Tar and I come back. We'll fix supper soon."

The day had gone by quickly and it was getting close to suppertime. The excitement of getting out in the fresh air and the anticipation of an exciting hunt had taken the minds of the hunters away from the hour. John knew it is a good time to look for a campsite and took his son to look for an adequate place.

Jeffrey still wandered around as the others waited for John and Tar to return.

"Hey, look at this?" said Jeffrey to Ephraim as he brought him a broken branch. "Isn't that hair on the stick?"

"Well I'll be darned, 'New York' you are getting purty darned good. That is hog hair and it looks as if the pigs have been through here today. See how the branch looks like it is freshly broken? I think the pigs will come to the water tonight. We can shoot them in the dark or follow them early in the morning. They will be easier to hunt then."

It wasn't long before Tar and his father returned to the group. Ephraim knew the land well and figured this was the best place to stay and camp. It would be the best place for protection from the elements and the pigs. It would be a place usually free of snakes and other unwanted varmints.

129

Grant Williams

"Bring you stuff," ordered John to the others. "Tar and I found a good place to stay for the night. Tar will get some wood. Ephraim's boys will feed the dogs and you men can relax while Ephraim and I fix you supper."

"Sounds like a good deal to me," said Walter.

"Me too," said Bill. "Do you need any help?"

"Not tonight fellas, me and the old man will take care of the food."

"We'll set up the tents," volunteered Walter. "Is over there by that fir tree all right?"

"Good place but try not to set up anything too near the water. The pigs will want to get to the water and may just go nuts if anything is in their way."

"Got ya," answered Walter, "Come on guys lets get this camp set up."

Washington and Johnny set their tent up away from the others and near the dogs. They understood that Ephraim would want them to look after the dogs and were not really invited to the camaraderie after dinner. It would be okay and accepted by the two men but would probably have to be explained to the Yankees.

Ephraim and John had planned a great meal and since the Yankees were paying for the hunt and important to feed those well so they would remember to tell their friends back up east for another hunt. Tar helped his father start the fire then put some potatoes in a pan and into the coals. John brought out some nice steaks for the crew and soon would put them on the grill to sizzle a while. There were plenty of the sweet Georgia onions that the Yankees paid big dollars for back home. There would be plenty of Home made bread baked at the McGregor house. There would be plenty of food to go around. They didn't have pork on the night of the hunt since it was a tradition in those parts of Georgia.

Soon the fresh meat was noisily sizzling on the grill. The potatoes were roasting in the pan in the coals and soon they would be ready. Ephraim had brought a few bottles of beer for the men and several bottles of root beer. Coffee was available but the men decided they would have the coffee in the morning.

130

The Boys from Hog Heaven

The sun over Western Georgia now setting and the night air became comfortable. The amazing burst of colors over the river thrilled the men as they looked toward the sunset. The brilliant purples and oranges lit up the western horizon. The men were happy and with full stomachs they sat around the campfire. Washington and Johnny cleaned up the dishes and cooking utensils and buried the garbage while the Yankees sat with the good ole boys and swapped tales of previous hunts. Some of the tales old Ephraim spun were probably not entirely true but brought the hair on the back of everyone's necks to attention. Of course Ephraim told the story of the most celebrated creature in the county. Ephraim had to tell tales of the big pig in the forest by the McGregor farm. He told the stories of the eaten children and the deathly screams at night near the farm.

The Yankees looked at John McGregor to see if he would verify the stories and watched in amazement as he nodded his head. Tar listened intently to the stories and hoped that the Yankees wouldn't ask to hunt in the forest by their farm. Tar knew someday he would kill the big pig and didn't need an organized hunt to do that. As the night got later and as the stories got grander the men heard a rustle of something moving quickly through the area between them and the river. The dogs started barking and jumping about.

"Is it the pigs?" asked Jeffrey excitedly.

"I think so," said Ephraim. "Grab your guns and we'll go toward the river. If it is the pigs we can see what direction they are going. I would suggest that we watch for the signs and go for the kill in the morning."

The moon had given enough light so that the men could see ahead on the river. The flashlights gave enough lights for the men to see the trail ahead. They all heard sounds of something in the water and slowly walked toward the sound. Soon there it was. Tar saw the outline of several pigs in the water. He pointed quickly to his father who in turn pointed to Ephraim.

Ephraim held up his hand and directed the sight to the Yankees and held a finger to his mouth as to indicate silence. He then whispered to the party.

Grant Williams

"Watch for the signs and which way they go. They won't go far tonight. We'll get them in the morning."

The three Yankees in their fancy hunting duds and the three southerners stood and looked at a sight not many people have ever seen. The differences in their culture and place of residence didn't matter at that moment. The pigs were thrashing around in the water as if no one was there. There was a large boar that seemed to be the leader and three other pigs enjoying the water. The boar had let the younger pigs into the water first and then he took over after he knew it was safe. The pigs' dark black bodies were now shining in the moonlight as if they were large fish each time they submerged, even Ephraim who had been on hundreds of hunts stood quietly and watched in amazement. Today they were playing like any family not knowing that tomorrow they would be a trophy and meat for the pig roast.

One of the blue tick hounds back at the camp let out a large howl. That sound seemed to alert the group of wild swine. The big boar looked around quickly and gazed back up the river before fleeing into the underbrush with his family running behind him.

Tar could sense the excitement but felt somewhat sad they would destroy the family tomorrow. He would hopefully get a shot and he would get his own pig but knew the Yankees would get the first shots since they were paying for this hunt.

Within minutes the hunting group was back at the camp where they assembled at the campsite. Jeffrey who could live in the city of New York without fear clutched his rifle as he sat in the countryside of rural Georgia. Here there is more fear to him about the unknown than the dangers and crime in the big city. The other men were excited and now were assured it would be a successful hunt.

Several hours passed before the fire died down along with the excitement they had just witnessed. Soon they would all be sleeping under the Georgia stars with the sweet smell of the peach blossoms and of course the aroma of the sweet Georgia onions.

132

The Boys from Hog Heaven

Tar felt safe knowing his father was nearby and feeling more like a man as each hour of the hunt went by. The Yankees, Walter and Bill had no trouble sleeping but Jeffrey sat for a long time in his tent clutching his rifle and listening to the sounds of the night.

John McGregor and Ephraim were up early and had rekindled the fire. Johnny and Washington had fed the dogs and packed up their tents. John had made a pot of coffee and the aroma of the liquid permeated their campsite by the river. Tar got up early too and had fetched some wood, enough for them to cook breakfast. Walter and Bill were up next and had packed up their tents. They all agreed all of the camping equipment, cooking equipment and utensil would be picked up later so everyone would stack up all items before leaving to continue the hunt. Ephraim would send the boys back later to get all of the items.

Ephraim had started cooking some country-smoked bacon and the enticing aroma awoke Jeffrey.

"Sleep well 'New York'?" asked Ephraim knowing that the wild became uncomfortable for his big city guest.

"I slept as well as you would have in New York City," said Jeffrey curtly. "Where is the coffee?"

Walter and Bill had to laugh seeing their friend still clutching his rifle. As Jeffrey approached the campfire Bill handed his friend a cup of hot coffee. With all of Jeffrey's fancy hunting duds he looked to him as a pimp in the woods.

"Jeffrey, are you going to shoot one of those wild boars or are you going to date one?" asked Walter sarcastically but in fun.

"What do you mean?" asked Jeffrey still not entirely awake.

"Those fancy duds. You look like an ad for the hunting magazine, just perfect."

"You guys will see. I'll probably shoot the first boar."

Walter looked at his other friend Bill and answered, "With your luck you probably will."

Tar watched this exchange and thought how different it is than conversations between him and his friends. For some strange reason he thought of Charlotte and wondered what she

133

was doing? He couldn't wait to see her in school next week to tell her about the hunt and maybe brag a little. He wanted to impress her and he wanted her to think he was now all grown up.

After breakfast the men stacked all of the gear and the hunt was again about to commence with Johnny and Washington leading the dogs, Ephraim, Bill and Jeffrey with John McGregor, Walter and Tar in the last group.

Ephraim was right; it would be easier to hunt in the morning. The dogs picked up the scent from last night and they saw signs of the pigs along the trail. The guns were loaded and the men anticipated a good day in the woods.

Suddenly up ahead a lot of activity from the two blue tick hounds broke out. Washington and Johnny now were having a tough time holding the canines back. The men could hear branches breaking up ahead and knew they were getting closer. Ephraim pointed to John McGregor to head off to the right and take Walter and Tar with him. He pointed to himself and to the other Yankees indicating he would continue straight up the trail and nearer the river.

Tar could now hear his heart beat and knew they were close to the kill. With each step he could feel each twig snap and each branch move. His senses now were extremely keen. Abruptly John McGregor stopped and pointed to the clearing ahead only protected by several Georgia pines held the prize. The men then saw the band of wild pigs with the big boar was standing in the middle of the group with several sows by his side. Two smaller boars were on the perimeter seeming to be soldiers and guarding the congregation. Slowly the men approached and John McGregor pointed to the large boar and then to Walter. Each step for Tar seemed like eternity causing him trouble breathing. The pigs seemed excited but were standing still. John gave the signal to Walt to ready for the kill. Walter slowly moved his gun up to his shoulder and a shot rang out through the Georgia wooded area.

The big boar went down still squealing frightfully while the other swine ran quickly away from their wounded leader and another shot rang out. It came from Ephraim's group of men.

134

The Boys from Hog Heaven

Tar didn't see the other pigs but heard more squealing in their direction. He knew another pig was down but still had his gun ready and would shoot if necessary. Tar then looked over to his father and John gave him the thumbs up to let his son know everything was all right. Tar had accepted the fact the hunt is for the Yankees and not for himself.

The trio walked slowly up to the downed pig. The boar rather large had tusks curled up in a devious way. The face still looked menacing and dangerous even in death. Walter had brought a small camera and had John take pictures of him and the pig. He took pictures of Tar and the pig and took pictures of his new southern friends. Johnny and Washington came over to the sight of the trophy. They knew they would have to bring it back later to the farm and it would be up to them to skin and gut it. They knew they would have to take the head to the old taxidermist to mount for the Yankee.

Ephraim came crashing through the brush. "I heard the shot and saw the old boar go down, good shot. You killed that old pig with one shot, nice going."

Ephraim looked over the pig and bragged to his guest shooter it was a fine trophy and he would have the head mounted and sent to him soon.

"We got another boar over yonder," said Ephraim. "Bill got off a nice shot when the pigs were running. I've got to find something else for old 'New York' to do. I don't think hunting in the woods is right for him."

"Grandpa is taking these guys fishing. Maybe fishing is his thing?" said John sympathetically, "I'll take him out target shooting with Tar next week. He might like that better than dressing up in his fancy hunting duds."

The men were happy with the kills and even Jeffrey was happy for his friend's success. They walked back toward Ephraim's place slowly talking and enjoying the landscape of the Georgia forest. Yankees aren't that bad thought Tar as he walked beside Walter

"Don't forget we will roast those pigs in a couple of days. Friday would be a good time to celebrate the hunt. I always give

135

Grant Williams

some of the meat to the church to distribute to the needy," said John, "If it is all right with you."

"Of course it is all right with me and how about you Bill?" asked Walter knowing what the answer would be.

"I would be happy to do what I can."

Ephraim piped in, "The boys will dress the hogs and I always give them a half for helping with the hunt. They'll bring them over to your smokehouse on Thursday."

"I'll have Miriam make up some food to go with the pigs and we'll eat Friday evening. We can invite some of the people around especially the hunters and have a good old time."

"Will there be any women there?" asked Walter hoping that he would see Betty again soon.

"There will be just family and maybe a few others, mostly just the hunters and some neighbors."

"Oh," said Walter now a little relieved. "It should be a great time John."

Tar was happy too and maybe his father would invite Bubba's family since they were neighbors. He didn't know since the last roast if that would be possible. Maybe since Betty would be with the guest of honor it wouldn't promote any problems. Tar hoped they could come and would ask his mother and father later if they could attend.

"Could we invite Will, Virgil and Junior?" asked Tar.

"Of course," answered John. "They will want to help cook the pigs."

"What about Bubba and his family?" asked Tar a little bolder.

"Well, I guess we should ask your mother, Tar. You know what happened last time."

"Daddy, Walter will have all of Betty's attention and mother really gets along with Bubba's wife. The girls won't get in Betty's way as long as she has a man around."

"Out of the mouths of babes," muttered John.

"What was that daddy?"

"Nothing son, we'll see. I hope they can come but mother should make that decision."

136

The Boys from Hog Heaven

That comment made Tar happy and knew his mother really wanted her neighbors to be at the McGregor functions. Maybe he could convince his mother to invite his friends; most of all make sure Charlotte is there. He would talk with his mother when they got home and try to convince her.

The hunt was successful and the Yankees were looking forward to a good old southern pig roast. Walter would see Betty, John could show off his family again, Grandpa could tell his tales, Ruth could exhibit her southern hospitality and maybe Tar could see his friend again. Ephraim would bring over the pigs for the roast and Miriam would be notified of the feast and invitations would be given out. It had been a good day as the men rode back in the pickup trucks feeling good and with anticipation of the weekend to come.

Monday the Yankees would be at Grandpa's mercy and hopefully would have a mess of striped bass at their mercy too. Carver would be allowed to miss school and he could spend the day on the lake. Tar would be happy at school where he could tell all of the other classmates about the hunt and about the Yankees. Tar would also be able to be with Charlotte and tell her all about his hunt. Tomorrow the Yankee men were all invited to church with the McGregors. Walter and Bill accepted right away and Jeffrey said he would try to make it but wondered if a man from New York would be accepted. After a little convincing from his comrades he told John McGregor he would attend also. Betty would be pleased that her father thought to ask the men from the north especially happy that she could see Walter again.

Chapter Twelve

Church and Other Things

Sunday morning is normally quite calm around the McGregor home whereas John, Grandpa and the boys would get ready after eating a light breakfast. Ruth and Betty would fuss over what they would wear to look good amongst the other parishioners. Ruth always felt that since the McGregor farm being such an important part of the community she and her daughter should also look the part of a successful family. Betty of course only wanted to look good for Betty and for her friends since she wanted to look like the southern Belle. Today became even more of an exception since John had announced the Yankees would be attending the morning services with his family. Betty couldn't seem to find the right dress to wear and the right shoes and hat.

As it got later and John finally called to his wife and daughter to tell them they would have to leave in ten minutes or they would be late. John said the Yankees would meet them at the church and would go into the service and sit with them. Ruth finally came down and said. "I just don't know what to do with that girl. She looks great and her clothes are perfect but she doesn't think she looks good enough."

"We're leaving in five minutes Betty," John hollered up the stairway. "We will leave without you if you are not down here."

"I guess I'll be there," Betty hollered back. "I just know I don't look ready."

With that statement Betty ascended the stairway and even Tar and Carver stared. Betty looked as if she came off the cover of a fashion magazine with her hair and hat perfect and her dress right for the occasion, respectful but feminine. Her makeup had been put on with much care and accented her lovely face.

The Boys from Hog Heaven

"Do I look all right, Daddy?" asked Betty desperate for some kind of compliment.

"You look like a million Yankee dollars."

"Thank you, daddy," said Betty finally with a smile and a big hug for her father.

The trip into town seemed always the same with John and Grandpa and Ruth tucked in between sat in the front seat of the shiny Buick. Betty sat by the window behind her mother with Carver in the middle and Tar sitting behind his father. The dusty road never seemed to dirty the Buick as it traveled toward the little town. Soon the family passed Bubba and Tess' place and Tar noticed the pickup truck not sitting in their driveway. Maybe they were at church too even though it wouldn't be their church. Tar also noticed the leaves on the trees in the forest now were covering up all the lifeless look of just tree trunks and underbrush. Someday he thought I am going to find that big old pig.

The black shiny Buick rolled into town and as promised the Yankees were waiting in front of the white church building. Walter came dressed like a big city lawyer and had neatly slicked back his dark hair. His tie tack would sparkle each time he would face the sun. Betty seemed happy and impressed. She had hardly looked at the other two men who also were dressed neatly in their pinstriped suits. Walter seemed to have interested Betty enough to pay attention even though she had been warned about Yankees. She would make sure Walter would escort her into the church building.

John and Ruth entered the sanctuary first with Betty on the arm of Walter. The other Yankees, Bill and Jeffrey walked in with the McGregor boys. They all seated themselves in the long wooden pews near the front of the room. The windows were slightly opened to let the warm Sunday morning air waft through the building and the sounds of birds chirping outside seem to warm the crowd for the sermon and the singing.

Walter who had been single and proud of it seemed happy to be with Betty in the church and glad the McGregor family had included him and his friends. He loved the part of the service when they would sing and he could hear the lovely voice of his companion. He would glance over at Betty when she wasn't aware of the fact he was looking. He then knew this hunting trip might be more than killing a pig and having a good time with his buddies.

Betty looked at Walter too when he listened to the preacher and saw a handsome man with a strong and virile body. She saw a man who although a leader was comfortable in a family situation. Maybe she would have a difference of opinion on all she had heard about the Yankees before the hunters went back home. She would have to find a way to be alone with him and knew the upcoming pig roast feast would be a good place to start.

Ruth McGregor looked at her daughter and the handsome Yankee and seemed to be very happy. She really didn't know the young man well but she knew that her husband liked him and respected him. She realized Betty no longer a child had her future ahead of her.

Tar and Carver watched the Yankees intently as the preacher told the congregation to beware of the devil and the devil came in different forms. The congregation seemed to look at the young men from the north as their beloved southern preacher made this statement. The men sang with the others and worshipped along with the southern community. Tar and Carver were glad the new friends came with them to this fine church.

After the service the family introduced the Yankees to all of their friends and to their pastor. Betty made sure she introduced Walter to her young female friends who were right at her side and seemed comfortable with the friend being with this cultured Yankee.

When time to go and Ruth made the suggestion that they could all meet for Sunday dinner but it seems that an old customer of Walter's company that lived in the next county had invited the men to their place to eat. They finally agreed the men would come over to the farm after supper for some homemade peach cobbler and ice cream. This idea and acceptance put a big smile on Walter and Betty's faces for at least they could spend a little time together. It gave Ruth a

The Boys from Hog Heaven

chance to entertain the guests from the north again to show them real southern hospitality. Grandpa seemed glad too since he would be able to fight the War Between the States over again with his Yankee counterparts.

Finally the McGregors left the churchyard and headed home down the dusty road. Ruth seemed pleased the congregation so graciously accepted the visitors and she knew her influence in the community highly thought of and sometimes she used it.

Her friends and neighbors knew if Ruth McGregor accepted the Yankees the entire town of Carver's elite would accept them. She seemed excited about a man of distinction even though he brought up a Yankee became interested in her lovely daughter. She saw for the first time a special light radiating around her young daughter. She was happy the Yankees had come to Georgia. She would with the help of Betty make the cobbler for tonight and have the men make the ice cream and not take her cook away from her own Sunday worship.

***

John McGregor seemed to be happy and he had a fondness of the men from the northeast. These Yankees were good men and were comfortable in a south they didn't entirely understand but enjoyed. It had been a pleasant surprise Betty and Walter were becoming good friends, since a relationship for Betty in the past became only a controlling issue or a trophy for her. He had been glad his daughter listened to Walter and his points of view and glad even though the hunters would only be in Georgia for a short time the two young people could get to know each other. John knew too, soon Betty would be off to college and would find other male interests.

Ruth and Betty were so happy to entertain and a Sunday night was not ordinary for this time of year with the children still in school but life always has exceptions. Betty had not totally been comfortable in the kitchen but not unlike her mother Ruth had a cook and companion could still whip up a mean cobbler or cook a meal when necessary. Ruth had taught Betty the basics of cooking and the part of domestic

Grant Williams

responsibilities she might someday need. Today would be fun and exciting for both Ruth and Betty especially the time they could talk about the young men and how much the visit the Yankees brought to them.

Tar and Carver loved their mother's cobbler and loved the fact that they could have some homemade ice cream and talk with the Yankees. Grandpa made sure he had his confederate literature around the parlor where the men would notice and he carried the buttons that Tar had brought him just for conversation. John smiled to himself to see his father revived and interested in the visitors and how he would try to convert them to good old boys.

After supper John and his boys got out the ice cream machine and checked on the ice. Ruth had made the cobbler and it was bubbling in the oven. She also had made the ice cream recipe and left it sitting in the refrigerator waiting to be poured and turned in the old hand cranked machine. The boys dressed in their school clothes for the guests while Betty had been in her room and in the bathroom for the last hour.

"Do you think that young lady will wear out that mirror?" asked Grandpa.

"She'll be fine," answered John. "She just wants to impress the Yankees."

"Okay," said Grandpa knowing John was aware of his idea also to impress the guests from the north. "They are still going fishing tomorrow?"

"As far as I know Carver is going too. I told him he could stay out of school tomorrow. He already knows more than his teacher anyway."

"Good, always glad to have some southern intelligence with us," replied Grandpa.

Carver looked at his father and saw the little wink knowing his father trusted him to go and happy he included him in the Yankee's visits.

"What time are we going?" asked Carver.

"I'd like to get out before it gets too hot but I don't know what time the Yankees get up in the morning," replied Grandpa.

"Don't you think they will be ready?"

142

The Boys from Hog Heaven

"I hope so since it is a little drive to the lake and we need to get the boat on the water."

"I hope we catch some big ones."

"All depends on if these fish like Yankees too."

"Really, Grandpa do you think the fish know the difference?"

Grandpa went on about how that sometimes fish don't want to be caught and it could be they knew who was sitting in the boat above. Carver looked at Grandpa curiously but somewhere in his soul he thought these things might be true even though his common sense told him it probably wasn't. John and Tar listened a while and then went back into the house to see if Ruth needed anything before the guests arrived.

It was just about seven o'clock when the family, now sitting on the porch saw the dust from the rented car come up the road. The Yankees were coming and they were on time. John and Ruth rose to greet the men as they descended the car. Grandpa still sat in his rocker with his grandsons standing beside him as Betty still primped upstairs but aware of the men arriving.

"Glad you could come this evening," said John.

The men greeted Ruth first and all thanked her for the invitation. Grandpa waved and the men in their best manners made sure that grandpa had been properly greeted and made to feel important. The men knew Tar and they spoke to each other before they all went over to shake Carver's hand. Walter looked around and didn't see Betty but knew it would not be polite to ask if she planned to be with them this evening.

John McGregor sensing Walter seemed to be searching for his daughter spoke, "My daughter Betty will be down in a minute but we can start churning that ice cream with a little help."

The boys got the churn and loaded it with ice and rock salt. Ruth brought out the recipe with the cream and sugar and poured it in the center container.

"Everybody gets a turn. You boys start cranking and maybe our friends would want to turn the crank a while too," said John.

143

Grant Williams

Grandpa looked suspiciously at the Yankees to see if they would help. He still had the impression they were all Prima Donnas. The conversation seemed to be light and the men talked about the visit to Walter's old friend's home. Grandpa became a little more comfortable knowing the men actually did know other people from Georgia. The men took turns and Walter took the lead and went first. John enjoyed seeing his sons talking and visiting with their guests. Ruth proudly watched her sons and seemed to be pleased with their southern manners.

Finally Betty arrived dressed in a simple but flowing dress. The frock fit her girlish figure and accented the right places. Her makeup put on to look as if she had little on but had been applied with the elegance of a New York salon. Ruth and John both looked at their daughter and smiled with pride.

The Yankees all stood up in unison and Walter quickly came to the lovely young lady's side. Betty quickly ushered Walter over to the loveseat placed the farthest away from the ice cream churn.

"I'm going to heat the cobbler and by that time I think the ice cream will be ready," said Ruth as she got up and went into the kitchen.

All of the men rose except grandpa when Ruth exited.

"I can see where you daughter got her charm and good looks," said Walter to John.

It sounded kind of corny to the others but to Betty and Walter it was a perfect statement. Betty smiled and quickly looked down to the floor of the porch while the others went on churning the ice cream freezer and telling tales. Grandpa had managed to get the War Between the States into the conversation but the Yankees seem to leave that subject alone and only agreed with grandpa. The boys were fascinated as Jeffrey pulled a couple of magic tricks on the boys and were promised, by Jeffrey, he would teach them both a trick before he left to go back home. Walter and Betty didn't say much but just sat together and listened to the others.

Soon the ice cream got firm and ready and Ruth had brought the cobbler out to the porch. Tar helped her bring out some dishes and Carver brought out the silverware. Ruth

144

The Boys from Hog Heaven

dipped out a large portion of the cobbler in a bowl and put a big scoop of ice cream on the top.

"Here you are Grandpa," said Ruth making sure the senior member of the family got served first.

Ruth then served her guests and had Betty help. The men felt very comfortable with the McGregors and happy to be sitting on the porch watching the sun go down and eating peach cobbler. The men mentioned the pig roast and John suggested they take a look at the smokehouse. Tar and Carver were invited along too as soon as they helped their mother clear the cobbler dishes from the porch. It became obvious to all Walter had little interest in the smokehouse but knew soon he could be alone with Betty. Ruth knew she would be close enough to be a fashionable chaperone but really wanted the young people to be alone.

When the others had gone their separate ways and Betty and Walter were alone. Betty finally spoke in her charming southern voice. "I didn't think we would ever be alone."

"Did you want to be alone?"

"I was hoping you could come over tonight. It would be shameful if we didn't have the courtesy to leave you gentlemen alone."

"I really like your family Betty. They are really good folks. Someday maybe you could come up to Philadelphia and meet my folks. They are a little different being from the city but down deep they are good people too."

"If they are like you Walter I'm sure they are fine people," answered Betty as she took out her little fan and fanned her face.

"Do you think we could see each other more during my stay here in Carver? Your Grandpa is taking us fishing tomorrow and we will be back sometime late in the day. Maybe we could go for a walk or just sit on the porch?"

"I'll be here at the farm when you' all will return tomorrow."

"Good, I mean I'm glad."

"I know what you mean," said Betty as she took her strong Yankee's hand.

145

Grant Williams

Walter looked back at her and responded by taking her in his arms and pressing his lips to hers not in a friendly way but serious and direct. Betty did not pull away but pushed the softness of her own lips firmly to his.

The two young lovers parted when they heard the noise of the men returning from the smokehouse.

"Before the men get back," said Betty breathlessly. "Would you escort me to the Country Club dance Saturday night? It is formal but I could get you a tuxedo and I could get dates and tuxes for your friends too."

"Of course I'll go and I'll ask my friends. They might just want to come stag if that is all right."

"I'm sure it would be all right with the country club people. They would be honored to have such distinguished guests as you' all. I'll let you know the details tomorrow when you return with Grandpa."

"Can't wait to hold you in my arms again," said Walter as the men approached the porch.

"Hush now you Yankee," said Betty as she got up and started into the house.

"Walter, you should see the smokehouse," said Bill O Hara. "Mighty fine set up."

John McGregor always proud his smokehouse received such accolades after all it is his pride and joy. The old building had roasted a lot of meat and the smokehouse had been the start of many celebrations. Grandpa was proud too that this farm carved out of the red land was such a wonder and such a place for love and fellowship.

Chapter Thirteen

Fishing with Grandpa

The Yankees met Grandpa and Carver a little before sunrise. Carver had actually been up for an hour before Grandpa knocked at his door and while lying in his bed thinking of how great it would be just to be with his Grandpa and the Yankees. Just down the hallway Betty lied awake too thinking about her new love and accepting the fact he is a Yankee.

The men were congregating on the porch with their fishing gear when Miriam arrived in the pickup truck driven by her brother Will.

"You' all going fishing I see," said Miriam as she walked toward the entrance of the big white house. "You' all bring a mess of fish back here and I'll cook 'em. You just clean 'em and I'll cook 'em."

"She can really cook," s aid Carver.

"I bet she can," s aid Walter to the young man.

"You going to let me catch any today?" asked Jeffrey looking directly at Carver.

"Yes, sir," answered Carver. "Those fish don't care if you are a Yankee."

Carver's face flushed for he didn't mean to say anything about being a Yankee or if it really did matter.

"I didn't mean it like that," stuttered Carver. "I meant."

"It's all right. I guess I don't care if they are rebel fish either," interrupted Jeffrey.

The men laughed with Grandpa being the most vocal because he knew his grandson is a true proud southern boy. Grandpa still had the fire to compete with the visitors from the north and even though he liked them they still were Yankees. The men saw this part of Grandpa's personality and felt sometimes they had to defend being from the north and being Yankees but they still liked and respected the old man.

Grant Williams

The men agreed that they would follow grandpa in their rental car because they knew the old pickup truck would be crowded and didn't want to inconvenience the old man. It would be more comfortable for all with this arrangement. Grandpa liked to get out once in a while behind the wheel also just letting everyone know he was still capable of driving a motor vehicle. Grandpa would take the men through the back roads and show them parts of Georgia they would have never seen otherwise.

The men all got in their vehicles and knew they would have an adventurous day. Jeffrey still looked like an ad for New York City hunting and fishing magazines with his brand new clothes. He really didn't care because he knew he stuck out like a sore thumb and looked different. Grandpa didn't care either because he could show everyone what a Yankee is supposed to look like. It had been a great adventure for Jeffrey and getting away from the city lights seemed to have agreed with him. Being in unknown territory had been the adventure he needed and it also had been good for the McGregors having such a city boy with them during his visit and the hunt.

The trip an hour from the farm and the lake is a place there would be plenty of activity for fishing. A popular place where there were areas pristine and seldom visited by land or boat. As the men drove the back roads, passed many small farms, small fields of cotton and sweet potatoes they were educated in some of the stark realities of the south and of Georgia. The leaves on the trees were almost completely out now and the greenery had become sight to behold with its slick look from the wetness of the morning dew. As they drew nearer the lake they saw the remnants of the morning fog that had protected the water. They heard the chirping of the birds now starting to build nests in the magnolias and redbud trees. The first sight of the lake amazed them for there was not a ripple on the water and the air stood still. The surface of the lake looked like a mirror reflecting the morning.

The men followed Grandpa up to an old dock made of strong cedar or pine that had weathered many Georgia days. The boat sat there as promised, left by the friends of the McGregors for such occasions.

The Boys from Hog Heaven

"See they left the boat for us," said Grandpa oblivious to the morning beauty.

"This is a beautiful place," said Walter. "How long have you been coming here?"

"I came here with my daddy when I was a boy and been coming here every year since," said Grandpa. "There is a lot of fish here."

"Even for Yankees?" prodded Jeffrey.

"Even for you 'New York'," said Grandpa looking suspiciously at the duds that Jeffrey wore. "Are you going to catch fish or charm them?"

"Whatever it takes, What ever it takes," answered Jeffrey as he waited his turn to get into the boat.

With the help of the men Grandpa got the boat loaded with all of the bait, tackle and the food and drinks. Carver followed his Grandpa closely so that he could sit by him when they cruised on the lake.

"Nice of the family here to keep our boat," said Grandpa as he sat near the motor. "Whenever we want to use it we just call a few days ahead of time and they bring it to the dock full of gas and bait for us."

"Great deal," said Bill O'Hara. "It seems typical of the southern hospitality we all have found here."

"It's just a way of doing things in the south," answered Grandpa with the pride of being a southerner oozing out of his conversation.

Carver watched intently as his Grandpa started the boat.

"Take in the lines," hollered Grandpa.

As the lines were taken in, the boat eased away from the dock and onto the lake with the fresh air in their face as the boat cut across the still water, which seemed so refreshing and comforting.

"Got some good spots?" asked Jeffrey.

"I've got a great spot for you 'New York'. You will be able to tell your friends back in the city that the fish just don't come from the fish market after you catch one of these big ones. I know a really good place on the other side of the lake in one of the inlets."

Grant Williams

Carver started getting anxious to throw his line into the water especially since he wanted to be part of the group and not just a little kid along for the ride. Carver, too, wanted his Grandpa to know he wasn't just a student but he could handle the outdoor life, just like his brother. He wanted to show the notorious Yankees that he could fish with the best of the southern boys.

Some activity had been starting on the lake. The insects were now patrolling over the still water and an occasional fish jumped to let the bugs know it could always dinnertime. The purr of the motor as it pulled the boat along became a pleasant beat, enjoyable to the occupants. It didn't take long before Grandpa pulled the boat into a little sheltered cove.

"Get ready for some good fishing," Grandpa said. "There is plenty of bait in the box and if you want to try some lures I have a few in that case over by the gas can."

Jeffrey watched the others bait their hooks and then he copied their motions. He had been fishing before but it had been a long time ago. He watched how deftly Grandpa threw out his line just to the right spot. He watched his friends also cast their lines into the crisp clear Georgia Lake. Even Carver had no difficulty putting his line in the water. Jeffrey finally cast his line and surprisingly threw it far enough away from the boat that it didn't embarrass him. He knew then he would enjoy the day.

Grandpa let the boat drift and as it drifted it moved a little further from the shoreline. The current in the lake had taken the boat in a perfect line and near the feeding areas of some of the bass.

It had been at least an hour and Jeffrey seemed disappointed that no fish were caught. Then suddenly they got a strike. The line on Grandpa's pole whizzed out from the reel and as he checked up the line the pole bent quickly on a sharp angle. Skillfully the old man brought in the taught line with the fish on the end fighting for its freedom to no avail. Grandpa landed the first fish, a bass and it was large enough to keep.

"There's one for Miriam," said Grandpa. "We need to catch his daddy," as he cast his line that he had again baited.

150

The Boys from Hog Heaven

"Nice fish," said Walter. "I hope I get one like that."

As proud as Grandpa seemed he told the group, "That was just average. We should get some bigger ones. They are feeding now."

Walter got the next strike and he expertly brought in the fish. It is a good fish too and similar to Grandpa's.

"We'll drift over toward that big oak tree on the corner of the cove," said Grandpa. "I've seen some big ones leave from there to deeper waters. Sometime they will hide in the weeds."

The fishing became a little better there and Bill O'Hara caught a nice fish and Walter another. Grandpa coached Carver and showed him where to throw his line and sure enough he felt a strike and the force and the surprise almost pulled Carver out of the boat. The men stopped their fishing and watched the lad fight the fish. They watched how the old grandfather worked with the boy but didn't do his fishing. The little beads of sweat on the fuzzy cheeks were popping out and running down. The men could see the little hands normally more comfortable with a pencil in school become red. The fish would run and Carver would gain advantage and the sequence would start all over. The boy started winning the battle but slowly. They knew this is not a little fish and would be something to brag about so they stood by with the net to capture this young man's dream.

Grandpa let the boat drift as Carver pursued his prey. The fish now started getting tired but so was Carver. This would be a fight to the finish and the boy would have to do it alone. The fish started to the surface and within fifteen feet of the boat jumped out of the water as its last hope for freedom. Carver skillfully as told by his grandfather kept the line tight and strong and maneuvered the fish to the side of the boat where Walter netted the catch.

The prize now pulled onto the boat and Carver with pride and amazement looked at his catch. He thought to himself 'it must be at least a hundred pounds'. Grandpa lifted up the fish in triumph and it looked large. Proud of his little grandson and happier than if he had caught the fish himself Grandpa smiled.

151

Grant Williams

"It must be twenty pounds. What a fish. Carver that was good. That was a great catch and you did a real good job landing that creature."

Carver beamed with pride for he had never heard his Grandpa brag about anything he had done before. Grandpa wasn't like his mother as she was always telling everyone how good Carver is in school. Grandpa, of course, extremely proud that the boy caught the fish while out with the Yankees.

The Yankees one by one pounded the boy on the back as a gesture of pride they had with his catch. Each one bragged how they had never seen a fish like his before. This too made the boy happy and proud, especially to hear the accolades from his new Yankee friends.

"Okay, Yankees, it is your turn to get a big one," said Grandpa still looking at his smiling grandson.

About the time that statement came out of grandpa's mouth Jeffrey's line whizzed out and finally Jeffrey got control of the reel.

"I think I got a monster too," said Jeffrey happy that he finally got a bite.

"Careful now, New York," said Grandpa "I'll bring the boat around slowly so you can bring her in. Keep the line tight."

Jeffrey not being the fishermen like the others listened to all of the advice. He intently watched the line waiting for the big fish to jump out of the water. The line stayed taught and Grandpa skillfully brought the boat nearer the end of the line.

"Bring her up," cried Grandpa.

With all of his strength Jeffrey gave a tremendous tug on the line and all of a sudden a snapping turtle emerged out of the water with Jeffrey's bait in its mouth. With the force of the pull from him the turtle landed in the boat and right beside Jeffrey. The two looked at each other for a moment and the turtle decided he too was unhappy with his captor. The slimy green amphibian moved quickly toward Jeffrey and about to take a bite of Yankee leg when Grandpa took a piece of the rope that tied up the boat and put it in front of the snapper. The turtle took the rope in its mouth and gave it a mighty chomp and at that instant Grandpa slung the turtle out of the boat.

152

The Boys from Hog Heaven

"Nice catch 'New York'" said Grandpa and then they all laughed including Jeffrey.

"I thought you were going to be a nice catch is what I meant," said Grandpa not wanting to let this moment go.

"Thanks Grandpa," said Jeffrey. "Not too many rebels would have saved me."

"Twern't nothing, I'd have done that for anyone."

"Still, thanks," smiled Jeffrey knowing this story would be told many times by Grandpa after they all went back up north.

The day went fine and the fishing got better. They ate their lunches of bologna and cheese sandwiches and drank their RC Cola. The heat of the day didn't deter these hearty fishermen as they constantly threw out their bait and reeled in the empty lines. As the afternoon moved on and the sun got higher it became obvious the fishing started getting slower and the fish had gone deeper into the colder water.

"Let's make another pass along the shore and then we can troll across the lake to the dock. I think the fishing have gone down to colder water. Maybe we should call it a day," said Grandpa and they all agreed.

It had been a productive day and the men all had caught fish. There were some big ones on the stringer and they were all happy except Jeffrey who had been shut out. Without his turtle incident he had not caught anything. They men and Jeffrey were resigned to the fact it wasn't his day and he would go home empty. So the boat passed the shoreline for the last time that day.

Grandpa turned the boat toward the middle of the lake and the men trolled their lines over the back as they headed toward the other side of the lake. Carver's face had now reddened by the sun and he seemed happy too, for it had become a very special day for him. The men talked about the day as the boat skimmed slowly across the water. They had enjoyed being with Grandpa and were appreciative he took them to his favorite spots.

153

Grant Williams

Even Jeffrey was grateful and happy as he started to reel up his line to put his pole away. As if out of a fairytale something struck his line. Excitedly he yelled to Grandpa.

"I got a bite. I got a bite."

"Not another snapper?" joked Grandpa.

"Really, Grandpa, I've got a bite. Really," said Jeffrey as excited as a schoolgirl on her first date.

Grandpa slowed the boat down and Jeffrey started working his line as he had seen the others do all day. Slowly he played out the line and then when he felt the line starting to slack he reeled it in quickly. He started to get excited for he knew it was not a little fish on the end of the line.

"Play her," directed Grandpa.

"Careful," instructed Bill.

"Watch for her to run," called Walter.

"Get her," encouraged Carver.

The fight lasted for what seemed like an hour but the struggle ended within fifteen minutes and the sight of the large fish in the net amazed them all. It amazed them such a large fish came from this lake and it amazed them Jeffrey would be the one to catch it. The fish bigger than Carver's but Carver still was happy for Jeffrey. The fish would someday be hanging on the wall of a New York office with the hopes someone would ask Jeffrey about it.

What a day, two big fish and a mess of fish to clean and for Miriam to cook. It had been a good day as the men climbed into their vehicles and headed back to the big farm and big white house. They would be able to relive the day and the stories for a long time.

The sun still high highlighted the red dirt of the Georgia countryside and accompanied them on they journey back to the homestead.

***

The men returned, cleaned the fish and were told that tonight there would be a big fish fry. They were going back to change clothes and then return to the McGregor farm. Jeffrey had been told where to find a taxidermist and he planned on

The Boys from Hog Heaven

taking his prize bass to get it stuffed. He didn't care what the cost might be since it had been the first thing in his life he had actually done by himself it would hang on his wall as a reminder. The fish fry would be a great get together and Walter would see Betty again.

***

Tar had told his father that he would find a way home from school and decided to walk. He had told all of his friends at school about the Yankees and the wild boar hunt. He told them how he had his gun but became only a backup to the men since they paid for the hunt. He explained the thrill of the hunt and the dangers that automatically added to his status amongst the other students. Charlotte listened to Tar but didn't interfere or take part in most of the conversations and made sure Tar was the hero he wanted to be. Tar finally managed to see Charlotte before their last class and ask if she was all right. He wanted her to be proud of him more than the others but worried she wasn't there most of the day.

They talked briefly and Tar told Charlotte that he had planned on walking home and if she would like for him to walk her home. Charlotte could catch up with her dad when he picked up Tara and she felt sure it would be okay as long as they went straight home.

The plan worked for Charlotte and she met up with Tar outside of the school grounds soon after class. Tar now happy not only that he would have company on his walk home but he could walk with his friend.

"Char why didn't you talk to me all day?" asked Tar as they started out of town and down the dusty road.

"You were busy with your friends and telling them about the hunt. I didn't want to bother you. Your friends might not have liked it if a girl was around."

"You always can be around. You are my best friend."

" I know but you really needed to be with just the guys."

"I missed not having you tagging around with me."

"Really, Tar. You did miss me."

155

Grant Williams

"Yeah I missed you. I missed you when I was on the hunt and I missed you all day today," answered Tar but not looking at his feminine friend.

"Sometimes at night I think about you too, Tar. I think about you growing up and killing the big pig in the forest. I think about you leaving and going away to college."

"I think about those things too," said Tar as he grabbed a piece of tall grass by the side of the road and placed it in his mouth.

"Do you think your sister will ever change and get along with my sister or me?"

"I don't know. Does it really matter?"

"I think it does to my sister but not that much to me. Your mother is very nice and gave us some nice clothes but I don't think your sister wants to be associated with us poor people."

"She's nuts but I don't think you will have to worry about her."

"Why is that?"

"She likes one of the Yankees."

"Really, do you think it is serious or do you think she is just curious?"

"Curious about what? The Yankees are a lot like us but only live in a different place. The war is over and things change. I like her new boyfriend too. He is a nice guy."

"Would you ever go out with a Yankee girl?"

"I don't know, Charlotte. I never thought about it."

"I hope you'll go out with me when I get older. I want you to take me to the movie show and buy me ice cream at the store."

Tar didn't answer but he too had that ambition. He wanted to be with Charlotte and didn't always understand why but he felt better when they were together. The little sharecropper's houses were coming in to view and Tar knew it would be time to leave Charlotte and head up to the big white house. He took her little hand as they only had to walk another few hundred yards and they didn't talk. They both were happy. As they came up to the front of Charlotte's house Tar let loose of her hand and told her his mother would probably invite them to

The Boys from Hog Heaven

the wild pig feed on Friday and he hoped they would come. She smiled and looked around quickly and gave her friend a little kiss on his cheek. She then ran into the house.

Tar stood there for a while before leaving. He left happy and whistled as he passed the forest. He knew there is a special bond between and his friend. Suddenly a loud noise came from the woods. It was a sound that Tar had never heard before. It sounded like a crazed animal and somewhat like a tortured human. His pace quickened as he passed the dark green forest. It had to be the big pig. It had seen him alone and would attack him. Maybe it was telling him to stay away. It didn't matter for soon Tar started running and only stopped when the sight of the trees were behind him. Soon he would be home.

Tar arrived in time to see the men cleaning the fish and he saw his little brother holding his big bass and his father taking a picture of the boy and his catch.

"Wow, Carver, What a fish," exclaimed Tar.

Carver looked at his brother proudly knowing he had pleased him very much.

"Caught it at the lake with Grandpa and the visitors," said Carver.

Walter looked up from his task of cleaning some of the bass and spoke. "Your little brother caught that fish all by himself."

The others piled on the praise and told the stories of the day. They told the tale of the turtle and Jeffrey. They talked about the big fish that Jeffrey finally caught on his last try. They laughed and all seemed to enjoy themselves. Even Grandpa decided 'those Yankee fellas weren't so bad after all.'

Chapter Fourteen

The Yankee Pig Feed

The Yankees were entertained all week by a few small bird hunts by John McGregor and Ephraim. They had come to the McGregor farm several times to visit and dine with the family. Betty became so overjoyed to see Walter her attitude had seemed to change especially towards helping her mother and getting along with the others. When the family and guests would sit on the front porch Betty and Walter would walk around the farm. Each invitation for Walter to come to the farm became special to Betty and to Ruth McGregor too.

Thursday afternoon the pigs from the hunt were brought to the farm and taken to the smokehouse. They were skinned and dressed now not looking so ominous. The heads had been removed and they would be mounted for the men to take home. The men were going to watch the process of the cooking and help. Ruth McGregor sent out the invitations to the friends and neighbors and after a long talk with Betty an invitation was sent out to Bubba's family too on the condition there would be no confrontations. Betty now more interested in Walter than worrying about the others on the guest list.

Will and his brothers stopped by and let John McGregor know they would be there through the night to make sure the pig would be ready for the feed the next day. John is happy Miriam and her brothers would be there not only for their help but because they were always such good neighbors. The brothers and John checked out the smokehouse and the wood supply and found it satisfactory. They looked at the two pigs and knew there would be more than enough food for the party. They knew too that some of the poor people in the area would benefit from this too.

The Yankees were happy too. Walter would be able to be with Betty and the others had tasted Miriam's cooking with the fish fry and chicken dinners knew that these pig pickings were a

The Boys from Hog Heaven

special treat in the south. They enjoyed being with the McGregors and even listening to Grandpa trying to explain the south actually did win the war.

They knew their time in Georgia was passing by quickly and this might be one of the last occasions to have everyone together.

Tar happy his mother is such a lady. He knew in his heart his mother would want all of the neighbors to come which would include Bubba's family. He didn't know how but even Betty didn't seem to mind. With all of the people there for the pig roast he would spend some time with Charlotte without being embarrassed he would be with a girl or had a girl friend.

***

Friday afternoon the tables were set for the guests and the pigs were being chopped up down in the smokehouse. The McGregors had dressed casually for the affair with the exception of Betty who still overdressed a bit for her new beau. Ephraim came with his two black workers Johnny and Washington, who had helped on the hunt. There were a few guests from town and all of the neighbors rich or poor and black and white. The Yankees were there early enough to help carry the platters of chopped pork to the tables and to help Miriam bring out the other side dishes. Miriam had grown to like these Yankees too but really didn't know what to make of them sometimes. Bubba and his family were strategically located far away from Betty and Walter. Tar asked his mother if he could sit with them and she agreed it would be a good gesture since the last time. Betty of course had to make a special entrance just before the time for her father to thank the guests for coming and to ask God's blessing on the food.

The tables were ready and even this time John insisted that Miriam sit down and everyone could pass the food around and she shouldn't have to wait on everyone. This pleased the long time cook for the McGregors and pleased her brothers too. They passed the food and everyone ate, talked and laughed. Betty sneaked a glance at Tara and whispered to her mother. "Isn't that my dress the girl is wearing?"

159

Grant Williams

Whereas Ruth replied, "Why yes Betty it is. I gave it to her since you never wear it anymore and you were going to throw it out. Doesn't she look nice?"

Betty didn't answer but turned her attention to Walter. Betty made sure everyone knew Walter is her date and her special friend not by words but by her actions. She didn't have time to worry about the sharecropper's daughter.

John McGregor introduced the Yankees to all of the people at the table and reminded his guest to thank the Yankees for killing the pigs they were eating. Grandpa even let everyone know he could tolerate these men from the north and even showed some kindness and affection to Jeffrey who he called 'New York' to everyone. Grandpa's gestures gave Jeffrey a warm feeling in his heart for the old man and didn't even mind the old man tell about catching the snapping turtle. Grandpa also bragged about the big bass 'New York' caught and bragged too about his young grandson catching a big bass at the lake.

Ruth and Tess caught up with one another while the dishes were being cleared from the table and with their wisdom had kept their older girls apart. Walter and Betty went for a stroll and Jeffrey who had spotted Tara during the meal now entertained her. John, Grandpa, Bill O'Hara, Bubba, Ephraim and the other men wandered down behind the barn to the smokehouse and tested some good old 'White lightning'. Usually the black men were not invited but this time they all went together. Jeffrey and Tara went out by the vehicles and sat on the tailgate of her dad's old pickup. Jeffrey carefully laid down an old gunnysack that sat in the bed of the truck so that Tara wouldn't soil her dress.

Jeffrey showed Tara some of his magic tricks and delighted her. She enjoyed being entertained by a man, especially a gentleman. They talked and laughed before finally Jeffrey told her he would pick her up for the dance tomorrow at the Country club but Tara said she couldn't go. Jeffrey didn't understand the class differences of Betty's crowd and Tara but insisted he would be there at seven tomorrow and pick her up. Tara thought what the heck, she would be protected by her date and for one night she could stay away from Betty McGregor.

160

She would show the girls in Carver she is as good as they were and would be there with a handsome young man. She would be happy to surprise Miss McGregor.

Tar and Charlotte sat alone at the table after all the others got up and went different ways. Even Carver found a friend and he was off to show his friend his fishing tackle.

"Tar," said Charlotte. "I'm glad we are finally alone."

"Shucks, Charlotte, there are all sorts of people around here."

"But they are not here with us."

"Did you like the pig feed?"

"It was really grand, Tar. Maybe someday you and I can sit together like your sister and the Yankee."

"Oh Walter, he is a nice guy. I like him and I don't even care that he is a Yankee."

"I mean we can sit together like a boyfriend and girlfriend."

"I don't know Charlotte, we're still just kids," said Tar trying to get out of this conversation but thinking he would like it. "Maybe when I kill the big pig we can have another roast and invite everyone and you and I can sit at the head of the table side by side."

"Oh, Tar, you are so grownup," said Charlotte looking admiringly at her friend.

"Some day soon we still need to read the rest of the book in the treasure box. We need to know if there is a treasure buried around here in Carver," said Tar finally changing the subject.

"We'll meet real soon after school. Oh, and Tar you will always be my boyfriend."

People were coming out of the house and up from the smokehouse and Tar didn't have to reply. He seemed very happy as he glanced at his companion with her little pigtails and big smile. He was happy he lived here in this part of what he considered his heaven.

The party now breaking up and people were leaving. Ephraim took a large quantity of the pig meat for the poor. Miriam and her brothers were told too to take some of the feast

Grant Williams

home too. Ruth McGregor made sure everyone had something to take with them as they left. Walter asked John if it would be all right when he took the other Yankees back to Mrs. Tucker's boardinghouse if Betty could ride with them and he would bring her straight home.

John looked at his wife and they looked at their lovely daughter and with a stern face agreed but not to stay out too late. This gesture made Betty happy and the McGregors knew that Walter being a gentleman and would do the right thing. Betty had forgotten about Tara and by being engulfed with her new beau. As the Yankees left with their daughter John and Ruth walked back into their big white house with John holding his wife's hand. It had been a wonderful night for all. They knew Betty would be home soon and they would leave a light on for her.

The Boys from Hog Heaven

Chapter Fifteen

The Country Club Dance

Betty McGregor had looked forward to the spring dances because it is very important to be amongst the privileged to attend the spring function at the Carver Country Club. Ruth McGregor had taken her daughter to the best dress shops to make sure she had the loveliest gown and would be one of the most sought after young ladies at the affair. It had surprised them both Walter Krucek would come from the north and sweep Betty off of her feet for it had been known Betty had been very fickle where the affairs of the heart were concerned. Now it became important to dress to impress the new man in her life and not to just be the belle of the ball.

The men folk around the McGregor farm knew whenever there was a social function their beloved Pima Donna would attend it would be time to make themselves scarce around the house. It had become such a traumatic experience for the entire McGregor household that it was amazing all of the things the men had to do without stepping foot into the big white house.

Since they had had the pig feed for the Yankees the day before, the drama wouldn't be so long this time. Ruth knew for her daughter to be in the right circles and to be part of the social circle of the area she must make sure the young lady would be ready to enlighten the influential members. She liked Walter but didn't know if this budding romance would ever go much further and knew too there would be other southern gentlemen at the dance who might be important to Betty long after Walter was safe back in Pennsylvania.

So Betty bathed, powdered, perfumed, dressed and adorned with some fine jewelry Ruth had bought her for such occasions. Even with all of the pampering Ruth would also make sure Betty would be fashionably late and made a grand entrance for her date and at the Country Club.

163

Grant Williams

Betty and Ruth did not eat with the others for the nerves wouldn't have let them enjoy any food anyway. The men ate quietly in the kitchen under the watchful eye of Miriam. Grandpa always enjoyed the histrionics of any performance his granddaughter and enjoyed the grand entrances, the makeup while thinking all along the performance should be put into a movie about the south. John was just proud of his daughter and her beauty and knew it wouldn't be long before Betty would be in college and then to marriage. Tar and Carver thought that their sister was spoiled but would never dare say anything derogatory about her in front of the elders.

Walter Krucek arrived on time and brought his friend Bill O'Hara with him. Betty would make sure that many girls at the dance would accompany Bill to the dance floor and would be entertained since her focus would be on Walter. Jeffrey's absence seemed conspicuous but it was explained he had a date and would see them at the affair. Betty had given him tickets earlier. Having one obstacle she wouldn't have to entertain out of the way was good for her and her time she could spend with Walter.

Walter and Bill sat silently waiting in the parlor. Walter had purchased a beautiful corsage of little roses and carefully held the package on his lap. After some time both men checked their watches only to find they were going to wait until it is fashionable for the Lady of honor entered the room. Ruth McGregor finally entered the parlor and greeted the handsome young men. She was happy they had found tuxedoes that fit well and looked so good. She made the normal excuses for her daughter's tardiness and did not let on it had more or less been planned.

"I think Betty is coming down now," announced Ruth to the men. The others hearing Betty coming down the stairs joined the group in the parlor.

The entrance by Betty was so grand and sophisticated could have been a scene from and old nineteen thirties black and white movie. Her hair was perfectly coiffed with each strand shining; her light blue gown that had billowy shoulders was cut to tastefully show just the slightest amount of cleavage and

164

The Boys from Hog Heaven

hung down in its taffeta splendor all the way to the floor. The jewelry that Ruth had chosen sparkled at every movement of her daughter's slender figure.

Betty walked confidently over to Walter knowing she had his entire attention and said in a demure voice.

"Are those flowers for me?"

"You look beautiful, these flowers are not worthy of adoring you," said Walter still mesmerized by his date.

"They are very beautiful, Walter. Thank you. Mother, Father we should be off now. It will be late when the dance is over."

"I'll make sure she gets home safe," said Walter to Ruth and John.

"You have a good time and enjoy the dance," said Ruth graciously and happy Betty would be with such a gentleman.

John even thought to himself 'I really like that Walter, Yankee or no Yankee.'

The McGregor family and even Miriam went to the porch and watched as Walter opened the door of the car for Betty and the three left down the dusty road. Even Tar and Carver were proud their sister is such a fine looking southern girl.

***

"You really look lovely, Betty," said Walter as they drove toward the dance.

"You do, and I agree," said Bill O'Hara from the back seat. "I hope there are some other lovely girls there too. You know maybe for me?"

"Don't you worry, Mr. O'Hara? You will have plenty of attention from my girlfriends. I told them about you too," answered Betty.

"We'll have to drop the Mr. O'Hara, Miss McGregor, or the girls will think I am an old man."

"You are an old man aren't you?"

"Just a couple of years older than you my dear."

"Is that in Yankee years or Southern years?"

"Is there a difference?"

"I don't know. Maybe you'll find out tonight?"

165

Grant Williams

Walter enjoyed the banter between his friend and his date. He looked at Betty several times as he maneuvered the vehicle down the road and amazed at her china doll complexion and how refined she really is. There is something about culture and breeding in the south and realized it is so important of the women of renown.

The huge circle driveway to the Country Club is something to behold. Guarding the sides of the black asphalt drive were mighty magnolia trees that now were in bloom. The grass manicured to perfection not shedding any light on the red dirt below. This is a different place where the people of influence could go and talk about their wealth and fortune but still give the impression of southern modesty. This is a place where the old cotton money and rich onion farmers could revel in their successes. It is a place where the professional men of the area could meet with their wives and comrades to enjoy the same interest. It is a place where race, creed and social standing did make a difference after all it still is a throwback to the old south. Still the differences were endured and accepted by all.

Walter drove the car to the front entrance where an attendant who opened the door for the lady Betty greeted them. The parking valet, a student who had most likely gotten his driver's license that spring, got behind the wheel of the car and took it to the backside of the large complex. Walter handed the three tickets to the guard at the front door and was given access as the large man opened the door for Betty and her friends.

When Betty and Walter entered the main ballroom people stopped talking to one another and watched the two enter the room. You would have thought that royalty had entered the old southern Country Club. It seemed most of the people were looking at the beauty and grace of Betty but the young ladies were secretly looking at Walter wishing he had been their date. Those young ladies knowing they would visit their friend Betty many times just hoping they could at least have one dance with the handsome gentleman.

Bill O'Hara got his share of looks not only from the young ladies but also from their mothers and the older generation matrons. Bill was ushered to the table with his friend Walter

The Boys from Hog Heaven

and Betty McGregor. Betty had made her female friends aware there is going to be an eligible bachelor for their entertainment too. His striking figure would garner many dances later on.

"Walter is Jeffrey coming tonight. I left him those two tickets?" asked Betty of the conspicuous absence of Walter's friend.

"He told me he met a girl and would be here later. He will be here. He always likes parties and dances. I'm sure he won't miss this event. Let's not worry about Jeffrey, my dear, this will be great even if it was you and I alone."

Those words were the words Betty loved to hear. She loved being the center of attention but more so from Walter. She enjoyed all of the women looking jealously at her date and the men longing to be with her but somehow with Walter it had become different. Being with Walter seemed to be more than enough.

"Walter would you get me some punch? I'm so thirsty," said Betty looking lovingly into Walter's eyes.

She had become really thirsty and she didn't ask for the drink just for Walter to walk across the room so the other ladies could look at him. The grand buffet had been placed also on the other side of the room and Walter asked if she would want anything from it while he was up by the punch bowl.

When Walter returned several of Betty's school friends were at the table waiting to be introduced to the handsome Yankee. They had heard so much in the last week about him they had to meet him. One of her friends, Louise, had already cornered Bill and had committed him to several dances throughout the night.

After things settled down and the band started playing Walter asked Betty to dance with him. The band played a very simple and lovely waltz and the two circled the dance floor as if they were walking on clouds. The older southern ladies loved the fact there were still gentlemen that treated the women the way God intended. They loved the grace and manners of Betty's date and soon forgot he came from the north. Bill O'Hara too, no stranger on the dance floor and was asked by many women from the ages of sixteen to seventy for a trip around the ballroom.

167

Grant Williams

Looking into each other's eyes Walter and Betty knew this would not be the last weekend together. They would find a way. Walter would be leaving the following week and going back home to his family's business and soon Betty would be going to college away from Carver. They could see a future for each other but tonight they would at least be together and make the most of the opportunity. Being a Yankee and a southern Belle seemed not to make much difference.

Walter and Betty finally had time to sit and enjoy some of the lovely hors d'oeuvres and canapés from the buffet bar. They enjoyed the punch but were warned that some of the college boys had spiked it with some Southern Comfort. They were at least able to sit for a while and relax. Little old widows and young impressionable girls were still dragging Bill to the floor. As humble as he normally as he seemed to be he enjoyed the fuss over him. Jeffrey still had not arrived.

Walter became a little concerned about his old friend not being there. Jeffrey had been very reliable and always on time. Betty could see the concern on her friends face and asked if everything is all right.

"Walter did Jeffrey say who he was bringing to the dance? I see most of my friends are already here. Is it a girl from Carver or somewhere else?"

"I really don't know, Betty? Jeffrey said he was glad to have the tickets and was bringing a date. He didn't say who she was or where she was from."

"We'll still save these seats for him and his date," said Betty a little annoyed at Walter's friend's tardiness.

The band struck up a slow dance and the lights were dimmed.

"Betty would you do me the honor of this dance?" said Walter in his most gentlemanly voice.

Betty smiled and took her date's hand as they proceeded to the dance floor. The music was sweet and comforting. Betty soon rested her head on Walter's shoulder and their feet moved magically across the dance floor.

They moved gracefully around the room and they were the envy of all of the other couples. As they maneuvered their

168

The Boys from Hog Heaven

way back toward their table Betty looked toward the door and saw Jeffrey. He was decked out in his rented tuxedo and looked handsome. He accompanied a young lady about Betty stature with strawberry blond hair. She looked familiar to Betty but she was still quite a distance away. Walter saw the couple and waved them over to their table.

As the couple moved toward the table Betty then knew who is with Walter's friend Jeffrey. It is Tara, Tara from the sharecropper's house, Bubba and Tess' girl, the poor girl from the other part of town. Betty inwardly upset but couldn't show this side to her beloved Walter so she sat at the table with all eyes on her as Tara and Jeffrey approached the table.

Some of Betty's girl friends now realized too who the new girl was. They couldn't believe the transformation. It had been like Cinderella. Tara's gown, blue and almost the same shade as Betty's hung seductively in the right places too. The shoulders were exposed and her strawberry blond hair sat softly on the exposed flesh.

She had only a single piece of jewelry that hung proudly around her neck and accented the cleavage of the young beautiful girl. The flowers Jeffrey had given her were tastefully worn on her wrist as a badge of acceptance.

"Jeffrey, we didn't think you were going to make it tonight," said Walter as he held a chair for Tara to sit between Betty and Jeffrey.

"I think I have met you before?" inquired Walter holding out his hand to greet the young lady. "I don't know if you know my beautiful date but may I introduce her to you. This is Betty."

Betty looked sternly but not obviously hatefully at Tara, "We know each other, Hello, Tara."

"Hello, Betty," said Tara. "You look very beautiful. You are the most beautiful girl here."

The icy stare from Betty melted for an instant and Betty replied, "Thank you, you look nice too."

"I am thirsty, Walter, where can I get some punch for Tara and me. Maybe you could get a drink for Betty too?" asked Jeffrey looking toward the punch bowl and buffet line.

169

Grant Williams

"If you ladies would excuse us for a moment we will get some punch and some goodies at the buffet for us," said Walter knowing his friend wanted to tell him something in private.

The two old friends walked toward the punch bowl and the girls were left alone. Many of Betty's school chums watched carefully as the girls were alone for the first time and when the men were out of earshot Betty indignantly asked Tara.

"What are you doing here? You know you are not a member of the Country Club? This is for all of the Professional people, people with money and people of influence."

"Well Miss Betty McGregor I was asked to come by Mr. Jeffrey Fitzgerald from New York City and I am here. I will mind my manners and you will mind yours unless you want your Walter to know what a spoiled girl you really are," said Tara looking directly into those big eyes of Betty.

Betty looked back in defiance and said directly to her adversary, "This is not the end of this."

"It can be if you mind your manners and I mind mine. You see we are not that much different anyways."

Perplexed by that comment Betty looked anxiously to see if the men were returning. She didn't seem comfortable and this subject usually had not been part of Betty's protected life.

"You do look nice Betty and I wasn't lying about that. You are the most beautiful girl here and I would admit it. Look at all of the jealous men looking over here. They would rather be here than as they would say 'That Yankee'."

"You look nice too, Tara," said Betty and the words coming out of her mouth surprised Betty as well as Tara.

"Does the gown look familiar?"

"Sort of."

"Your mother gave it to me and my mother made some changes. I hope you didn't mind that I wore it tonight?"

"The dress is pretty and I guess if my mother gave it to you I have nothing to say about that."

"I will give it back to you if you want me too after the dance," stated Tara looking for something from Betty.

"It's yours. I don't need it anymore," answered Betty looking for an answer or something to say.

The Boys from Hog Heaven

Sitting together at the Country Club it didn't all of a sudden feel like they were adversaries. They were not cut from the same cloth but both had Georgia roots and sensibilities. They knew their lives might cross at different times and they really didn't need to be friends. They were with men who were friends and if they wanted the affection of their dates at least for tonight they would have to be amicable toward each other. They could take their differences somewhere else but tonight would test their character.

The men returned soon with crystal glasses of punch and some delicious canapés. Tara seemed amazed at the creativity of the chefs and the affluence of the food. She tasted a few of the treats only after watching her refined neighbor devour a few of the tidbits. The punch felt good of the girl's parched throats. The conversation between them seemed to dry their mouths and parch their young throats.

"Isn't it grand to be sitting here with the two most beautiful girls in Georgia," said Walter and directing his conversation to Jeffrey.

"I think we should dance and make these southern gentlemen jealous," answered Jeffrey as he extended his hand to Tara.

The couples were the hit of the dance. The old southern ladies and gents watched as the youngsters flew gracefully around the dance floor. They must have had some flashbacks of their youth as every once in a while you would see them smile as if they were reliving some special moment in their own lives. The couples changed partners for a few dances but Betty didn't seem quite comfortable with Tara dancing with her Walter. She didn't know why and didn't have any reason but something still seemed not comfortable about the girls being together. Bill O'Hara still dancing with most of the other girls but finally it had become appropriate for him to dance with his friend's dates too. So on and on the music played and the young people danced. To some the Southern Comfort kicked in and they were escorted out to their vehicles to sleep it off for a while. The older couples started leaving as the night got later and later. Soon it was just young couples and the chaperones.

171

Grant Williams

The band had been asked to liven up the music and fast modern dances were played and the couple danced and played into the late night. Soon it would be over and the young people would have to go home where the young ladies could dream of the men and the wonderful spring dance. As the night got later the rivalry between Betty and Tara lessened and the tension seemed to have disappeared. Tonight they had learned to live together and if they didn't see each other socially again they were at least friends for the moment.

Bill O'Hara went outside to get some air while his friends and their dates continued dancing. The coolness of the night air felt good on his face. With all of the dances he had broken out a sweat and was glad to feel the coolness on his person. He noticed that some of the young single men had congregated outside of the front entrance and under the pergola that covered the front doors. The Southern Comfort showing its courage in some of the youthful men and they were looking for trouble. Bill trying to avoid any problems tried to duck back into the hall but was grabbed by a big good old boy and took back to the others.

"Look what I found?" said the big southern boy pointing to Bill.

"Hey, I don't want any trouble," said Bill in a rational voice.

"You're a Yankee aren't you?" asked a skinny young man who looked like a weasel.

"I'm not from here but was invited to this dance," stated Bill. "We don't need any trouble. The women would be upset if we had any problems."

"We don't appreciate you Yankees coming down and taking our girls."

"I didn't have any girls here. I danced when I was asked to and tried to be a gentleman like I was supposed to be."

"Are you saying we aren't gentlemen?" asked the bigger man.

Bill having enough of the posturing blurted out. "Where I come from men don't act like little boys so if you want to act like little boys I guess I'll treat you like little boys."

The Boys from Hog Heaven

With that statement there was a crash across Bill's back and a pine board broke as the pain went through the guest from the north.

"Little boys, eh, I'll show you little boys," said the weasel like character and he raised his right foot and swiftly crunched it in Bill's exposed stomach.

Bill went down in a heap. The pain on his back was excruciating and feeling of a foot in his stomach stirred his anger. He noticed the other men or boys were only following the lead of their weasel and large friend so Bill with his strength picked up the half of the pine board that lay at his feet and swung it mightily at the big southern boy and hit him square in the face. Blood flew everywhere and the big man went down. The man that looked like a weasel came up to Bill knowing his comrades were behind him and took a swing at the big old northern boy and missed. Looking back and seeing most of the others had gone the weasely character tried to run but Bill caught him by the hair and swung just one time and hit the man. As the man dropped to the ground the others left quickly getting into their cars and pickup trucks.

Security came quickly but only to see the three men, Bill, the big man and the weasel all looking worse for wear. The southerners were escorted off with help from some of the locals and the security guard took Bill back into an isolated bathroom and helped him clean up.

"I think you should leave too," said the security guard, "for your own protection. These men down here always have revenge on their minds and it might be a good time to get out of here. I'll notify the local sheriff and he'll make sure you have no other trouble."

"Thanks" said Bill wiping off his face and now combing his hair. "would you please get my friend Walter and bring him back here and then we can leave."

"Sure thing. Are you going to be all right?"

"I'm all right and it wasn't the Country Club's fault it is just a couple of men who couldn't hold their liquor."

"I'll get your friend," said the security guard as he left the men's room.

Grant Williams

Bill explained what had happened. Walter then tried to make Bill as presentable as possible so not to upset Betty. They could leave as soon as the sheriff arrived to assure the safety of the group. They would make sure that Jeffrey would follow them and they would try to make things as comfortable for the ladies as possible.

So with Bill safely in the back seat and Walter and Betty in the front they drove back down the dusty road with the sheriff following them to first Bubba's little house where with a brief goodnight kiss Jeffrey dropped off Tara. Then the group went up to the big white house and Walter escorted his beautiful Betty to the door.

"Thanks for a wonderful time, Betty," said Walter looking into her eyes.

"I had a wonderful time, Walter. Do you think Bill will be okay?"

"Bill will be okay. I promise."

Betty moved closer to Walter and reached up to his neck and pulled his face to hers. She kissed him like she had never kissed anyone before. She melted into his arms and didn't want to break the moment.

"We've got company Betty. You know your local Sheriff. I really have to go. We will see each other again before I go."

"I love you, Yankee."

"I love you too my sweet southern Bell and frankly I really do give a damn."

Betty went into the house and heard the cars leave. She knew Walter would be back before he would have to go back to Philadelphia. She would tell her mother about everything at the Country Club and how she loved Walter.

Down the road in the front room of the little sharecropper's house Tara is sitting still dressed in her beautiful blue gown and telling her mother of the wonderful evening. She told her of the wonderful building, the big band and their music. She told her mother of the wonderful food and the punch served in crystal glasses. She told her mother of her time with Betty McGregor and told her mother how much she enjoyed being out

174

The Boys from Hog Heaven

to a fancy place. Tess seemed so happy knowing sometimes you can even live your life or see happiness through your children.

Grant Williams

Chapter Sixteen

Saying Goodbye to the Yankees

Word spreads fast in small towns and Carver is no exception. The news of events at the Country Club traveled fast. To the young girls the news had been Betty's date and Tara coming to the Club with a Yankee. To the older women the news had been the handsome and polite young men from the north. The men had been embarrassed by the fight in front of the Country Club and the inappropriate behavior of the southern boys. John McGregor had been aware of the events and his concern centered around his daughter and her feelings toward these events. He normally let Ruth take care of those matters but today he would talk with his lovely daughter.

The sheriff had come by early and met John in the fields before he left to get ready for church. He explained what had transpired and told John his daughter had never been in danger. He also told John that the Yankees were actually good men and he had been embarrassed for the behavior of the local boys. He told John he would keep an eye out for any suspicious events and watch over the men until they headed back up north.

Ruth talked with her daughter for quite sometime before church in Betty's room where Betty told her mother she loved Walter and didn't know how she would handle the situation when he went back up north. Betty told her mother of the events at the Country Club and told her mother that she wouldn't be surprised if Walter would never want to come back to Carver again. She also told her mother Tara looked good in the dress given to her by her mother. She told her mother that Tara wasn't so bad after all but don't expect her to start running around with her. Ruth smiled and listened to her daughter who seemed to be growing up and thinking like an adult. Soon Ruth knew Betty would be going away and then maybe she would start to forget about her handsome Yankee. She told her daughter it is normal and all right to be in love. Betty hugged

176

The Boys from Hog Heaven

her mother and surprised Ruth for it had been a long time since they were that close.

John told his boys Tar and Carver they would have to say goodbye to the Yankees today since tomorrow is a school day and the boys would have to get back into the school days and their education. Betty had permission from her mother to go into town and say goodbye to Walter tomorrow and see him and his friends off. The whole family would miss the Yankees, even Grandpa but at least Grandpa had the turtle and the fishing stories to tell about Jeffrey or 'New York' as he called him. Miriam liked the men too and always seemed so happy to see them. Ruth too was glad they came even if Walter went home with Betty's heart.

At church that morning they all had different things to pray about. John prayed about his family, Ruth prayed about all of their happiness and safety, Betty prayed that she would see her beloved Walter more after he left the south, Grandpa prayed that his family would stay together and live in Carver, Tar prayed that someday he would kill the big pig and Carver prayed that he would continue to do well in school.

After church and after Sunday dinner John sat on the front porch of the big white house and talked to his daughter. They talked a lot about her growing up and now ready for college. John also talked seriously about how it had been a good thing she had met Walter and how he personally liked him very much. He told her things have a way of working out and if a further relationship with Walter is to be that she would ultimately know. John told his daughter how proud he had become of her and now going away to school would be a big step. He told her if she ever needed anything or to talk, she could always come to him for help or advice.

Betty appreciated she had the talk with her father especially since lately they seemed to be drawn apart.

"Thank you, Daddy. I know I can always come to you or mother if I need anything. I love you both," said Betty as she hugged her father.

"You will always be my little girl," said John McGregor with the sign of a tear in the corner of his eye.

177

Grant Williams

"Will you come to see me when I go away to college?"

"Only if you ask me," stated John.

"Good idea but don't forget about me."

"I hope Tar will go on to school. I think he is more interested in the farm."

"The farm is good for you isn't it, daddy?"

"It is a wonderful place but I want all of my children to have all of the advantages"

"Don't worry. Tar has a good head on his shoulders and he still is young."

"I guess you are right. I do know I won't have to worry about Carver for he is already lining up schools where he can go to medical school or law school."

"You know we probably will all come back to Carver and live here. It is a wonderful place even with the red dirt and the onions."

"Looks like a car coming up the dusty old road?"

Betty stood up to see if she could recognize the vehicle.

"I think it might be Walter, at least I can hope it is him," said Betty anxiously.

"I think you are right and you can wait for him while I go in and see if your mother needs anything," said John as he left the porch with his lovely daughter looking at the approaching vehicle.

Betty waited patiently as the car came up the road swiftly. Her heart began beating a little faster knowing Walter is here and is coming to see her. She wondered what purpose he had in mind and if they would be alone at least for the final hours they would be together. Her blood pressure increased as the car rolled to a stop in front of the big white house.

"Hi Betty, " hollered out Walter as he climbed out of his rental car. " thought you might want some company this afternoon?"

"Hi Walter, come on up and sit on the porch. I'll get some lemonade if you would like?" asked Betty with her southern hospitality still shining above her actual feelings.

"Not now, maybe later," said Walter "I just wanted to see you before we had to leave tomorrow. I thought if your Mother

The Boys from Hog Heaven

and Father didn't mind we might take a ride around the area. You can show me more of the Carver area if it is all right?"

"I'm sure Mother and Father won't mind if we take a drive. They like you and they trust me."

"Well, I hope they trust me too," said Walter knowing he would get a reaction from Betty.

"I'm sure they trust you even if you are a Yankee," laughed Betty. "Let's go in and ask them anyway."

The couple walked into the front room where Ruth had been talking with John and Carver.

"Mother, Father, Walter and I would like to go for a drive. May I go?"

"I want Betty to show me more of Carver so I'll have it all to remember when I'm sitting in an office in Philadelphia. I hope you won't mind if we go out for the afternoon. I will have her back early."

Ruth looked at John knowing it would be his place to speak.

"Why don't you youngsters go out and see the sights. I also heard they have good food at the old roadhouse on route forty-nine. Walter I think it would be nice for you two to have dinner there tonight and we'll see you later."

"Thank you Daddy," said Betty as she gave her father a hug and then went over to her mother and hugged her too. "Thank you mother, we'll be back after dinner. I love you."

"I'll bring her home after dinner," said Walter to John and shook his hand. "See you later this evening Mrs. McGregor. I'll keep our precious girl safe."

The couple then walked back out the door to the rental car arm in arm. Ruth and John watched from the doorway and waved as they got into the car. Then the McGregors looked at each other and smiled happy for this day even though they had dreaded it for so long. Today had been the day their little girl became a woman and left the old house with a man she adored. They knew thing were changing and probably would never be the same again in her life. Today is a day to build memories.

"Where would you like to go?" asked Betty soon after the car went down the dusty road.

179

Grant Williams

"I just wanted to be with you. I really don't matter. Maybe we will just ride for a while."

"I know a place by this little pond. It is private and a place we can be alone."

"Is it far from here?"

"It is a place my daddy took us kids when we were little. We could catch sunfish and you can even swim there. It is private and peaceful. It has always my favorite place of peace."

"Just show me the way, my fine southern lady," said Walter as he smiled at his beautiful date for the day.

"We'll have to open a few gates and when we shut them I would have captured my Yankee prisoner."

"I surrender."

As Betty said, it wasn't far from the McGregor farm and after going through some gates and shutting them behind they approached the little pond. The big weeping willow tree hung out over the far side of the water as portraying itself in a Monet painting. The dogwood trees protected the side where the young couple approached.

"Walter let's sit here where we can overlook the water," said Betty. "Do you have something to sit on?"

"I think there is a blanket in the back. Jeffrey had put it in there when your Father took us hunting."

Walter carefully placed the blanket on the high ground facing the water and then helped Betty to sit down. Soon they were not talking but looking out into the stillness of the little pond.

"Betty I really don't want this to end," said Walter trying to catch his breath.

"You are going home tomorrow," replied Betty waiting for Walter to find an answer.

"Soon I will be busy running the company again but it just won't be the same. I really like it here but I really will miss you."

"Oh Walter," said Betty as she took him in her arms. "I will miss you too."

"Won't you come back to Philadelphia with me?"

"You know I can't, at least not now."

180

The Boys from Hog Heaven

"I'll come back before you go on to school."

"Let's not talk. Let's just look at the water and hold me Walter. Hold me."

The pond looked so beautiful and occasionally a fish would break the surface of the water only to return to its home below. The pine trees nearby gave off their fresh aroma of the forest. The little water lilies that guarded the lake seemed to have blossomed just in time for the young couple's visit. Romance now in the air and the birds aware of the visitors welcomed it with their songs.

Betty now lying on the old blanket with her hair spread out framing her beautiful face.

"Walter, would you really come back to see me?"

"I don't really want to leave but I will be back."

"I love you Walter."

"I love you too, Betty," and he leaned over her young body and kissed her.

Betty took Walter's hand and put it on her young breast.

"I want you," said Betty. " n ow Walter."

Walter removed his hand from her supple young body and took Betty in his arms.

"I love you Betty but this isn't the right time. If we love each other we will find the right thing to do. Now is not that time. We just need to be with each other and not let our vulnerabilities overtake our good sense. I want you too, but now is not the right time."

Betty turned her head away from Walter for a moment and looked out over the calm water. "You are right and I know it but I just wanted to show you that I loved you."

"I know, my darling Betty, I know."

They caught their breath and walked around for a while. They didn't say much for all had been said and they knew now just being together is more important. This time would be etched in the memories over the summer or until they saw each other again. Betty knew she had college ahead and would be away from home. Walter had to run the family business but would come back again before Betty left. It would not be the end of the

Grant Williams

world but these memories would help ease the lonely nights that would be ahead for both of them.

"We need to go Betty," said Walter. "I think we should take your Father's advice and find that roadhouse for dinner."

"Just a few more minutes, I want to remember this place with you," said Betty as she again pulled Walter's face toward hers and kissed him.

Soon they left and closed each gate behind them as if they were metaphors. The sun is now setting as they drove toward the roadhouse with the windows down and the wind blowing gently into the automobile. They would have a wonderful supper and Walter would take Betty home knowing he would be leaving the following day. They would kiss goodnight on the porch of the big white house promising to see each other the following day.

***

Betty had a difficult time sleeping and looked out of her window most of the night while lying in the safety and comfort of her bedroom. Walter was doing the same at the boarding house. They knew today they would say goodbye for a while not knowing their future or if they really had a future together.

The McGregor family arose early as usual and John took his boys to school right after breakfast. There had not much been said at the breakfast table as the family looked at Betty looking so forlorn just sitting there picking at her food. Even Miriam didn't have much to add to the morning conversation. She too knew somehow today would be a milestone for the daughter who had been such a Prima Donna now humbled by a romance for now had a doubtful ending.

As soon as John left with the boys Ruth and Betty went off together to dress for the day. Betty sat solemnly at her dressing table thinking of yesterday and wondering about tomorrow. Ruth sat silently in her room looking in her mirror hoping she would have the right advice and the right things to say to her daughter today. Ruth could remember how much she loved John and how much see wanted to be with him before they were married. Ruth still hoped if this romance would develop things would turn out as well for Betty as they had for her.

The Boys from Hog Heaven

John returned home after dropping the boys off at their school. He waited anxiously wondering how his precious daughter would feel when they would leave for town. Ruth got ready first and assured John everything would be okay. John felt much better and pleased Ruth is going with them. Grandpa told John he would stay home and watch the farm. John knew his father didn't like to say goodbye to anyone and surely wouldn't have wanted to show any emotion to a Yankee. He handed John a prized lure from his fishing collection, told him to give it to 'New York' and give him the message it was not to be used on turtles.

Betty soon came down and looked very good even though her eyes were a little red from crying but now she seemed to be upholding her strength as a southern lady. She prepared for the day and she would be strong.

The Yankees were waiting in front of their rental car outside of Mrs. Tucker's boardinghouse. Walter came quickly to the door of the shiny black McGregor Buick when it arrived and opened the doors for Ruth and for Betty.

"Good morning. I'm glad you could come to see us off," said Walter first looking at Ruth and then at his lovely Betty.

Bill O'Hara took Ruth's hand and escorted her over to their car.

"We have something for you and your family," said Bill as he brought Ruth and John together. "It is just a token of our appreciation for making us feel so welcome."

The gift was two feet by three feet and wrapped in brown paper.

"Open it," said Jeffrey. "It is from all of us Yankees."

"John, you do the honors," said Ruth gesturing to her husband. "Betty come see what the young men gave us."

John opened the paper and inside was a wonderful picture of the farm. The Georgia farm never looked so good with its big white house and farm buildings.

"You have a wonderful place and we wanted you to have something from us that said we appreciated being with such good and hospitable people. Thank you for taking us in like you did. We had a great time here in Georgia."

183

Grant Williams

"Thank you all so much," said Ruth. "I just love it."

Walter took Betty back to the other side of the Buick and John presented Jeffrey with the lure that Grandpa sent with the message. They all laughed and shook hands and hugged. John told the men the trophies from hunting and fishing would be sent north when they were completed and told them all to come back.

While all of those events were taking place Walter had his chance to say goodbye to Betty. He to had a gift for her and pressed it in her hand and told her to look at it when he was gone. He then gently took her in his arms and kissed her gently.

"I will be back," he said.

"I will be waiting," answered Betty.

"Time to go Walter," said Bill. "long drive ahead of us today."

The family from the south said their goodbyes and hugged for the last time. Walter got in the passenger's side of the car with Bill behind the wheel and they drove slowly off toward Atlanta.

Betty stood beside her mother and waved to her Yankee as the rental car disappeared out of town. John finally turned to his wife and daughter and calmly said.

"It's time to go home," They all got into the big black Buick and headed down the dusty road. There were no tears for they all seem to know that the Yankees would return.

184

The Boys from Hog Heaven

Chapter Seventeen

Onion Festival

Things were getting back to normal around the McGregor farm. The Yankees had been gone for almost a month and Betty has been getting ready for college. The onion crop is extremely plentiful whereas the farmers and sharecroppers sent many boxes and bags of onions to the big city and truckloads out for distribution to go up north which made John McGregor happy. His neighbors; Bubba's family and Miriam's family had made some extra money this year thanks to the extra plants John McGregor had given them. The town of Carver had been blessed and rewarded by a small carnival coming to their town for a festival of the onion harvest.

Tar and Carver looked forward to the yearly event, loved to ride the rides and to play the Carney's games of chance just to win a kewpie doll or a whistle. Betty would normally go with a boy from town and parade around the carnival but this time she would go with her parents. Walter had been on her mind every day and she thought about him as they wrote each other often. Walter had been busy also with his family's business and as Betty prepared for school some of the energy went into those endeavors. The peaches were forming nicely on the trees and if everything went well there would be another festival in the fall at peach picking time.

Grandpa loved to come to the carnival and watch his grandson's ride the rides and play the games. He told everyone the reason he had to go was to make sure the Carney's didn't take advantage of his young ones but everyone knew grandpa love the caramel apples and the funnel cakes with the powdered sugar and of course he had to test them to make sure that his family wouldn't get food poisoning.

Tar had been happy too because with all going on in Betty's life any attention to him now would be rather remote and he liked it that way. He too felling more attached to his friend

185

Grant Williams

Charlotte decided he would ask her to go to the carnival with him and his family. With Tess and Ruth now closer friends the two family's relationship had got better. Betty even included Tara when she wanted to talk about the Yankees and the letters they got from their northern male friends. Bubba even worked a few days for John when they sprayed the peach trees, which made Tar happy the families now got along much better.

"Mother, may I ask Charlotte to go to the carnival with us?" asked Tar one afternoon when he got home from school.

"I think it would be all right. Have you mentioned it to your father?"

"I thought I would ask you if you thought it was proper."

"You ask your daddy and you can tell him I think it is just dandy."

"Thanks mother, I have some money saved up for us to ride the rides and play the games. I won't need any money from you or daddy."

Ruth smiled thinking how grownup Tar seemed to act sometimes and knew it wouldn't be too many years when he would leave the nest. She also is proud Tar would think to take their neighbor even if she was just a sharecropper's daughter.

"Tar, I think it is great you asked Charlotte. She seems like such a good girl and I think she likes you a lot."

"We are good friends. She isn't like the other girls. She seems to understand some of the guy things and she can climb trees too."

"You check with your daddy and if he says it is all right. You ask her and her parents in the proper way. You understand."

"Yes Mother, I understand and thanks."

Tar knew exactly what his mother meant with her comment in the proper way. For it is in the nature of the southern males to be taught manners and patience around women and as they grew they also learned the good points of Southern Comfort, a good hunting dog along with a great hunting rifle. It is a rule of manners and protocol Tar would follow the rest of his days.

The Boys from Hog Heaven

The days coming up to the festival were going slowly for Tar and his little brother. It seemed as if took forever for the festival to start. Tar had permission to take Charlotte to the event with the rest of his family in the big shiny Buick. Tar carefully took his money and put it in his pocket. He had plenty of cash for him and Charlotte to play lots of games, ride lots of rides and have plenty of festival food.

Tar became very nervous as any young man and decided to wait until after school and all of the other children had gone on their way to ask her. As Charlotte and Tar were standing in front of the old school building waiting for their rides home Tar finally screwed up the courage to ask her to go.

"Charlotte," said Tar looking at the ground in front of her.

"Yes, Tar," answered Charlotte looking directly at her friend.

"I want you, I mean could you or would you," stammered Tar.

"What is it Tar?"

"You know the carnival is in town this weekend. I mean would you go to the festival with me Saturday. My Mother and Daddy will pick you up. Oh, I will be there too," continued Tar still not looking at the girl in her pigtails.

"Mr. Tarleton McGregor, I would be delighted to go with you. I will ask my Mama and my Daddy and let you know tomorrow," smiled Charlotte.

Tar then looked at his friend knowing that he hadn't been rejected, "Char, I'm glad you want to go with me. I've got money for the rides and the games. I even have money for the food. Do you like the funnel cakes?"

"I don't know if I ever had one."

"I worked for my daddy and he paid me to work in the fields so we will have plenty of money to have fun together. I want you to go with me. You are my best friend."

"Are you my boyfriend?" asked Charlotte coyly.

"I guess so. I do like you a lot."

It seemed at that instant things came much easier for Tar in this relationship with the girl with the little pigtails. This is

187

Grant Williams

his first relationship with any of his female friends that was more than just friendship.

"I like you a lot too. I'm sure my Momma and my Daddy won't mind if I go with you after all you are a McGregor."

"Not only a McGregor but your boyfriend."

About that time Bubba's pickup pulled up with Tara sitting in the front seat with her father. Tara looked at Tar and smiled. Tar's face became red and he started getting nervous again for he knew too he had a secret with Tara too. Charlotte got in and sat between her sister and her father. Their old pickup then left and Tar watched it disappear with Charlotte's pigtails dancing in the back window.

***

Saturday finally came and the family all got together for the event. Miriam had been told not to come over so she could go the event with her brothers. Betty would go and would walk around with her parents. Grandpa made sure he got ready on time since he would have to check out the safety of the food especially the funnel cakes and caramel apples.

Even John didn't mind going since he was always a big part of the onion production but really it was another opportunity to show off his beautiful wife and show off his family. Everyone had been told to make Charlotte comfortable and welcome especially since Tar invited her.

The Buick had been shined and cleaned and looked so nice. It made Tar happy he could take his date to the fair in such a fine vehicle. John drove proudly down the old road and to Bubba's house and parked in front. Ruth told Tar to go to the house say hello to Charlotte's parents and then escort Charlotte back to the carriage awaiting, the big shiny Buick.

Charlotte ready and waiting looked so clean and scrubbed. Tar was polite to Char's parents before he escorted his girl back to his family car. Tar could sense the slight aroma of magnolias in her hair as she climbed into the vehicle. Bubba and Tess watched from the porch and waved at the McGregors and their own little daughter as they pulled away from the little

The Boys from Hog Heaven

house. It would be a fun day and everyone seemed happy Charlotte came with the McGregor family.

John parked the big Buick not too far from the fair entrance and they all walked in together. John, Ruth, Betty and Carver told Tar that they were going over to the little midway first to put Carver on some rides and they would meet at the entrance at ten if they got separated. Tar told his mother he and Charlotte would be all right and would play some games and ride the rides. Ruth reminded Tar to make sure Charlotte got fed through this course of events. Grandpa said he would just mosey around and see if he would run into some old friends but everyone knew if he did they would have to be at the funnel cake concession stand.

"See you later," said Tar as he grabbed his date's little hand.

"Bye Mr. and Mrs. McGregor and thank you for bringing me with you," said Charlotte as if she had been practicing the comments all day.

"We are glad you could come," replied Ruth, "Now you young people go and have a good time. We'll see you later."

Tar didn't seem to care if his schoolmates and friends saw him with Charlotte. He seemed so happy and so glad she could come with him. He wanted to make sure she had a good time.

"What do you want to do first?" asked Tar.

"I don't know, do you want something to eat?"

"Let's ride the rides or play the games first."

Tar happy Charlotte wanted him to take control and felt so confident she had such faith in him.

"Let's see what games they have. Here Charlotte let me win you a kewpie doll at the shooting gallery," said Tar wanting show his prowess in his shooting skills. After all he had told her he is going to shoot that big pig someday and he would want her to know he is a good shot.

Tar plopped up his quarter on the counter and the greasy Carney handed him an air rifle that looked like a .22 caliber.

"Watch this, Charlotte?" said Tar as he lined up his first shot.

Grant Williams

Bang, Bang, Bang and so on until he emptied the rifle. The old Carney knew he had a good mark and brought back the target to show the two the score. Tar had hit the target with all of his shots and was given a little stuffed pig.

He handed the pig to Charlotte and smiled "I'll get the big pig for you someday."

"Try again only a quarter. You are a marksman young man. Win another prize for your girlfriend."

"We'll come back mister," answered Tar. "We'll be back."

Tar seemed so proud of his score and Charlotte is so happy to have her stuffed toy but more proud she came with Tar.

"Come on Charlotte, you should play the games too," said Tar pulling his little date along by the hand to another game.

They knocked down milk bottles, threw rings on things, spun wheels and had a great time. They won some little prizes and were happy to be together. They passed by Carver having fun too accompanied by his parents.

"Hey Charlotte, want to ride the rides?"

This is the excitement they had heard about all through school. The Octopus had been the thriller and the Ferris wheel was great where you could see all over Carver. To ride the rides always had been the ultimate reason to go to the Carnival. Charlotte wasn't quite sure if she would be able to ride without being afraid but knowing Tar is with her seemed to overcome that idea.

"Over here," said Tar as they approached the line for the Octopus. "This looks like fun."

Charlotte wasn't quite sure that this is what she really wanted to do but being with Tar seemed to make it Okay. As they stood in line they noticed a few of their classmates too were going to ride the famous Octopus too. Charlotte tightened her grip on Tar's hand not knowing if it is her anticipation of fear or just to let the other classmates know she is with Tar.

The entered the ride and the young Carney tightened their seat belts.

"Hang on sweetie," said the young Carney showing his half rotted front teeth as he looked at Charlotte.

190

The Boys from Hog Heaven

Tar gripped his dates hand to let her know he is there for her and to protect her. The big mechanical ride began to turn slowly and Charlotte looked at Tar with trepidation. The ride turned faster and faster, around and around and soon it was tilting and going so very fast. The fear slowly turned into fun and Charlotte now laughing but her grip on Tar's hand was still tight but now more because she just wanted to hold his hand.

The ride ended and the young couple exited with the others. They saw their schoolmates and they all talked quickly on the thrill of the ride not even thinking Tar had a date with him. They knew this was a big event in their lives and they would talk about the ride at school for months.

"How about another ride Charlotte?" asked Tar trying so hard to please his friend for every instant of the evening.

"Let's take an easier ride if it is all right with you, Tar?" implored Charlotte.

"Would you like to ride the Ferris wheel?"

"Is it scary?"

"It's not like the Octopus but it does go way up in the air?"

"Okay but you'll hold my hand if I get scared, won't you?"

"Okay, Charlotte, but you won't be scared."

They walked over to the Ferris wheel hand in hand with Charlotte still clutching her stuffed pig in the free hand. Tar got the tickets and they waited in line. Charlotte watched the wheel come around then as the riders embarked they seemed to disappear up into the night sky. Maybe this wasn't such a good idea she thought. Soon it is their turn to get on and with Tar as her safety net she boarded the ride and slowly too is whisked up into the night sky. She felt a funny feeling in her stomach as the wheel lifted the two into the air but soon felt good with the air on her face and her boyfriend beside her. Round and round the wheel went slowly but with enough speed to feel the sensation of the movement. Charlotte seemed thrilled by this ride. She could see the entire town of Carver but in the distance she saw Tar's farm and her little home. She saw the rivers and the forest and also she saw the stars.

"Do you like this ride better?" asked Tar.

191

Grant Williams

"Oh Tar, this is wonderful. I can see your farm and I can see my house. Look over there. You can see the school and the town. This is so great. Thank you for bringing me. I love this ride."

Tar was very happy and he too was glad they were on this ride. They were with many other people but were alone too. What a paradox, so many of their friends down below or in separate gondolas on the ride but ultimately they were alone for the first time that evening.

The ride started slowing down and step-by-step the riders were let off. Finally it became Tar and Charlotte's turn to be on the very top of the ride. They could see way out into the night and they could see the stars and the lights of the town.

Tar looked at Charlotte and she knew it is a special moment. He didn't hesitate or ask but just kissed her and it wasn't a childish kiss or a peck on the cheek. He pressed his lips on her soft lips and felt the special moment course through his soul. Charlotte didn't resist and seemed so glad for this moment. It would be special between them forever and no one else would probably ever know. The wheel then jerked and they started ascending back toward the group below. They looked at each other now knowing nothing would ever be the same between them.

The Carney stopped the wheel and let the young couple out but smiled as if he had been let in on their secret.

"Tar, could we get something to eat? I think with all of the excitement I forgot I didn't eat much today."

"Let's go over to the food court and gorge ourselves. I am starved too."

They walked slowly hand in hand still remembering the moment on the Ferris wheel but afraid to comment thinking it would break the spell.

Soon the young couple found themselves sitting on a picnic table and after devouring a hot dog, French fries and a coke they were working their way through a couple of funnel cakes.

"Grandpa loves these funnel cakes. He won't admit it but I think it is why he comes to the fair."

The Boys from Hog Heaven

"Oh, I love them too. I can't wait for next year and have another."

"I can't wait for next year either." Said Tar and they both knew it wasn't just because of the food.

As they were finishing off their food suddenly they heard a commotion over behind the game tents. It sounded as if several men were arguing and it seemed to get more and more vocal. Tar and Charlotte with the same youthful curiosity looked at each other and without a lot of words started over toward the back of the tents.

"What do you think is going on?" asked Charlotte.

"We had better stay in the shadows. It might be dangerous and I wouldn't want to put you in harm's way."

"You know I'm a big girl and not a scaredy cat."

"I know Charlotte, but we need to stay out of sight, Okay?"

Quietly the two moved closer to the noise and the arguments. They silently stole up to near the tents without being seen. Tar put his index finger to his mouth indicating to stay quiet.

In the dim light they could see several men standing and pointing fingers at one another. There were several Carnival workers, a skinny weasely looking white man with a large white man and there is Junior, Miriam's little brother and Washington who worked for Ephraim and was on the hunt with Tar and the Yankees.

"You black son of a bitch, steal my money in a crap game," said the weasely looking character.

"I didn't steal anything. If anybody stole anything it was these Carneys," said Junior trying to verbally defend himself.

"Don't accuse me boy," said the Carney looking straight a Junior.

Tar looked at Charlotte and again held his index finger to his mouth.

"I won my money fair and square," said Junior now not sounding so confident.

"Give me back what you stole and I'll leave," said the weasely character.

193

Grant Williams

"You heard him," said the big man with the weasely man.

"I ain't giving back anything I have my own money and it's staying with me. Come on Washington let's get out of here."

"You ain't going anywhere until we get our money back," said the big man and he smacked Junior across the face.

"I said you go to hell, I didn't take your money," and Junior swung back and hit the big man.

The big man didn't move but just looked Junior in the eye. "This isn't over yet, you hear."

Junior now scared ran quickly away with Washington at his side. Tar and Charlotte saw him running toward the entrance. They didn't move and watched the Carneys and the two men still talking loud and still angry. The young people knew there had never been any love between most of the whites and blacks in the area but really had never seen it so belligerent and so up close before. Tar had grown up with Miriam and her brothers and Charlotte always had black neighbors but they knew too what they had seen was probably not the end of the ordeal but just triggered more hatred.

Tar motioned to Charlotte that they need to leave quietly and without being noticed. They walked quietly until they reached the midway and heard the noise or the rides and games of the fair.

"I'm sorry Charlotte we had to hear all of that."

"Do you think it is over?"

"Who knows, most times it just causes more hate and nothing more is done but more separation and more words."

"I hope not. Those men were sure mad at Junior."

"I know Junior is not a thief. He likes to drink and gamble a bit but a lot of his friends do too."

"Let's see what your Momma and Daddy are doing? It is almost ten o'clock and we are supposed to meet them."

"Charlotte, I had a great time with you. I am so glad you could come with me. Want to get together again soon and we can look at George McGregor's book again."

"Maybe sometime next week."

The Boys from Hog Heaven

They walked hand in hand until they saw Ruth, John and Carver in the distance. They then quit holding hands as they walked toward them.

"Where's Betty?" asked Tar.

"She went with some friends to a get together in town. She will be home later," said Ruth, "did you have a good time?"

They didn't say anything about the argument behind the tent or the kiss on the Ferris wheel but proceeded to tell Tar's parents all about the rides, the games and the food. Carver too had a couple of prizes he had won on the midway and had a big strawberry stain on the front of his shirt from the treats at the food court.

"Where is Grandpa?" asked Carver.

"He went to the car a few minutes ago," answered John, "I think the funnel cakes and Caramel Apples got the best of him."

They all laughed as they headed toward the big shiny Buick for they all had a good time and were tired. Now it is time to go home and time for Tar to walk Charlotte to her door and say goodnight.

After the McGregors had dropped off Charlotte and on the way home Ruth said to all in the car. "I like that girl. She has a real air of confidence about her I really admire and she is very pretty too."

Tar didn't reply but just looked out of the window into the Georgia night and smiled for he already knew what his mother said is very true.

Grant Williams

Chapter Eighteen

Trouble

What a night! Tar still so excited about the carnival and the Onion Festival and was so glad that he took Charlotte with him and his family. The thoughts of the incident behind the tents with Junior and the other men still concerned him. He didn't want to worry his family so he didn't mention the confrontation to his father of his mother. He just wanted to lie on his own bed and recall the evening. He wanted to remember the shooting range, the Octopus, the Ferris wheel and the food but most of all he wanted to just think about Charlotte. Carver had fallen asleep as soon as his head had hit the pillow and probably was dreaming about the carnival and like Grandpa the funnel cakes. Tar heard Betty arrive from town but was with some girls. Tar still amazed with all of the activity Betty still remained so interested in Walter.

Tar's eyes were filling with sleep when he noticed that the sky became abnormally bright. He quickly got out of his bed, went to his window and looked out over the forest and it looked as if it was coming from the area of Miriam and her brothers' sharecropper farm. It looked as if the place was on fire. Tar ran quickly to his parent's bedroom door and pounded on the door."

"Daddy, wake up. Wake up I think there is something wrong over at Miriam's place," hollered Tar as he kept pounding on the door.

"What is it Tar," said John McGregor as he opened the door already dressed in his work pants and holding his shoes in his hand.

"I think there is a fire over at Miriam's place. I see a lot of light over there."

"Get dressed and meet me in the pickup truck. They might need some help," said John as he tried putting on his shoes.

The Boys from Hog Heaven

Quickly Tar ran back to his room and dressed quickly and was waiting in the pickup truck when his father arrived.

"Does look like a fire, son. Let's go and see if we can help put it out," said John to his son as he started the pickup truck and put it in gear.

It took little time to get down the dusty road and past the forest. They could see there is a fire at the little sharecropper house. It looked as if some help already had arrived for from a distance they could see men running around the front of the house.

They got closer and it wasn't just men but men in white sheets. They had pointed white hats covering their faces and they seemed to be dancing around and screaming.

"Get down;" ordered John to his young son, "there might be trouble here. Get down now."

Tar had heard of the group who lived in the south and carried out their hatred toward different races and creeds of people but had never seen this up close. He knew something had to be wrong when his father became so concerned about his son's safety. The pickup slowly drove up toward the little farm but much more cautiously. Tar peeked out of the window and saw the men quickly leaving in various cars and trucks but he still could see that the fire was still burning at the small homestead.

"Tar I said stay down," ordered John now in a much louder voice.

"What are those men doing?" asked Tar.

"I think there is trouble here with the brothers. Whatever you do, stay in the truck. Do not get out. Understand!"

"Yes Daddy. I'll stay in the truck."

"I think they all left when they saw us coming but you never know about that group. Just stay in the truck."

The light burning brightly and Tar could hear Miriam wailing and crying. Will and Virgil didn't recognize John's pickup at first put soon they knew there neighbor had come to help. Tar could see that Will and Virgil were throwing water at a large cross burning on their lawn. Tar could also see something he would never forget. He could see the limp body of Junior hanging from the burning cross, lifeless and charred.

Grant Williams

Tar saw his father help the two black men take down the still body of their brother and lay him on the red Georgia dirt. By that time Bubba had arrived and helped put out the rest of the fire but he didn't stay after the fire was out.

Tar now stared at the solemn faces of the three men standing as neighbors over the burned body. Their heads were hung down and they didn't look at one another but were experience grief in their own ways. Junior was lying dead for just being a black man. Tar then remembered the argument in back of the tents at the festival. He remembered the threats and the hatred the different races had for one another. He knew the men had returned to take care of the matter and to show Junior his so called place in their society.

John stayed with his neighbors for quite a while and they covered the burnt lifeless body of their brother or their friend with an old blanket. John tried to comfort Miriam who had become hysterical with pain and grief. They prayed and sang a couple of spirituals. John promised Junior's death would not be forgotten and he would go directly to the sheriff while Will and Virgil would take the body to the old black church.

John shook his neighbor's hands and hugged Miriam assuring them he would be at the sheriff's office directly. Tar still watched this ritual of love and kindness but also saw the hatred that could sprout its anger at anytime there in his beloved countryside as he looked at the covered body of his neighbor lying there on the ground.

John got into the pickup truck and looked at his son and seemed helpless in what to say and how to explain what had happened.

Tar looked at his father who was trying to speak and just simply said, "I understand, daddy, I really do understand."

***

Father and son drove to the sheriff's office that night and the deputy called the sheriff. John and the sheriff sat around for quite some time talking. Tar who was sitting in the waiting room could see his father gesturing with his hands as if he was explaining the cross and the fire. Tar had heard his father say

The Boys from Hog Heaven

many times how fair this sheriff is and how he took his job seriously and would protect all of the people of the community. Tar knew his father would do his best to help his neighbors get justice in this time of grief.

Tar waited and looked at the guns that were locked up in the big glass front cabinet. He looked at the certificates and pictures of the law enforcement officers hanging on the walls. He looked at the entire official looking paraphernalia all around and wondered if anyone would be found who was involved in the death of Junior. He knew it wouldn't be easy there in this part of the world and this part of Georgia.

It was late when John and Tar arrived at home. Ruth had got up and wrapped herself in her terrycloth bathrobe and had put a pot of coffee on the stove. When John and Tar came into the kitchen she came over and hugged them both knowing something is dreadfully wrong.

The three of them sat at the kitchen table and with cups of coffee, Tar's with plenty of sugar and milk, talked about the terrible event and what they should do to help the grieving family. They knew it would be a long time before Miriam could come back and they knew she needed to be with her own brothers in this time of sadness. The sun now coming up soon reminded them it is a school day. Ruth told her eldest son he would not have to attend school but Tar knew he would have to work out his feelings his own way and wanted to go to school whereas Ruth and John did not object. There would be plenty of things to do today and it would start with Ruth. John would do what he could but he needed some time to try to erase the horror from his mind too. Ruth knew that too so she would visit Miriam that morning by herself.

Grant Williams

Chapter Eighteen

The Aftermath

Tar was very tired at school and kept to himself without drawing attention. Charlotte knew something had to be wrong and she also knew something dreadful had happened at her neighbor's place the night before. She wanted to be with Tar and talk about the Carnival and the festival but seemed to sense she should wait until the right moment would arise. Tar stayed in for the first recess and went to the small library. He needed to be alone but went there under the pretext of doing some research. Charlotte knew this is not like Tar and wanted to help him if he needed her.

Finally after lunch the two young people met alone and outside near the old swings.

"Tar are you all right? I missed you at the first recess."

"Oh Charlotte," said Tar and he grabbed her and just hugged her. "Did you hear what happened last night?"

"My daddy told us there was trouble at the little farm next door and Junior was dead. He didn't say much more but to be very careful."

"I was there. They hung him on a cross and burned it with him on it. It was awful. I saw the whole thing."

"Oh my dear Tar," said Charlotte. "It will be Okay. We are together."

"I know, my dearest, I will always be safe when I am with you."

"I know."

"There were men in white sheets. They did it. I know they did it. I heard about them before but I didn't know they were here in Carver."

"Tar, they are all over the south, they were a lot of them in Jackson County when I lived there. My daddy wouldn't join and finally that was why we moved."

The Boys from Hog Heaven

"They were running around as if they were crazy. They had torches. It was awful."

"They won't hurt you. Did you see the body?"

"He was all burned up. I couldn't recognize his face. He was all charred and burned. I saw the look on Will and Virgil's faces and I saw the fear. It was awful."

"Did you see Miriam?'

"She was hysterical. I saw her looking to the sky for help from God and waiting as if something would happen just then and Junior would rise up. She was in bad shape. My mother is going to be with her today."

"My momma is going there too. Miriam needs help to get through this ordeal."

"Miriam helped raise me, Char. She is so important to all of us. I hope she will be all right."

"Tar, do you think it was those men who were arguing with Junior at the Carnival?"

"I don't know but maybe we should tell the sheriff?"

"Should we? You should tell your daddy first and see what he says."

"I will, Charlotte."

"Tar, I will never forget Saturday night and the carnival. Thank you for asking me to go with you," said Charlotte trying to change the subject and cheer up her best friend.

"I will never forget the Ferris wheel ride," said Tar with a devilish grin.

Charlotte looked away with her face flushed, "Oh, Tar. Will we be friends for a long time? I will never forget just being with you."

"We will still get together soon. I'm sure we will all go to Junior's funeral."

"I know but we still need to read more about George McGregor. We still need to know more about your treasure."

"We'll get together soon. You know sometime after the funeral. We had better start getting back to class the bell should ring real soon. And yes we will be friends for a long time."

The two of them walked together back to their class side by side, not holding hands as they both wished they could do.

201

Grant Williams

***

Back at the big farm Ruth had packed a basket with food Miriam and her brothers could eat without much preparation. She also included a little bible for Miriam to console herself with. She also slipped in an envelope from her, John and Grandpa to help with the funeral. She knew Miriam would not want to accept a handout but with the card enclosed she would have to accept the monetary gift just for her brother's memory.

Back at the little sharecroppers house Tess also had put together a basket of food for her neighbors. They were not real close but not having a lot of worldly provisions Bubba and Tess knew some of the hardships of living the life that their neighbors did. The reminder of things that transpired in Jackson County and how close the evil was to her simple domain it was apparent that she would have to be strong and help her neighbor through this ordeal.

John and Bubba both went to their own separate fields and worked the land. It became important for them to get away by themselves and pray the evil would leave the area and maybe things would return to some order. The weeds being removed from the red dirt seemed to be consoling to both family men.

Grandpa sat alone in his room and as much as he believed in the southern tradition he could not stomach the atrocity that occurred so close to his hallowed ground. He did not have the blinders on he had been given as a youth and now it is not a black and white issue it is family. It was his beloved McGregor family and the neighbors who always were there to help in time of need.

Betty also had heard of what had happened and suddenly wanted to see Walter again and feel his strength. She who had been always so much about herself found she had compassion for family who is more than neighbors. She knew Miriam would not ever overcome the tragedy and wished she could console her longtime nanny and friend but didn't even know how.

Betty went to Miriam's home with her mother and comforted Miriam while Will and Virgil were at the church preparing for the funeral of their younger brother. The women

The Boys from Hog Heaven

sat and talked mostly about Junior and his life here on earth and his time in Carver. Tess and Tara who had walked over to their neighbor's simple home joined the ladies. They both saw the burned grass on the front lawn area with the outline of the cross a reminder of the evil that had sprouted the night before. Miriam pleased to see her closest neighbors there with her in her time of trouble and to see Betty and Tara sitting together in the same room with the same purpose. Miriam whispered under her breath 'The Lord works in mysterious ways.'

Soon Will and Virgil returned home and announced that the funeral would be on Wednesday and Junior would be buried in the Negro Cemetery behind the little church. The ladies left together after again giving their condolences to the family for they understood the saddened family would need time to be alone.

"Tess, would you come up to the house on Thursday," asked Ruth deep in thought. "It would be good for us neighbors to see each other more often."

Betty interrupted and interjected, "Won't you come too, Tara? We should be friends too."

Tara nodded to Betty but still overcome with the grief as they stood on the land of the poor black family that only wanted to be good neighbors and to be an example of God's own people.

***

That night after dinner Will and Virgil came to visit John McGregor. They walked privately outside and walked toward the land that overlooked the little sharecropper's home. They talked and walked for quite a while and out of his bedroom window Tar saw his father shake hands with Will and Virgil. The three men slowly walked back to the house where the two black men got back into their old pickup truck and drove back down the path and the dusty road. John just watched for a while and turned back toward the house as the pickup truck disappeared around the curve by the forest. John knew there would be several difficult days ahead for his friends. He looked tired as he came into the house and went straight to his bedroom. Sleep would feel good tonight.

203

Grant Williams

The funeral became a show of solidarity in the black community and the injustice that had been done would not go quietly. The sheriff had his deputies watch the area around the little white church and would make sure nothing else would occur to heighten the grief of the family. John McGregor and his family sat in the pew directly behind Junior's family. Miriam dressed solemnly in a straight black dress sat between her brothers and held their hands for strength. The plain pine box sat just below the preacher's pulpit and looked so meaningful with its lid closed and a single bouquet of flowers adorning the top.

Bubba there too with his family sat near the back and even Old Ephraim with his true old time southern attitude attended the service for he too knew it is not the general conscientious of the Carver people that thugs could do such things to its people whether they were black or white.

The service seemed to last a long time but there were songs to be sung and eulogies to be heard. Tears had to be shed and Junior would have to be sent off to heaven in the most appropriate way. The congregation slowly walked together hand in hand to the cemetery of cold mossy stones, some with just a name with no dates. Some even could have been slaves from a long time ago.

Tar and Carver had only attended one other funeral and that was of an old uncle who had been buried in the white cemetery in a fancy box. The look in Miriam's eyes brought tears to the boys for Miriam had raised them and loved them as her own. Now she hurt and saddened by her brother's untimely death and there seemed as if there is nothing they could do. Tar saw Charlotte walking with her family and wished she was with him but now was family time for her too. The interment was short. The McGregor family walked by Junior's family and spoke to Will, Virgil and hugged their dear Miriam to let her know their prayers were with her that day. They would see her later.

It was a solemn ride home from the old cemetery that afternoon. No one spoke for there is nothing else to say. It is a

The Boys from Hog Heaven

day they would all remember and a day that changed the lives of all of the McGregors.

That evening after dinner and the family sitting on the front porch a car drove up into the driveway and to the big white house. It was Miriam, Will and Virgil. Miriam came up to the porch and sat beside Ruth. Will and Virgil walked with John toward the smokehouse. Tar and Carver sat on the edge of the porch in front of their Grandpa who was smoking the pipe Carver had given him for his birthday. Betty sat close to her Mother and joined in the conversation with Miriam.

"I've got to run up to my room," said Grandpa knowing the women folk wanted to talk.

"Mr. George," said Miriam. "We are leaving tonight. We are leaving Carver. I want to thank you for all the years you let me work here and to be part of this family."

Grandpa didn't expect this for he thought that Miriam would be there forever. She had fed them and watched after them for so many years. She had been more than a cook and a nanny; she is part of the family. But Grandpa understood as he looked at her sad eyes for nothing there in Carver could ever be the same for Miriam and her surviving brothers.

Grandpa walked over to Miriam. "Thank you for all of your years. I will miss you too."

He hugged the big black woman, turned quickly and left the porch. Tar and Carver could see him take out his old handkerchief and wipe his eyes as he walked through the front door.

"Tar, Carver, You heard. I'm leavin' for Atlanta and I'll be staying with some kinfolks there. It will be best for me and Will and Virgil. You boys be good. You hear. Now come along and give old Miriam a big hug. You two have grown up to be good young men. Take care of your Momma and your Daddy."

They hugged and cried then hugged some more. Ruth and Betty had tears on their cheeks too as they watched the boys try to give Miriam a little of the love she had given them through the years.

"Now you two young'uns git along. I need to talk to your Momma."

205

Grant Williams

Tar and Carver left the porch and went to the safety of their room.

"Miriam, You don't have to leave. John and I can move you up here," said Ruth after the boys had gone, "You know you are part of this family."

"We have to leave. God will watch over us. I don't think we could ever live again in our house and I need to be with my brothers. I will miss you too."

Ruth knew there would be no convincing Miriam to stay and she could understand. Betty had seen more reality in the last few days and knew she would have to act more like an adult and be more of a part of the family. They loved Miriam and depended on her. They not only would miss her wonderful cooking but would miss the love she gave to everyone of the McGregor clan.

"What do you need, Miriam," asked Ruth.

"Ms. Ruth, I have enough worldly things. You have provided me well through the years. I do want to ask you to do something for me."

"What is it?" asked Ruth looking directly into her dear friends eyes.

"When you go into Carver would you look after Junior's grave? He wouldn't mind if you would put flowers on it once in a while. He was the most sentimental of my brothers."

"I would be honored, Miriam. I will make sure he has flowers too."

The men were coming back toward the house and Ruth turned to Miriam and asked her, "Could I put up some food for you to take with you on your trip to Atlanta?"

"No, Ma'am, I put up a basket this afternoon."

"Evenin' Mrs. McGregor and Miss McGregor," said Will when he got into earshot of the two ladies.

"Good evening Will and good evening Virgil," said Ruth as they approached the porch.

"We've got to leave soon Ma'am," said Virgil "But we had to say goodbye. Thank you all for being such good neighbors."

The Boys from Hog Heaven

"We will miss you," replied Ruth McGregor in her most proper southern manners, "I hope you will have a good trip to Atlanta."

Miriam left quickly holding a white handkerchief to her face as she quickly got into the car whereas Betty at that point fled the porch and disappeared into the big white house. Will and Virgil followed hastily to the car after shaking John's hand and quickly the only thing to be seen was the taillights going down the dusty road.

"Ruth, I have something to tell you," said John after their old friends had gone.

"Yes, John."

"I bought their place. I bought the little farm from Miriam's brothers. They convinced me they would not return and they would need the money to get a new life in Atlanta. I did promise them if they would ever come back I would help them find another place here in Carver. They would never be able to live with the memory of Junior's death at the present farm."

"What are you going to do with it?"

"I was thinking if you agree. I want to give it to Bubba and his family to farm free of any money. They can farm the land and live make a better living. If Miriam and her brother's aren't ever coming back then they can have the farm free and clear after two years. Bubba can help me and maybe you can get Tess to help you around here. They could use the money raising the girls and other things."

"Let's tell our family after you talk with Bubba. Oh, John I love you so. This is the right thing to do. I know Miriam and her brothers would approve. And I know Junior would have approved too."

"Let's go in, my dear Ruth. It has been a long day."

207

Grant Williams

Chapter Nineteen

Bubba's Family's New Wealth

Thursday Tess came up to the big farm. Bubba didn't mind taking her since he couldn't get his mind off of the terrible events that had transpired. The children were at school and grandpa had taken the McGregor pickup to the lake for some fishing and some time alone. John and Ruth were sitting in the kitchen when they heard their neighbor's old truck rattle into the driveway.

"I invited Tess to come up today, John. I thought it would be good for her and I to try to forget about the last few days. I also had planned to ask her if she would help me around here a couple of days in the week until we get things sorted out after Miriam's departure."

"It would be a good idea. She could help with the household duties at least until Betty goes away to school. I know you like her and it would be good to have someone here for you during the day."

"I think it is what I need. Miriam and I were together so long. She was always there to talk to if I need to talk to someone."

"I'll invite them in and we can get this matter over with about Miriam and her brother's farm."

"I'll make some coffee."

John went to the porch and invited the neighbors in. Ruth and Tess were very comfortable with one another but John and Bubba were more distant since most likely Bubba felt John McGregor is a very important man in the community and he is just a sharecropper.

"Here have some coffee and sit down," said Ruth. "There is some sugar and cream if you'd like."

"Thank you Ma'am," said Bubba as he sat down next to his wife.

"How's the sweet potatoes, Bubba?" asked John.

208

The Boys from Hog Heaven

"Doing mighty good and we have lots of tomatoes this year too. Hope I can sell some after Tess puts up what we need."

"I think there will be a lot of peaches this year too. I could use some help if you have time later on. How are the girls doing? I hope they like living here."

Tess smiled at Ruth and answered. "Things are getting better. Tara seems to be getting along better now and you know Charlotte is always happy."

"Good and how do you like it here?" asked John.

Bubba looked at Tess and Tess answered for the two. "We like it here a lot. Carver is so much better for us than Jackson County. We've got a lot of work to do but this year we have been blessed."

John McGregor looked at Ruth and told the couple about his idea. John told them he wanted them to have the land that he had purchased from Miriam and her brothers. The land is adjacent to their property and the sweet potatoes and some other crops were already up. John told them he didn't want any other neighbors around and he would be honored if they would farm the other land.

"What do you want for the land?" asked Bubba. "You know we don't have any extra money."

"The only thing I need is some help in the spring planting onions and some help in the fall until all of the peaches are picked. I will sign the land over to you and if you decide to leave I will have the first option on buying the land back. Tess can come up and visit with Ruth and we can get to know each other better."

Bubba taken totally unaware didn't know how to act for such kindness and generosity since he had never been given anything like this before and what little he had he worked hard for. He looked at Tess for some words but Tess was sitting there with tears in her eyes too.

"Don't say anything and I will bring the papers over sometime later on this week. We want to do this for you," said John.

Grant Williams

"Yes we want to do this because you are our neighbors and it is the right thing to do," said Ruth putting her hand on Tess' arm.

The neighbors drank coffee. Soon Bubba started talking and telling John about his plans around the farms. As Bubba became more excited John and Ruth felt so contented. Ruth mentioned that she could use Tess' help around there for a few weeks until they got used to not having Miriam around all of the time. Tess knew she had been happy to be asked not only that she could help pay back the kindness of the McGregors but that she could be with Ruth.

"We haven't told anyone yet but tonight we are going to tell our family," said John. "We wanted to let you know first. I think our children will be very happy too."

"So will ours," said Bubba. "Thank you Ms. McGregor and John, we will try to repay this kindness."

"I know you will," said John. "We are happy that you are our neighbors."

"And Bubba," said Ruth. "You can call me Ruth."

"And my name is Tess," said Bubba's wife.

They all laughed and drank coffee before they all walked out on the porch and looked out over the land. Bubba and John pointed out the new acreage and walked together for a while. Bubba looked over to Tess and told her he would be back later then Ruth and Tess excused themselves for they had a lot to talk about.

That evening both families was told of the decision about Miriam and her brother's old farm and even Betty seemed happy their neighbors were expanding and would be so much better off with the new property. Bubba's family was so happy some of the worries would no longer affect their family. Charlotte was happy for she knew now she would stay there in Carver for a long time. Tar was happy since he now would be able to see Charlotte more often. Ruth told them too Tess would be coming up to help for a while and they should treat her with kindness just like they did Miriam.

That evening Tar walked out and looked down the dusty road. He could see the lights at Bubba's house and could

210

The Boys from Hog Heaven

imagine how happy they were with their newfound wealth and happiness. He still could see the trees from the forest casting ominous shadows. Now the only thing between him and Charlotte is the forest but knew he would someday still go to the forest and kill the big pig and the families would celebrate together especially him and Charlotte.

***

The next day Tess came up to the farm right after the children were in school. John had already started working down in the orchard with grandpa and Bubba had begun cultivating the crops at his place and his new place.

"Tess I am so glad you could come. Please sit down and have a cup of coffee and a sweet roll," said Ruth to her neighbor.

"Don't you want me to do some work around here to help you?"

"That will wait. I just want to talk. I don't have any other women folk to talk to and now that Miriam left for Atlanta I only have Betty and Betty loves to talk about Betty."

"Betty has changed a lot. I noticed she changed a lot after the Yankees came down here to hunt."

"I think it is serious with Walter but she still has to go on to school first. We already have her enrolled."

"Do you think she will run away?"

"Sometimes she gets lonely but I think she is just in love. How are your girls?"

"Tara is so much happier now that she is included in some of the things at school. I think things changed a lot for her too when the Yankees were here. I hope she decides what she wants to do soon. When I was her age I was already married and she was on the way."

"Does she hear from Jeffrey?"

"They write but I think they are just friends. Tara loves to hear about the big city and the excitement of things she has never seen. I think Jeffrey had a great time here in Carver and wants to come back again."

"You know Tess I really didn't mind that they were here and I never thought of them as just Yankees."

211

Grant Williams

That day they two women did the laundry for the McGregors and hung the clothes on the line to dry. They had lunch together and planned to be together again the next day. It was the beginning of such a good thing since Ruth now had a friend so close by and her days would be so much better. Tomorrow they would go through some of Betty's old clothes and Tess would have some pretty dresses for her girls. It was a good thing for Tess too since most of her life it had been just work and take care of family. Now it is good she has a friend too. Both women were happy as they put their families to bed that night. They both closed their eyes and thanked God for the blessings.

The Boys from Hog Heaven

Chapter Twenty

Peaches, Pigs and Friendship

Tar and Charlotte met at school as usual. They always made some time together before their friends would come around. Charlotte would get so excited and could hardly wait for the first recess an when the bell rang and the class went quickly to their free time Charlotte ran to Tar, grabbed him by the hand and led him to a place just outside the schoolhouse front door, quiet and private.

"Oh Tar, what a wonderful thing your family did for mine."

"My mother and daddy wanted your family to be happy. With all of that commotion with Miriam's brothers they wanted our farms to be safe again. I'm so glad too, maybe you can come up sometime with your mother and we can read more about Old George McGregor and the war?"

"I'll try to let her bring me up on Saturday. I think she said something about Tara and her were going to come up and try on some more dresses."

Tar's face flushed at the thought of Tara again but managed to go on with the conversation. "Maybe we can go back out into the field and see if there are anymore things out there?"

"I'll try to come up Saturday morning."

"It looks as if we'll be neighbors for a long time," smiled Tar.

"Will you still be my boyfriend?"

"Oh, Charlotte, here comes the other kids. We'll see each other on Saturday."

John McGregor and Grandpa were spending quite a bit of time in the orchard. The trees were trimmed and the pathways under the trees were cleared and the brush taken away and it looked as if they would have a good peach crop this year. The fence between the forest and the orchard had been repaired but

213

Grant Williams

for several days. John noticed it had been moved again and there was a hole that needed to be repaired again.

There were little green peaches now forming on the stout branches. In some of the trees the weight of the new fruit would eventually bend the branches toward the ground but it seemed as the branches would never break but just bear the fruit. On the trees near the fence by the forest John noticed there were quite a few green peaches on the ground as if an animal was knocking down the green fruit just for food. This had become a concern to John because a deer or possibly a large wild pig could cause havoc to the harvest. So everyday John and Grandpa would faithfully check the fence by the orchard and make repairs as necessary. There were also the sweet potatoes to harvest soon and the tractors were ready for the task. It wasn't so hard anymore with the equipment turning over the ground and actually bringing the potatoes into the wagons. The sweet potato harvest didn't last long and sometimes John would take the crop to the city himself. A lot was going on around the farm.

Saturday morning Tess came to the McGregor farm with her two daughters. Tar sat in the kitchen anxiously waiting for his friend to arrive. John had already gone to the fields with Grandpa and Carver sat upstairs in his room reading.

Ruth saw her neighbors coming up the driveway and welcomed them at the door.

"Good Morning," said Ruth "c ome on in I have made some coffee and we have some sweet rolls."

"I brought some peach jam that I made last year," said Tess.

"Good morning Mrs. McGregor," said the girls in unison.

"Good morning Tar," said Tara as she smiled at the young man knowing they had a secret.

"Morning," answered Tar.

The women and Tar sat in the kitchen for a while until Ruth noticed that her son seemed a little uncomfortable with all women.

"You may be excused Tar," said Ruth.

The Boys from Hog Heaven

Charlotte looked at her mother for the same help, "Charlotte you may go too," said Tess. "Don't go too far we may need you later."

"Yes Momma. Thank you Ms. McGregor for the sweet rolls they were delicious."

The two friends felt like they were let out of captivity as they went out on the porch. They noticed Betty coming to the kitchen when they left and were happy to be outside.

"I didn't think we would ever get outside today?" said Tar.

"I think our Mommas are becoming good friends. I even think that our sisters are getting along. I'm glad to get outside too. Can we look at the book again?"

"Sure Char. We can get it from the box in the barn and we can sit outside and read it. It is too hot there in the barn."

" I'll just wait for you here," said Charlotte. "I just want to look at the land."

Tar smiled for he knew how the extra land would help Charlotte and her family and the land is so visible here on the hill by the big white house.

In a few minutes Tar came back with the box and the book and motioned to Charlotte to come and sit under the big old oak tree that held an old swing.

"You can sit on the swing Charlotte; I will just sit here on the ground."

Charlotte is so happy Tar is such a gentleman.

Tar opened the box and a Charlotte said "Tar your Great-Great grandpa really loved Mary Ellen. It is so beautiful what he wrote."

"Let's look at the map. I think it might be something about the farm or this land," answered Tar trying to change the subject.

He pulled out the old book and turned the pages until he got to the page where the map is located.

"Look Charlotte, I think there is something else on the map other than the land. It looks like there was something over here," said Tar pointing to the smaller 'x' on the page.

215

Grant Williams

"If that big 'X' is by the farm, the little 'x' is in the forest. See Tar it is about the same distance from the water as it is from the farm?"

"I think you are right. Do you think it is guns or money?"

"It might have been since the battle here near Carver was won by the Yankees. Maybe your great-great grandfather wanted to hide something so the Yankees couldn't get it."

The book went on to say the "the land by the river was fertile and would make a good home. I will take my bride Mary Ellen and build a farm here where we will have peace with God our Father. The forest protects many things and will be a comfort to us. The trees will grow and keep what is good safe. We will put markers in the woods to notate our land and our future. A simple cross with the letters GM will do."

"Do you think he is leaving a message?"

"I don t know Charlotte. We need to find a marker," said Tar.

"But it is in the forest where the big pig lives."

"We will have to plan where we will go and I will bring my rifle."

"Should we tell our daddies about this?"

"I reckon not yet, Charlotte. We need to find what is in the forest and by the markers."

Charlotte swung slowly in the swing on the old oak tree. "Tar do you think there really is a treasure in the forest?"

"I'll read on. 'The men in the blue uniforms are not very far away and we are outnumbered here. I will fight for what is right my dear Mary Ellen but I will not put our dear men in harm's way. We will be together after this horrible war is over and all of the atrocities of war have past. We will live on the hill and I will build you a white house overlooking the land and the river. Our house will be one quarter mile from the turn in the river and will be one quarter mile from the forest all connecting.'"

"Tar, I think there is a plan. I think your great-great grandfather had a big triangle and something at each place is significant."

216

The Boys from Hog Heaven

"I think so too. We need to look at the river and the forest. Don't tell anyone about this book or what we know. Please Charlotte?"

Charlotte knew too this information could cause a frenzy around the farms if got out to the local people. There had always been rumors about there is money buried around the Carver area by the Confederate Army before the battle. Any hint of a treasure or even just written word would cause a massive upheaval of lack of respect for neighbors and friends.

"I promise, Tar, I won't tell a soul. It is our secret and we will find out if it is true. I promise."

"We will have to make a plan. We need to take out time and think this out. I will draw a map for us with the river the farm and the forest. You can see if you can find anything in the school library. I will clean my gun and we will be ready for when the time comes."

"Tar read more to me. I want to know more about Mary Ellen and your great-great grandpa. He really loved her didn't he?" said Charlotte looking directly at her young boy friend.

"Gee Charlotte it is kind of mushy sometimes don't you think?"

"No it isn't. It is special. Please read more?"

Tar went on with the dialog in the book. "My dear, Mary Ellen, I think of you every day as we walk many miles through swamps and over the red clay on the land. I think only of the time we will be together. The sun is setting over the dreamland I envision for us as I sit by the river and look up to the hill and over at the forest. I see the same triangle as our love with you on one side, me on the other side and the war separating us. Tomorrow we know there will be a battle and I now am burying this box with some of my private buttons and an old pistol. I am burying this book too and hopefully I will return to find it. But if I perish in this war of brother against brother I would hope that someday someone would find this and let you know how much I love you.' It is signed George McGregor Lieutenant Confederate Army, First Division of Georgia. There also is a picture of a cross and the letter 'G' on one side and the letter 'M' on the other. Wait there is something on the back cover."

217

Grant Williams

"What is it Tar? Is it a map?"

"No Charlotte there is a small cross put in the back cover of the book."

"Let me see," said Charlotte as she jumped down off of the swing.

Tar took the small cross from the cover of the book and handed it to Charlotte to look at. The cross was dirty from the apparent years covered in the old onion field.

"Tar this is beautiful. Do you think George McGregor was going to give this to Mary Ellen when they got back together?"

"Probably was. He probably buried it along with the book so the Yankee enemy wouldn't get it. It is beautiful."

Charlotte took the small cross in her hand and looked at Tar as if she is Mary Ellen and he is George McGregor. Tar saw the look and wasn't embarrassed for Charlotte is his girl and he was happy she is here to share this moment.

"Char, I want you to keep this cross."

"I can't Tar. It is so important to your family. You should give it to your mother."

"No Char, I want you to have this. We are together now and it is important to me that you have this."

"I will always keep this close to my heart, Tar. It is so special."

"Do you think we should go back to the house now?" asked Tar.

"Oh I think our mother's trust us together. If they need us they will holler," said Charlotte hoping they could stay together a little longer.

"I need to put the box back in the barn."

"Okay but I'll meet you here when you get back."

Tar walked slowly to the barn and Charlotte looked into her little hand at the dirty little cross. It is so special to have such a monumental thing in her life and especially as a gift from Tar. He is only a boy but as he walked to put the box away Charlotte thought he had grown a little taller and got a little older.

When Tar got back to Charlotte they went and sat on the porch and watched John McGregor returning from the fields.

The Boys from Hog Heaven

"Hello, Miss Charlotte," said John in his typical southern greeting.

"Hello, Mr. McGregor, have you been working in the peach orchard?"

"Yes I have and it seems every day there is a hole in the fence and some green peaches have been knocked out of the trees and eaten."

"Do you think it is a wild pig?" asked Tar.

" I know it isn't a deer or a little varmint. If this keeps up we'll have to go hunting again."

"You mean I can use my gun?" said Tar excitedly.

"You know Tar has a new gun don't you Charlotte?"

"Yes sir, Mr. McGregor, Tar told me that you got him a new rifle to hunt with."

"Are you afraid of guns, Charlotte?" asked John, knowing that most girls would shy away from any firearm.

"Oh they are all right for you men folk," answered Charlotte.

John McGregor laughed "You are quite a girl, Miss Charlotte, it is no wonder that Tar likes you for a friend."

Tar seemed so glad that his father had added for a friend to his sentence. He really liked Charlotte as a more than a friend but felt a little uncomfortable saying anything like that around his father.

"Well have fun," said John as he turned to go into the house, "We'll all have lunch together later on."

"I should go into the house too," said Charlotte, "I should ask my Momma if I could help too."

"I think you should. Maybe we can go for a walk later on in the afternoon," said Tar hoping they would be able to spend some more time together.

Tar started thinking he wouldn't tell his little brother about the map and the possible treasure but later he would be the first to know. It would be better now just for Charlotte and him to know about the book and the map. Tar sat there on the front porch by himself just thinking about his great-great grandpa and what he thought as he prepared for battle. He wondered what he would feel like if he had to go into battle and

219

Grant Williams

leave Charlotte forever. He looked down toward the river and then to the forest. He almost could envision the marching of soldiers some wearing gray but some wearing blue. He could envision his great distant relative leading a charge and going down in defeat but still a hero.

The Boys from Hog Heaven

Chapter Twenty-One

Sweet Potatoes, Peanuts and Peaches

Charlotte and Tar were investigating the maps and the history of the battles around the town of Carver. Their teacher was so happy that they were taking such interest in the schoolwork not knowing they had an ulterior motive. They spent a lot of time in the library with their noses in history books and learned a lot about the area and the war.

Bubba and John were doing well on the farms and it was now time to harvest the sweet potatoes. It made a lot of sense to both farmers to pool their labor and they would dig up the potatoes with the tractors and harvesting equipment together. Bubba with the extra land and the potatoes that Miriam's brothers had planted had quite a harvest this year too.

Tar was even asked to help and he could do whatever was necessary. Sometimes he could drive the tractor or help unload the wagons. He knew too he could see Charlotte when he was working. Sometimes Charlotte would ride on the tractor with her father. Tar would see them together and think how close they were just like him and his father. The crop was good and it seemed that they had been blessed again with the better than average onion crop and now a very good sweet potato crop. Tar was not only happy for his family's bounty but was happy that his neighbors were now experiencing a bountiful year too.

Soon they would be digging up the peanuts and they were looking good. He would help his father and grandpa sack the peanuts and then they would roast a few sacks for themselves. Peanuts were becoming more important to the economy of this part of Georgia and the profits would help sustain the family farms in the area. This year Tar was hoping that his father would have him travel with him to Americus to drop off the peanuts at the buyers. There wasn't much to do in Americus but it was different and he could get something at the five and ten

221

Grant Williams

cent store. Maybe they could go up with Bubba and they could all ride together.

The peaches were getting bigger and just starting to change from the dark green little balls to a sunshine color. It would be a while before they would pick peaches. Most of the time Will, Virgil and Junior would help with the picking but now they were gone Tar knew he would have to help. John would probably have Carver help a little this year.
Also Bubba had committed to help John as a payment for the land and the help would be appreciated. Maybe there would be some help from town too. It would be a fast two weeks of picking and later another two weeks.

Tess and Ruth were getting along like sisters and Tess helped out a lot at the big white house. Tara and Charlotte helped out a lot at their place in their mother's absence but enjoyed being able to help. Sometimes they would come up to the big white house and help too. Tara would always smile at Tar until his face turned red. Charlotte and Tar would somehow always find time to be together. It was amazing the transformation of Betty and how her and Tara got along. They had a lot in common with their friends from the north and the letters.

Life just seemed to go along at an easy pace. The summer months were now upon them and Betty's graduation was now a thing of the past. Betty received a wonderful gift from Walter and he told her he would be back before she went on to college. She was very happy for the first time in her life. The family missed Miriam but also had received a letter from her that told them she and her brothers were all right. Miriam told them she had got a job working for a white woman in a big house in Atlanta and her brothers worked at a big peanut factory. She said she missed them all but knew this is what God wanted her to do.

The sweet potato crop was good and when it was harvested Bubba was sending a check to Miriam and her brothers. He knew it was right because it was those men who planted the potatoes and started them growing. Bubba mentioned to John that he had done that and wanted to know if

222

The Boys from Hog Heaven

it was all right since John had given him the land to farm. John was happy especially since he had another good neighbor.

Tar and Charlotte got to see each other quite a lot during the sweet potato harvest. They even got to spend some time together plotting their next move and to explore the legend of George McGregor. Tar noticed that Charlotte now wore the little cross on her neck. She had put it on a strong fishing line so it wouldn't get lost. Tar noticed how it shined on her skin. He was so happy that she had this gift.

" Hey Charlotte, after we get the peanuts in we should plan on going to find what George McGregor was indicating on that map." Said Tar.

" We should go before it is time to pick the peaches. I think we need to draw our own map and maybe we can pace off the other distances before we go into the woods."

" We can look at George's plain map and try to figure what he meant again."

" I think he wanted to put markers, that is why he mentioned the cross and the GM initials. If we find the cross we will find the treasure."

"Do you think it was guns or money?"

" I rightly don't know Tar. It didn't say anything in the history books other than a lot of money was brought up from the gulf coast to pay for the war and a lot of the money traveled through Georgia. Sometimes the gunrunners would meet the Confederates and sell their guns to them in little towns and backwoods locations. It could be guns."

" Let's pace off the other distances from the farm to the river bend first. Then we can figure out where to go from there. We can then pace off the distance from the river to the woods and the farm to the woods and find out where they cross. Are you going with us to take the peanuts to Americus?"

"I don't know. I'll have to ask my daddy."

" I'll mention it to my daddy and tell him it would be nice it I could have company. You helped and should go."

Tar helped with the peanut crop. The peanuts were sacked and put on the back of the truck it looked as if there would be at least two trips to the buyers.

Grant Williams

" Tar, I'm going to take a load of peanuts to Americus tomorrow. You will have to go to school but we will take another load on Saturday and I already have asked Bubba to go and invited his daughter along too. You can go too but will have to sit on the some of the sacks in the back."

" I do want to go daddy, I don't mind sitting in the back. It is only an hour or so to Americus anyway."

"We'll leave early Saturday morning and pickup Bubba and his peanuts. You be ready."

Tar couldn't wait to tell Charlotte when he got to school. Charlotte was happy too. She could sit on the peanut sacks with Tar and they could go to the bigger city together. Maybe they could go to the five and ten-cent store or maybe they could even get lunch at a restaurant. Charlotte had never eaten in a restaurant before. School was winding down two and there was only one more week until the summer break. Everything was working out.

The two friends still went to the library at school and studied more about Carver and the War Between the States. They had found a lot of information about the history of Carver and some of it pertained to George McGregor. They would have a plan to find the marker as soon as school was out and they would have more free time.

Betty was out of school and was preparing for college. Walter was planning to come to Carver in a few weeks to see her before she left for school. Tess became a very faithful friend and helper for Ruth but they still missed Miriam. Bubba would send tomatoes and other fresh vegetables with Tess on her visits. Tara helped around their farm and sometimes would come to the big farm with her mother. Each time Tara would see Tar she would smile to let him know she still had their secret. Grandpa and John had the peach crates ready for harvest but were still having problems keeping the fence repaired between the orchard and the woods. Life was good and peaceful at that time.

Tar was up at sunrise on Saturday morning he had washed his face and already combed his hair before John showed up with the truck loaded with peanuts.

The Boys from Hog Heaven

" Are you ready to go, Tar?" Asked John looking at his son who was dressed in his school clothes.

John didn't mention how good Tar looked all washed and combed but was happy that he could go along. It wasn't often that they would go out of town and it would be a good experience for his son.

" We will have enough room for Bubba's peanuts and you an Charlotte can sit on the blanket in the back too unless she wants to sit up front with us?"

That thought never entered Tar's mind. He just assumed that she would sit with him.

" She probably would sit back here so you and Mr. Bubba can talk." Said Tar justifying the fact that Charlotte should sit with him.

" You might be right but we should ask her. It is a little more comfortable in the front seat."

" We can fold the blanket on the peanuts and it will be comfortable too."

" We should ask anyway." Said John as they pull ed up to the pile of peanut sacks in front of his little house.

" Morning Bubba, We've got plenty of room in the back. Tar can help us stack the peanut sacks on the truck."

The two men left Tar on the truck to stack the bags and they threw the bags up to him. He carefully stacked the peanuts knowing they had a long trip ahead and didn't want any to fall off.

" Is your daughter going with us?" asked John.

" I thought she was right here. Just a minute, I'll look and see if she is coming." Answered Bubba.

'Not coming?' thought Tar. It would be a lonesome ride without her company.

About that time Charlotte arrived and she was dressed in her best blue jeans and cute little blue shirt. Her hair was freshly combed and her pigtails were just tied. Tar was so happy to see her and for the first time realized that she was a beautiful young lady.

" Do you want to sit in the front with us?" asked John. " Or do you want to sit on the blanket in the back with Tar?"

Grant Williams

" Oh, Mr. McGregor, I think I'll just sit in the back with Tarelton so you and my daddy can talk." Said Charlotte and then smiled at Tar.

Bubba helped his daughter to the back and Tar made a comfortable place to sit on the blanket for her and for him.

They were off and down the road toward Americus they went slowly in the morning sun. Char and Tar didn't have much to say for a while but looked at one another and so happy they were together. Every once in a while the sun would dance off of the shiny pigtails of Charlotte and light up the morning. The little cross that hung on the fishing line around her neck could be seen as they bounced down the road.

As the trip proceeded and they came upon different landscapes and scenes they talked about the treasure and the history they were uncovering. They talked about their plans to find whatever was in the forest that was left by George McGregor. As they go closer to Americus they talked about the five and dime and where to have lunch. It was so good to be together.

Upon entering Americus the large warehouses were lined neatly on the west side of town. They passed several other farmers carrying their peanuts to market too. Soon they would be able to unload the truck and they could go to the five and ten-cent store. There were several trucks lined up before John McGregor's so he and Bubba helped the youngsters down. They put the blanket in the cab and the children walked beside the truck as it approached the warehouse.

Tar and Charlotte waited outside of the large building while their fathers made deals for the peanuts. The large man with his pants cinched high over his belly and wearing a white straw hat seemed to be the man in charge and the buyer.

The youngsters could hear the greeting from the large man and it seemed that he knew John McGregor and had done business with him before. Bubba was introduced and the man opened several bags of peanuts and looked at the contents. He made an offer to John and then to Bubba and it was accepted and the handshakes were all around when the deal was completed. Two large black men then unloaded the peanut sacks

226

The Boys from Hog Heaven

on the scales and after they were weighed handed John and Bubba a piece of paper.

" You' all take that paper to the man behind the windows and he will pay you." Said one of the black men.

John pulled the truck out from the warehouse and parked in front of the office. He and Bubba went in with their weight sheets and soon returned with their money in their pockets.

" Price was good this year." Said John to Bubba with a big smile on his face. "Mr. Carter is a fair man to deal with. He will always treat you right."

" I think we did well, Mr. McGregor, I mean John." Said Bubba with a wink to John. " I think we should take the youngsters to the five and dime. Don't you?"

" I think they wouldn't mind a bit."

The two proud fathers went to the department store and to Charlotte it was amazing. She had never been in such a big store before. Tar was so happy for her when he saw the excitement in her eyes.

" We have got to go to the farm store next door. Tar would you look after Charlotte while we are gone. Here is some money for you and for her." Said John McGregor as he handed his son some money.

" Charlotte you mind your manners and be polite. You hear." Said Bubba as he too handed his little girl some money. " You have a good time we'll be back shortly."

They watched their fathers leave and looked into the large store. Where would they go first?

" Tar I want to find something for my Momma and my sister. Would you go with me?" asked Charlotte nervously.

It was really what Tar wanted to do but how could he refuse. The two looked over the feminine items with hundreds of hairpins and barrettes. There were hundreds of feet of ribbons and bows.

" I think I'll get Tara some ribbons and maybe I'll get my mother some candy. She just loves candy."

" What are you going to get for yourself?"

227

Grant Williams

" Oh I don't know. I need to get my daddy something too. He works so hard for us. Maybe I'll get him a big red handkerchief to tie around his neck when he works in the fields."

"What are you going to get Tar?"

" I'm going to get my Mother something too. I think I will get her a lace handkerchief and I'll get Carver something too. Maybe I'll get him a comic book or a mystery book. I think I'll even get Betty something too since Walter is coming back down soon, maybe I'll get her a bow for her hair."

They wandered all over the store and found the items they wanted to buy for the others at home. Tar left Charlotte at the candy counter while he had to make another purchase that he had forgot about. The soon were looking at the candy piled inside of the display windows of the candy counter. There were chocolate drops and cinnamon sticks. There were rows of black licorice and mints. There were gumdrops and hard candy, peanut brittle and divinity. There were choices that any youngster should not have to make. Charlotte and Tar both got their bags of candy. Some was to be for the family back home and some was just for them.

The two young persons were just leaving the store when John and Bubba showed up.

" Did you find anything?" asked Bubba to his daughter.

" Daddy you wouldn't believe all of the things in that store. I would like to take Momma here sometime. She would love all of the things I saw. Do you think next year we could bring her?"

" Sure Charlotte, I think we could." Smiled Bubba so happy that his daughter was always so generous in her thoughts and deeds.

" How about you, son?" asked John.

" I found a lot of things too but we only bought a few things."

" Are you hungry?" asked John realizing that they had not eaten anything that morning.

" I am hungry." Answered Bubba. " And I bet the young'uns are starved too. I'll buy lunch today. After all you paid

The Boys from Hog Heaven

for the gas up and back and hauled our peanuts here with yours."

" That's a good deal." Said John appreciative of his neighbor's thoughtfulness. " I know a real good place to get some hamburgers and French fried potatoes and a RC Cola to wash it down."

"Sounds good to me." Said Bubba.

" We can walk from here." Said John. " Tar and C harlotte do you need to drop off you sack at the truck."

" No, Mr. McGregor, I want to keep mine with Me." Answered Charlotte afraid to let loose of her new found treasures.

" I'll keep mine with me too." Said Tar.

"Well let's go." Said John and he started walking down the sidewalk toward the end of the block.

They could smell the aroma of hamburgers and onions cooking on a grill as they approached the humble little restaurant. The smell reminded them that they had not eaten that morning. John got there first and opened the door for Charlotte, Tar and Bubba. Charlotte couldn't believe the booths along the wall and the counter in front with the little stools lined up as if they were protecting the items behind it. She noticed the two women in their white uniforms and little white hats taking orders from customers around the place. There were glass cases with pies stacked in them and a little window behind the counter where she could see a man cooking with his tee shirt and little white paper hat sitting precariously on his head. This was so fancy to Charlotte for she had never been in a restaurant before. Charlotte was ushered into a booth beside her father and Tar sat to the inside of his father on the opposite Charlotte.

The waitress came over to the table and put down four glasses of water.

" New around here?" she asked as she looked over the group. " Here are some menus. I'll be back in a minute to take your order."

Charlotte picked up the menu and it had so many things on it she didn't know what to order. John didn't even look at his menu but announced.

229

Grant Williams

" I know what I want. I want a hamburger with fried onions and some of those French fried potatoes and a RC Cola."

" I think I'll have the same thing." Said Bubba.

" Me too." Chimed in Tar.

Charlotte looked for some help with the menu but decided to be safe she would order what the others had ordered.

" I'll have the same thing with those French fried potatoes too and I'll have a RC Cola too." She thought how exciting potatoes from France, so exotic and so romantic.

The waitress soon came back to get their order and they all said what they wanted. She carefully wrote down on a little pad the order with the pencil she pulled out from her hair and under her little white hat.

" Peanut business?" she asked the men.

" Yes, ma'am." Answered John. " We are from Carver."

" Lots of peanuts this year. Lots of business for us too." Then she looked at Charlotte and said. " You save room for some of our famous pie, you hear."

" Yes, Ma'am." Answered Charlotte in a bashful way. " I will."

It was only minutes until the waitress returned with their order. She brought all of the food at once and it amazed them all how she could balance everything including a bottle of ketchup. The food smelled really good as it sat in front of the hungry visitors from Carver. Charlotte couldn't wait to dig into her meal but watched carefully how to approach this event. She didn't want to embarrass anyone with improper manners.

The four diners ate their hamburgers and fries and washed it down with the ice-cold RC colas. Charlotte thought she was eating at an elaborate restaurant and it would always be in her memory. The hamburgers seemed like filet mignon and the potatoes to her did seem like they came from an exotic place like France.

" Charlotte, how about a nice piece of pecan pie." Asked John McGregor noticing how much his little neighbor enjoyed the meal and the restaurant.

The Boys from Hog Heaven

" Yes, sir, I guess so if it is all right with you daddy?" said Charlotte as she looked over at her father hoping he would want a piece too.

"We are all going to have some pie, aren't we Tar?"

" Yes, sir, I would enjoy a piece of pie but I want a piece with the cream on top."

" Pie with cream on top for you and for you Charlotte?" asked Bubba.

" I want cream on top of my pie too."

" I'll still have pecan pie." Said John happy that he was there with his friends and neighbors.

When the waitress came back they all ordered pie and again she pulled the pencil out from her hair and under her hat.

"Would you men like some coffee with that pie?"

" I'm fine." Said John.

" I'm Okay too." Responded Bubba. " I guess we'll just have the pie."

As Charlotte watched the waitress efficiently work around the tables and pick up the tips left by the satisfied customers she thought someday she might go to a bigger city and become a waitress. She thought how much fun it must be meeting new people and making them happy by bringing them their food. She thought they must make a lot of money since she saw the waitresses pick up a lot of change from the tables.

After the fine lunch the four left the restaurant full and happy. Bubba paid the bill and John left the waitress a nice tip for her services. Charlotte couldn't wait to get home to give her mother her candy and tell her about the restaurant and the fancy potatoes from France and the wonderful pie with the cream on top.

When they got back to the truck Tar made sure the blanket was folded up where they had something soft to sit on. He put it on some of the empty burlap sacks that help make a cushion. Then he and Charlotte climbed back onto the bed of the truck and sat on their now cushioned seats. The trip home wouldn't be so bad knowing they would be together again.

Grant Williams

As they pulled out of Americus Tar reached into his bag from the five and dime store, took out a light blue ribbon and handed it to Charlotte.

" I thought you would look good in this shade of blue and I wanted you to have something from me from the trip."

" Oh, Tar, you shouldn't spend all of your money on me. It is beautiful. Thank you." She replied as she took the ribbon and tied it around her neck.

" I see you still have the cross around your neck?"

" I will never take it off. It is very special especially since it was from you."

" Here Charlotte, " said Tar trying to change the subject. " have a licorice twist."

Charlotte took the candy and sat closer to her friend. " Thanks Tar, I've had a wonderful day."

Tar didn't answer but looked out over the Georgia red countryside as they chugged down the highway and headed back home to Carver. 'Yes it was a good day' thought Tar but everyday with Charlotte was always a good day for him.

The Boys from Hog Heaven

Chapter Twenty-Two

Time for the Treasure

School was out and it was still a month before the peach crop would be harvested. They always had an early harvest in Carver since they were so much further south than a lot of the Georgia orchards. John McGregor and grandpa had all of the equipment ready and had put together a lot of crates for the crop to be shipped in. Betty was getting ready for her move to college and Ruth was helping her. Carver had joined a club at the library in town that met several times a week and Tar had a lot of free time.

He had been given permission to go to Bubba's farm as long as an adult was there and he could only go in the daylight hours. This was good since at least one day a week Charlotte came up to the big white house with her mother to help with the laundry. Those days Tar and Char usually had some time together and they studied the book and the map. They even practiced the distances between the triangle of the woods, the farm and the river by what should be the stride of a Confederate soldier. The only things to do now were go to the forest and try to find the marker.

Each night Tar would go over the map in his head and the number of steps. He knew also there was danger in the woods and the big pig would not be too happy with someone infiltrating his domain. He would have to take the new rifle and protect himself and protect Charlotte. He would have to be careful that his father wouldn't get upset with him taking the rifle out without an adult present. But he justified in his mind that his father would want him to be able to protect an innocent girl and himself. He and Char could safely walk in the forest if he had the gun. They wouldn't be able to take Carver this time for it might be too dangerous to watch after three people and Carver didn't know about the last part of the map.

Grant Williams

The plan was made and the young people wouldn't be missed for Tar would tell his mother that he was going to visit Charlotte and Charlotte would tell her father that she was going to the big white house with her mother. They would have the freedom to search for George's treasure and walk the steps on the map.

So on Tuesday morning after everyone was busy in his or her morning routines Tar walked toward Charlotte's house but met her at the bend in the road near the forest. They had already established a marker by the river. It was a pile of stones with a little wooden cross. It looked like an old grave but it was a significant place to start for the young people.

"Do you think we will find the treasure? Is the gun loaded? Do you think your daddy will be mad if he finds out you took the gun?" asked Charlotte excitedly.

" Whoa, easy Charlotte, one thing at a time. I hope we will be able to find the marker in the woods. Secondly my father would want me to have protection for you and me if we went into the woods and yes the gun is loaded but the safety is on and it won't go off unless I take the safety off."

"Oh okay, will we start at the river marker?"

" We will start at the river marker and walk two hundred steps and into the forest, just like we planned. Then we can leave a marker and walk the distance from the point by the farm and the lines should meet."

"What if they don't meet?"

" They will meet somewhere. We just need to make sure we are careful." Said Tar as he put down his rifle and showed Charlotte the map. " See we will start at the river point."

Tar felt so grownup and so self-assured he was leading this hunt and he would be protecting his favorite girl friend. He felt as if he was George McGregor leading his Georgia boys and protecting the treasure.

The two young people met at the river marker and looked toward the forest.

"Remember Charlotte, we need to take big steps just like George McGregor did when he buried the treasure?" Said Tar as he put the map away and picked up his rifle.

The Boys from Hog Heaven

The two marched slowly making sure their steps were bigger than normal. They reached the woods and slowly walked into the trees counting every step. As they got deeper into the forest they abruptly stopped when they hear a loud crack of a dried branch. Tar looked over to the area just in time to see the white of the tail of a deer fleeing to a safer place. They marched on and at the two hundred paces they stopped and looked around. There was no marker but Tar marked the area anyway with several loose stones and put a stick with a red rag securely into the pile of rocks.

" Tar there is no marker from George McGregor here." Said Charlotte disappointedly. " Do you think the map is a hoax?"

" Charlotte my dear Charlotte, we still need to pace off the steps from the point on the hill near the farm. We might be close but when we pace off the other steps it might put us closer. After all it has been almost a hundred years since George buried whatever he buried and it might take some time to find it. No one has found any treasure yet have they?"

"Tar you are right. You are so smart." Said Charlotte looking with such pride at her young man.

Tar felt so grownup and so important. Charlotte always made him feel important. He was always happy when he was with her. He would find the treasure if just to repay the confidence Charlotte had in him.

"Let's get up to the other marker on the hill by the farm. We'll start from there. Okay Charlotte?"

" You are right. I guess I expected just to walk in a pick up the treasure off of the ground."

They turned and started retracing their steps back to the dusty road when they heard a sound that frightened them both. Tar grabbed his gun tighter and pointed it at where the sound was coming from. It was hideous and almost sounded like a child screaming and then a sound someone would associate with a demon. There was a squeal and it was very loud and frightening.

"Let's get out of here right now Charlotte. Run. Go right back to the road. I will be right behind you. Run. Go." Shouted Tar.

Grant Williams

Charlotte ran and Tar was right behind her. The sweat was now pouring down their cheeks but not from the heat but from the fear of the unknown. The branches from the brush stung their cheeks as they rushed to the safety of the dusty road. They finally could see the road and didn't stop running until they were on the opposite side away from the forest and the evil sound.

" Oh Tar I'm scared." Cried Charlotte.

" Everything is all right now." Said Tar as he dropped his rifle and put his arm around her. "Everything will be Okay."

The sat for a few moments and looked at the woods. They didn't hear anymore sounds. They now felt safe.

" What was that sound?" said Charlotte. "I have never heard anything like that before."

" I think it was the big pig. I think he didn't want us near his home."

" Do you think it will be safe to go back in there?" asked Charlotte.

" We will pace the other steps and if we hear any noises we won't go in the forest. I will watch out for any danger and I will have my gun." Said Tar trying to reassure his friend and continue the adventure.

"Are you sure we will be all right?"

" Don't you trust me, Charlotte?" asked Tar and he looked directly into her little face. " I wouldn't let anything happen to you."

Then and there Charlotte knew they must go on and she did trust him and felt so secure with him.

" Let's go on, Tar. George McGregor I think wants us to find whatever he buried. I think we should go to the marker on the hill."

The two walked slowly up to the top of the hill by the farm. Tar was carrying his gun just like the Confederate soldiers must have done almost a hundred years ago. The two youngsters now with the red marks on their cheeks from the branches hitting them as the fled the forest looked more confident and knew there must be a reason why they must go on.

The Boys from Hog Heaven

" Okay Char, this is the marker we decided to start from. Are you sure you want to continue? We can do this again another day."

" No Tar, we must go on. It is important that we go on. I will be just fine." Answered Charlotte with the determined look on her face that Tar admired.

"Well let's go. One.Two.Three." said Tar as they started pacing off the distance to the forest.

Charlotte was close behind and the marched slowly down the path and across the dusty road. Soon they would be back in the forest and they would be a step closer to finding what was so important to George McGregor. They paced the long steps and soon they were back at the edge of the forest. Tar looked at Charlotte and she nodded to him that she was all right and they again entered the heavily wooded area.

" Stay close to me, Char." Said Tar. " We will go slowly. Keep your eyes open for anything unusual."

Charlotte didn't answer and didn't need to. Tar knew she would be close to him. The slowed their pace and tried to walk as silently as possible. It was now getting a little darker as the branches of the trees held out a lot of the sunlight. Charlotte kept looking at Tar for her inspiration and continued on not complaining about her fears. Tar just gripped the gun a little tighter and marched onward still counting the paces.

Soon Charlotte heard Tar say one ninety-nine and then two hundred.

"We are two hundred paces from the point on the hill." Said Tar to Charlotte. "Do you see the other marker?"

" No, do you think our calculations are way off?"

" Let us look around. Quietly and slowly, Okay? We will mark this area too so we can come back." Said Tar as he made another marker of stones and a red rag.

The walked silently back toward what little light they saw in the distance. They knew it must be the dusty road.

" Look!" said Tar as he stopped suddenly. " See all of those branches are broken on the brush. I think we broke them when we ran last time. Let us follow that trail back the other way."

Grant Williams

Slowly and cautiously they watched the broken limbs and found their way back to the other marker.

"There it is!" Shouted Charlotte. " I see the marker. Over there, Tar, to your right."

" Okay now let us walk to the right and we should meet the other marker. Be careful and go slowly. I think we should only be about a hundred feet away."

The brush was extremely heavy. The brambles and the briars slowed down their progress but they continued on brushing the obstructions out of their faces and eyes.

" I think we are close, Char. Are you Okay?"

" I'll be fine, Tar." Answered Charlotte rather abruptly not appreciating the fact that he thought she could be just a wimpy girl.

"Stop, Look." Said Tar as he put up his hand and pointed at some briars near the ground. " See? Look? There are some black hairs on the briars. I think the pig had come through here recently. Be careful and keep looking. I'm going to take the safety off the gun just in case."

Charlotte looked at the bits of hair and didn't find them menacing. They were just some hair she thought not even conceiving that it came from the dangerous animal. They walked on slowly until up ahead Charlotte saw the red rag from the second marker.

"What do we do now Tar?" asked Charlotte. "There is no marker with a cross on it. Do you think we were wrong and there is nothing from George McGregor. Or maybe he came back and dug it up himself later?"

" Char, we are going to walk a big circle around the last marker and start at ten feet we could be close if there is anything here."

They slowly walked the circle and found nothing and then started a bigger circle walking slowly through the underbrush and brambles. They found nothing again. Tar thought maybe Charlotte was right and George McGregor came back and dug up his valuables. They continued walking the circles and slowly they came to the other marker. Nothing was found.

238

The Boys from Hog Heaven

"Charlotte let's make one more circle back to the other marker and if we don't find anything we will go back home and study some more. Okay?"

It was all right with Charlotte since she was tired sweaty, thirsty and scratched up from her ankles to her face.

" One more circle, Tar. We will walk one more circle and then go home." Answered Charlotte now with defeat in her voice for the first time.

Slowly they walked looking ahead at what seemed like just more briars and underbrush. Each step now seemed closer to defeat and not the joy they had expected. The humidity in the woods seemed to also be taking away some of the joy of the adventure. Tar was still trying to be as determined as he was a few hours ago but the anticipation of victory was eluding him now. He knew Charlotte was tired and he should take her out of here soon. They could look again another day.

Charlotte stumbled and Tar was quickly at her side. " Are you Okay?"

" I'm okay. I just tripped over this rock. I really will be all right. Just let me sit here a minute."

Charlotte looked down and noticed the rock she had tripped on had a little cross on it. Could it be the right one? Tar saw the sign at the same time and the looked at it carefully and Tar started digging around where the stone was in the ground. There were other stones and finally after they dug for a while they had uncovered several other stones that also had the mark and then they uncovered the small stone that was actually the little cross.

The looked at each other with their little dirty faces and laughed. They were tired, hot and miserable but they had found what they were looking for. They knew they might be close to what ever it was that George McGregor thought was so important to bury here in the Georgia woods.

Slowly they started digging up the ground around the little cross. It was difficult digging and they would have to stop every so often and rest a while before continuing. The ground in the forest was not as red as the surrounding Georgia soil and it was covered for years with the decaying leaves of the tall trees.

Grant Williams

Slowly they removed more of the dirt and leaves until they hit something solid. It was a metal box and only about the size of small ladies jewelry box.

" Open it, Tar. Open it!" said Charlotte excitedly as she wiped the sweaty dirt from her forehead.

Tar didn't say a word but reverently looked at the little box that had been buried for almost a century wondering what was so important for his Great-Great Grandfather to bury. The hinges of the metal box were still intact but had rusted shut. The lid was securely attached but with a little prodding and prying Tar opened the box.

The two young friends looked into the box and only to find one piece of paper or parchment.

"What is it?" asked Charlotte not taking her eyes away from the opened box.

Tar took the parchment from the box and carefully opened it where they could see the writing.

" It's the deed to the farm and the land around here. It must have been the original deed and he didn't want the Yankees or the others around here to have it. This land was so important to him and to the McGregors to come. We got the land anyway later on but this was so important to him to assure we would live here and see the beauty of this place for a long time after his death."

" Wow, I think I know how it feels now that we have a bigger place thanks to your family."

" We need to take this back and give it to my father." Said Tar looking reverently at the paper.

" This is very important to do this. I know it will bring a lot of happiness to all of your family."

"Wait Charlotte, what is that in the ground under the box."

" Where Tar, I don't see anything."

" I think I see another outline of another container. Quick, help me dig."

They dug for a just a few moments and there was another box and this was a little larger. It looked as if it was metal too.

240

The Boys from Hog Heaven

" Here Charlotte, help me get this out of the ground. It is really heavy."

It was heavy and it was quite a struggle for the two young people to get the larger box out of its grave of a hundred years. Finally when the box was resting on the ground beside the pair the two just looked at it a while before saying a word.

" Shall we open it?" said Tar. " Or sho uld we just take it back to the farm?"

" Open it Tar, please open it."

There was an old rusty lock protecting the lid and the contents and with a swift whack with a rock the lock sprung open. Tar and Charlotte carefully pried the lid open and to their surprise and wonder inside of the box was some money. It was different and didn't look like any money that they had seen before. Tar knew right away what it was and explained the Confederate money to Charlotte.

" We're rich, we're rich." Exclaimed Charlotte. " Look at all of that money. We can change it into our money and we will be rich."

Tar quietly and calmly explained that the Confederate money was useless to spend but some museums would like to have the money as part of the southern history. Charlotte was disappointed but was still happy about the deed in the other box. They decided to come back for the big box of Confederate money and would try to move it a little closer to the dusty road. The old box was very heavy and they only could move it a few feet. Tar looked back in the box and couldn't understand how the box could be so heavy until he noticed a false bottom to the box.

" Charlotte, the box has another compartment under the money. Look." Said Tar as he moved some of the currency away from a corner. Then he slowly lifted the false bottom and there on the bottom were four rather large bars of a metal and right away he knew. It was gold. He knew gold sometimes was used in the purchase of supplies or guns for the rebels.

" Charlotte we are rich. That is gold on the bottom of the box. We better tell our parents and get some help."

Grant Williams

Charlotte grabbed Tar and hugged him tightly as big tears streamed down her dirty little cheeks. " Oh Tar, You still are my best boyfriend even if we are rich."

"We better get out of here and get some help. Follow me. We'll be at the road real soon."

" Take the paper Tar, don't forget George's paper."

" I won't" said Tar as he carefully put the paper in his breast pocket. " Let's get out of here."

About the time they turned and started for the light there was a loud squeal and a loud haunting sound very near to them. It seemed as if it was coming from the area ahead of them and between them and the dusty road. Charlotte stopped and looked into the area ahead and saw nothing. She saw Tar going into the light   and   hollered   at   him.

" Tar wait for me. Please wait for me."

" Hurry Char, please come to me. Hurry."

Suddenly the two friends heard a crash and in between them came the sight of a huge animal. It was larger than a dog or a normal pig. It was hairy and had two twisted tusks protruding out of each side of its foamy mouth. Its eyes were extremely red and had the look of the devil in them. Its teeth were sharp and looked as if they could tear a person apart with one bite. The animal stopped and looked first at Tar and then at the helpless Charlotte and then pawed viciously at the ground.

Tar looked at Charlotte and saw the fear of death in her eyes. He saw the animal between him and Charlotte. He raised his new rifle but couldn't shoot because Charlotte was in the line of fire.

" Sing Charlotte, Sing." Shouted Tar. "Junior told me that he was trapped by the big pig once and he sang loudly. Then the pig went away and didn't harm him. Please sing."

Charlotte could only think of a song from her Sunday school and started singing "Jesus loves me, this I know. For the Bible tells me so."

" Keep singing and I'll move around to get a shot."

"Little ones to him belong, Yes Jesus loves me."

The big pig slowly moved away from Charlotte and looked at Tar. Tar could see what looked like steam coming from the

242

The Boys from Hog Heaven

nostrils of the wild beast. The pig was much bigger than he had expected and knew if he shot at it, he would have to make the shot count. The tusks were so long they looked like twisted spears of bone snarling their way out to past the tip of its nose. The eyes were as if Satan had put them in the beast himself.

"Keep singing Charlotte." Said Tar "I think it is coming over toward me now. Keep moving toward the dusty road so I can get a good shot."

Charlotte kept singing and moving. Tar kept the gun pointed at the beast and watched its every move. His hands were now sweaty with anticipation and with some fear but he didn't waiver. Charlotte was now safely nearer the road and Tar knew soon he would have the shot and would have to make it count. Then abruptly the big pig turned and let out a loud cry and charged toward Tar. There was a crack of the gun as it fired a round straight at the wild boar. The boar stumbled but continued toward Tar and Tar fired again and again. The pig kept coming and when it made its last gasp to reach Tar he fired once again and this time the big pig laid silently at Tar's feet with its red eyes looking up at him.

" Are you Okay Tar? Speak to me. Are you all right?" cried Charlotte as she ran to her young hero.

She reached him as he still stood silently over his kill. Tar was in some kind of shock and when he heard Charlotte near him he turned to her and grabbed her and they hugged. They hugged for what seemed eternity. They now felt safe. Then as suddenly as the pig appeared they heard a noise coming from the road Tar quickly picked up the gun fearing there was more of the wild herd of pigs coming for their slain leader.

"Tar it's your daddy and it's my daddy coming too." Screamed Charlotte.

Within seconds the two fathers were holding their beloved children in their arms. Now all was good. They all walked out of the forest together. Not even waiting for the stories or explanations. There would be plenty of time to tell all about the treasure and the wild pig. Charlotte and Tar sat on the old pickup truck and stared back into the forest. They were

Grant Williams

waiting to tell their fathers of the events of the day but now they just looked at each other happy they were safe and together.

The Boys from Hog Heaven

Chapter Twenty-Three

Heroes and Families

After several hours of explanations and tears Bubba's Family and John McGregor's family found out the truth about the treasure. They listened while their children told the story of the book and the map. They heard the story about the old buttons and the pieces of the old confederate pistol that Tar had found in the field while he was learning to drive the tractor. The two children told of how they studied the history books in the school library and found out a lot of information about the War Between the States and about the town of Carver. Tar explained why he took the new rifle with them and he wanted always to make sure Charlotte was safe.

The most important thing was that the two young friends were safe and back at home. Later in the day Bubba and John went back to the forest, dragged the big pig to the dusty road and loaded it on the old pickup truck. They also loaded the old box on the truck too and took both up the hill to the big farm. It was a sight to see since the wild boar was so large part of it hung out past the lowered tailgate. The two men took it back by the smoke house but hoisted the carcass up on a sturdy branch on the old oak tree where they could attend to it later.

Tess and Ruth were there at the big white house and cleaned up their children. Ruth gave Tess a pair of Carver's blue jeans and a shirt to dress Charlotte in until they would go home. Tar too scrubbed his sweaty, dirty body and changed his clothes before they all met in the kitchen.

John and Bubba had brought the old box and put it on some old newspapers that were lying on the kitchen table. Then in front of both families they opened the box. They carefully took out all of the confederate money and put it in neat stacks. Some of the bills had dried out and were a bit crumbly. Then they took the false plate off of the bottom of the box and took out the four

Grant Williams

bars of gold and laid them on the table beside the stacks of worthless confederate currency.

"We must keep this find a secret." Said John McGregor. " We can take the gold bars to the government in Atlanta and they can dispose of it. They can determine its worth and give us real money for us to put into the bank. I say we split the money evenly since Charlotte and Tar found it together."

" Mr. McGregor, I mean John, the box was on your land. It was in the forest which is your land." Said Bubba. " Your family should have the box and the bars. You have given us more land and have taken care of us."

Ruth McGregor spoke up which in most southern families was unusual for the wife to take over the family conversation.

" This money will be split up evenly. In my heart I know that George McGregor knew there were more important things than wealth and power. According to some of his comments in this book he wanted to have this part of Georgia for his family and the love around a family was more important. Yes, we are neighbors and Yes our name is McGregor but you are in a way our family and part of this Georgia dream of George McGregor."

Tar looked at his mother and was amazed with her wisdom. It was right for Charlotte and her family to share in this newfound wealth. He looked at all of the people around the room there was Betty sitting next to Tara, Ruth and Tess were together as if they were sisters, Charlotte was standing between her mother and father, Grandpa was sitting with Carver standing by his side and he was standing next to his father so proud that they were all there together as a big family.

So it was decided that John and Bubba would take the gold to Atlanta. They would put their shares in the bank. Bubba told everyone he wanted to officially buy his land from the McGregors and build a proper house for his family. John said he would use their share of the money to send the young people to school. This was the plan and they all agreed and then they prayed together and held each other's hands while doing this.

The Boys from Hog Heaven

***

The next day it was crazy around the big farm. There were many townspeople coming out to look at the big pig. It looked so ominous hanging from the sturdy branch on the old oak tree. The tusks were the largest ever seen in the area and the teeth still looked dangerous protruding out of the half closed mouth of the monster. There was a newspaperman from the county that came over and took several pictures of the animal and also pictures of Tar and Charlotte standing next to the black hairy carcass. The notoriety of the wild boar spread around the Carver area and many times later in Tar's life when people would see him they would always say that was the boy who shot the big pig.

John McGregor sent out the word there would be a big pig feed again at his place. He and Bubba skinned the carcass but John had sent the large head to the taxidermist to save for the McGregor family. When the men gutted the large animal to their surprise they found some other buttons similar to the ones that Tar had found in the box with the George McGregor book but these had different initials on some of them. They also found a small girls hair barrette. These items were given to Tar for safekeeping and to be his secret that he would share with Charlotte.

The families shared the cooking of the big pig. They cooked it for hours in the old smokehouse until the meat now was not tough but tender and succulent. They greeted the community with platters of chopped meat and the neighbor all brought their covered dishes to share. The families sat together and made Tar and Charlotte tell their story about the pig many times but they would never tell the group about the treasure and the gold for that was their own special secret.

The night was now approaching and many of the people had left for their homes in the town and in the Georgia countryside. Grandpa was now sitting on the porch smoking his new pipe and telling Carver about the fish that was waiting for them at the lake. Ruth, Tess and the two older girls were tidying up around the kitchen. John and Bubba were outside by the

Grant Williams

pickup truck looking over the valley talking about the farmland and the peach crop.

Tar and Charlotte managed to slip off and were sitting on the back porch looking out over the land and over the dark trees in the forest down below. They looked at each other while holding hands not knowing what their futures might be but knowing that they might someday be a big part of the history and the lore of that sweet part of the red dirt country of western Georgia. They would be able to tell their children and grandchildren about the Yankees and those men in white sheets. They would be able to tell them about the treasure and the big pig but most of all they would be able to tell them what it was like to fall in love for the very first time.